In the
SHADOWS

OTHER BOOKS AND BOOKS ON CASSETTE
BY LORRAINE TAYLOR:

Last Words

In the
SHADOWS

a novel

LORRAINE
TAYLOR

Covenant Communications, Inc.

Cover image © Digital Vision/Getty Images

Cover design copyrighted 2004 by Covenant Communications, Inc.

Published by Covenant Communications, Inc.
American Fork, Utah

Printed in Canada
First Printing: April 2004

12 11 10 09 08 07 06 05 04   10 9 8 7 6 5 4 3 2 1

ISBN 1-59156-458-1

To my sister Ava and my niece Jessica.
Thank you for a lifetime of loving memories.
Mere words can never express how much
I love and appreciate you.

"Peace I leave with you, my peace I give unto you: not as the world giveth, give I unto you. Let not your heart be troubled, neither let it be afraid."

JOHN 14:27

Prologue

The drumming of falling rain drowned out the sound of the truck's engine. The storm deluging the mountainside cast the small house into an illusion of isolation, and as the man pulled up behind it, he stared at the water streaming down the outside of his windshield.

It was the perfect night for the perfect plan. Tonight would be the culmination of all his dreams. He crawled out of the cab, inured to the cold rain soaking his head and drenching his clothes. He crept up to the window and smiled. It was still unlatched. Signs of his earlier entry had gone unnoticed. He pushed the window up and agilely climbed into the house. He could hear the TV blaring in the front room. The children were still up.

That was good.

Shivers crept down his spine, and the hair on the back of his neck tingled with excitement. First, he'd get the children out of the way. Then he'd come back in and wait for her to come home.

Tonight was his night. She was coming home to him tonight and every night hereafter. He wasn't ever going to be alone again. She was his, and they'd be together forever.

He smiled, aching with the pain of his love for her as he stealthily moved through the house. The children were watching TV, and they wouldn't have a chance to escape.

In spite of their struggling, he carried them out the way he had come in and secured them with ropes, hiding them in the back of his pickup beneath several layers of weatherproof canvas. He then re-entered the house, clicked off the television, and turned off the lights. He unlocked the door and opened it, leaving it slightly ajar.

There! She'll come home to an open door, and I'll be waiting for her! She'll be so frightened and so worried about the children, she'll fall into my arms. Don't be afraid, my darling. I'm here now.

Imagining her surprised response made him shiver with glee. With a laugh of anticipation, he stepped into the back hallway, hiding in the shadows, away from the strobelike flashes of lightning occasionally lighting up the room. *It wouldn't do for her to see me too soon. Now, all I have to do is wait. She'll be home soon. And then, my darling, we'll be together. Just you and me. Together. And you won't ever have to be afraid again.*

Chapter 1

"Bree, I'm hungry . . . Ouch!" Six-year-old Brock Nelson slapped at his sister Shari, older by one year, for kicking him in the leg.

The plaintive voice of her brother caused Gabrielle Nelson to flinch. Wearily pushing aside the curtain of auburn curls that swung against her delicate cheek, Bree knelt on the floor next to the rickety cot that served as a bed for Brock. "I know, baby. Dinner wasn't very good, was it?"

Brock's silence confirmed Bree's statement. She saw wisdom beyond his age reflected in his chocolate-colored eyes. A few tears trickled down his cheeks. She heard his tummy rumble, but he smiled valiantly in an apparent effort to disguise his discomfort.

Seeing his tears and misunderstanding their source, Bree choked on a sudden surge of sadness. Reaching to him with a gentle, loving hand, she ruffled the closely cropped red hair and said, "Let me go see what I can find for you, buddy."

"I'm okay, Bree. I'm not hungry anymore."

"Are you sure? I might be able to find you a piece of bread. And I think we have a little jam left."

Bree felt tears well in her own eyes as Brock solemnly stated, "No, thank you. I'm really okay. I think I'll just go to sleep now."

"If you're sure . . ."

Brock nodded, and Bree leaned forward and placed a quick kiss on the freckled cheek. She reached across him to tickle the quiet girl lying next to him. "How 'bout you, sunshine? You hungry?"

Shari smiled at Bree and said, "I'm good. I love you, sissy."

"I love you too, sunshine," Bree answered. "You too, buddy. Love you bunches."

Bree echoed their whispered good nights, extinguishing the small lamp that sat on the floor by the cot. She rose and tucked the one thin quilt closely around the two children lying huddled in the bed. The room was chilly from the early spring night, but she was grateful that at least winter was over. Many cold nights Brock and Shari had huddled with Bree on the lumpy couch in the front room, preferring to be cramped and warm to lying shivering by themselves on the cot.

Bree wandered out into the sparsely furnished living room and gazed unhappily at the cheerless interior. She ached knowing that Brock and Shari had to go to bed hungry. She was an adult and could handle the discomfort, but they were so young and so dependent on her. She felt as if she were failing them.

Bree pushed the heavy curls off her face once more. She usually loved the way her hair swung and bounced as she moved. But sometimes, like tonight, when weariness and despondency threatened to overwhelm her, the mass of auburn curls was more a burden than anything.

Bree walked into the tiny kitchen and opened the refrigerator. With a grimace she stared at the meager contents. The bread bag looked like it held three or four thin slices, and the jar of grape jelly was almost empty, with only a smear clinging to the glass. There was an egg and an apple resting on one of the shelves. She didn't even bother to open the cupboards. She knew that they were just as bare as the refrigerator.

Ignoring the ache in her empty stomach, Bree quietly closed the refrigerator door and shuffled out to the front room. After making sure the flimsy door to the apartment was locked, she turned out the overhead light, plunging the dismal room into darkness.

Bree welcomed the black obscurity. It masked the disheartening sight of their cheerless home. She collapsed onto the uncomfortable couch that served as her bed. Pulling the thin, woolen blanket over her shoulders, Bree turned on her side and nestled her head on her bent arm. She tried her hardest to turn off her mind, to block out the memories, to forget the desperate circumstances.

How could they have ended up like this? Bree felt her sorrow rise, and the flood of tears she had been holding back suddenly broke through the dam of her resolve. Burying her face in her hands, Bree cried from the grief and heartache.

Six months earlier, her parents had been involved in a tragic accident. They had both been killed instantly, leaving eighteen-year-old Bree responsible for her little brother and sister. Vicki and Seth Nelson had always provided the basic necessities of life for their small family, but their lifestyle was carefree, and they had given little thought to long-range goals or financial security. As a result, they were unprepared for the unexpected. Their car was uninsured, as was the vehicle that ran a red light and hit them head-on. Seth and Vicki had no life insurance, no savings, nothing to pass on to their children that would provide for their future.

Bree had grown up sharing their carefree lifestyle but often shouldering the responsibility of Brock and Shari. She loved her little sister and brother with a devotion that sometimes amazed and always amused their parents. Vicki Nelson had recognized the maternal side of her eldest daughter the moment they brought tiny Shari home from the hospital, and she had gladly allowed Bree to mother and supervise the youngsters.

After the accident, the income provided by their father vanished, but their needs didn't. The children were quickly outgrowing their clothes. They lived in a tiny, drafty apartment that barely offered them shelter, and their food was almost gone.

Bree, a senior in high school, was determined to finish her education. She worked part-time at a fast-food restaurant on the weekends and after school, making just enough to pay their rent and to buy the barest of essentials. Graduation was two weeks away, and after that she would be free to find full-time work.

But they were out of food now, and though she knew she would be paid in a few days, she also knew it wouldn't go far. Rent was also due soon, which meant that very little would be left over for groceries.

Bree knew that they would make it through the next two weeks. They would have to. It would be hard, but then, the last six months had been hard. She was so lucky that Brock and Shari were good-natured kids. They rarely complained, which was why Brock's whispered plea earlier that night had been so hard to hear. If he was willing to voice his hunger, it meant that the void in his belly was truly great.

With a sigh, Bree wiped her face with the back of her hands and closed her eyes. Tomorrow. She would think it out tomorrow.

Before she could go to sleep, however, Bree suddenly knew that there was an answer. She worked at a fast food restaurant, and there was always food that they threw out at the end of each shift. Bree sat up. She knew that her friend and boss, Melanie Russell, would help her. With a flash of unexpected insight, Bree saw how her pride had ended up hurting the children. They were hungry. They were out of food. It was time to abandon the pride that had kept her from asking for help.

Tomorrow! She would talk to Mel tomorrow. Soon the children would have plenty to eat. A grin appeared across Bree's face, dispelling her earlier sorrow. She jumped off the couch, tossing aside the blankets.

She went back into the kitchen and removed the food from the refrigerator. She busied herself toasting the bread, scraping enough jelly from the jar to spread a thin layer on each piece of toast. She scrambled the egg and then sliced the apple. She then set it all on the table on one plate. She laid three forks next to the plate and smiled in anticipation, knowing how surprised Brock and Shari would be.

Creeping into their room, Bree listened for a moment. She knew both children were awake and smiled when two tousled heads raised off the pillows and two sets of wondering eyes stared at her through the darkness.

"What's wrong, Bree?" Shari's voice was quiet.

"Nothing is wrong, sissy. I just have a surprise for you!"

Brock scrambled out of the bed, his bare feet hitting the floor with a slap. His eyes shone, and his freckled face was alight with a smile. "A surprise!"

Bree walked across the room and grabbed Brock's hand. She then pulled down the covers with her other hand and urged Shari out of bed. "Yes, a surprise. Now come on . . . hurry!"

Brock and Shari followed Bree out into the kitchen and stared at the food sitting on the table. "C'mon. Sit down," she prompted, nudging them toward their seats. She then sat in an empty chair and said, "We're having us a midnight feast!" She glanced at her watch. "Even though it's only 9:30!"

Ten minutes later, Bree supervised Shari and Brock through a second round of teeth brushing before herding them back to bed. They had polished off the food, grateful for its filling satisfaction, and Bree was finally able to go back to bed with a sense of peace in her heart.

Chapter 2

"C'mon, you two . . . scoot!" Bree prodded Brock and Shari out the door of their apartment. "Do you have your meal tickets for school?"

"Yes, Bree. For breakfas' and lunch."

Bree smiled at Brock's answer, grateful for the special program that allowed her brother and sister to eat both breakfast and hot lunch at school.

She waved at the children as they boarded the school bus, then turned and made her way down the city block. Their apartment was only four blocks away from Boise High School, and Bree found herself scurrying down the street, anxious to get to school and start the day.

She enjoyed her classes and was looking forward to graduation. While she had a secret hunger to go to college, she was realistic enough to know that her plans would have to be put on hold. For now, she needed to find full-time work. She and the children couldn't go on much longer in their current situation. She was eager to get through the day's classes and get to work so that she could talk to Mel about giving the children some of the restaurant's leftovers. Bree found that she was excited at the prospect of presenting her siblings with a plateful of hamburgers and French fries for dinner that night. She could only imagine their smiles and hear the pleasure in their voices. She would do anything to make them happy and keep them safe.

Later that day, Bree sat beside Melanie Russell, a middle-aged woman who was round and cheery, with prematurely gray hair and bright blue eyes. She watched as the older woman wiped at tears.

"Bree, honey . . ." Mel paused. "I don't know whether to hug you or shake you. I am so sorry that you've been going through this. But I'm also angry with you for not telling me sooner!"

Bree smiled sheepishly. "I'm sorry. I just thought I could do it on my own." Her voice dropped to a whisper. "I was afraid."

"Afraid of what?" Mel asked, a frown of surprised concern creasing her forehead.

"I was afraid if word got out about how bad things are . . ."

Mel nodded as the realization dawned. "You were afraid someone would come in and take those two youngsters away from you."

Bree nodded twice, blinking furiously to hold back the tears. It hurt to hear someone else mention the possibility. "I don't know what I would do without them. And they need me, too. We can't be separated."

"Honey, you don't have to ever worry about that—not as long as you work for me. You can have all the leftovers you want. Them youngsters might get pretty tired of hamburgers by the time you get on your feet, but they won't be going to bed hungry at night!"

Bree stood up and went over to Mel, leaning down to put her arms around the plump older woman. They hugged for a few seconds before Mel pushed Bree away and said, "All righty then. Time to get to work."

The next two hours passed quickly, and soon Bree was preparing to leave, a sack of hamburgers, fries, and cookies grasped tightly in her hand. She was shrugging into her sweater when her friend and coworker Chuck Laird came into the small office. "Are you headin' home, Bree?"

"Yep, I need to get home to Brock and Shari. Our neighbor is only able to watch them until her husband gets home at 6:30."

"Do you have to pay her for babysitting?" Chuck blushed when Bree glanced at him, surprised by his question. "I'm sorry. I shouldn't have asked. I just know how hard things are for you right now, and I was worried that you were having to try and pay a babysitter. I mean, on top of everything else."

Bree's eyes softened at the tone of genuine concern in Chuck's voice. "No, I don't have to pay her. I usually watch her little girl on Sundays. We kind of trade babysitting."

"Oh, that's good." Chuck paused, and when Bree turned to leave, he hesitantly said, "Uh, Bree?"

"Yes, Chuck." Bree tried to hide the underlying tone of impatience in her voice. She was eager to get home to the kids. She missed them and was excited to see the sparkle in their eyes when she showed them their unexpected treat.

"I-I-I . . . um, I was wondering something."

"What?"

"Well, I should have asked a couple of weeks ago, so I'm sorry for the short notice."

"What is it, Chuck?" Bree found her impatience tempered by curiosity.

Chuck smiled, his brown eyes suddenly twinkling. "I was wondering if you would go to prom with me Saturday night?"

Bree was stunned. Prom! She hadn't given it a single thought. She had no intention of going, mainly because she didn't have a boyfriend, never mind the issue of a dress, shoes, or what to do with the children.

"Well? What do you think?" Chuck's smile faded with Bree's silence.

"I don't know, Chuck. I mean, I appreciate the invitation." Bree's eyes looked sympathetic. "It would be fun. I just don't know what I'd do with the kids. And I really don't have anything to wear."

Chuck smiled. "My sister, Jillie—she'll babysit."

"But . . ."

"Don't worry about paying her, Bree. She owes me a wad of money. She used up her allowance a couple weeks ago, and I lent her some money to buy a couple of new CDs. She'll sit for you. I've already asked her."

Bree felt breathless with a rush of pleasure. Prom! She was going to prom! She smiled brightly, realizing that she had made up her mind. "Yes! Thank you, Chuck! I would be happy to go to prom with you!"

"All right!"

Bree laughed out loud at his enthusiasm. She bit her upper lip, the wheels in her mind turning. Maybe she could visit a thrift store or two and find a secondhand dress that wasn't in too bad of shape.

"Okay, you two, I need a cook to get busy at the grill, and Bree, those burgers are gonna be dried out before you get them home if you don't get going." Mel smiled at the two teenagers, softening her stern words. She waited until Chuck left before continuing. "And Bree, don't you worry about a dress. I have an idea or two. I'll talk to you about it tomorrow."

Bree left work, her heart full of a song as she almost danced down the darkening street. Her feet felt light, and for the first time in months, she felt young and carefree. She hummed to herself all the way home and actually started singing as she approached the small apartment complex.

Shari and Brock were eagerly awaiting her homecoming, and they walked home with her, full of questions about the bag she held and curious about the happiness they saw reflected in her eyes.

"Hamburgers!" Brock shouted when he saw the food.

"Prom!" Shari squealed when Bree told her about the high school dance.

The evening was filled with happy chatter and laughter as the Nelson family munched on hamburgers and talked about plans for Bree's upcoming date. Later, Bree tucked the two children in bed and crawled sleepily under her own blanket. She closed her eyes and fell asleep that night with a smile on her face.

Chapter 3

"You look beautiful tonight, Bree."

Bree blushed with pleasure as she danced in Chuck's arms. He was holding her with a gentle but firm hold as they swayed to the music. So far, the night had been magical. The decorations, the lights, the music—all added to the sense of fantasy, and Bree felt like she was floating as she danced with Chuck.

She felt confident in the lovely dress Mel had given her. When Mel pulled the dress out of its bag, its clouds of blue and aqua chiffon flowing, Bree had been speechless. Mel had told her that the dress had belonged to her middle daughter, who had left home the year before.

Bree had held the dress up to herself, unable to tear her eyes away from her reflection in the mirror in Mel's office. "It's beautiful." She had thanked Mel with a hug and tears. Now, as she danced in Chuck's arms, she was filled with gratitude for Mel's friendship and generosity.

Bree felt Chuck's hands tighten their hold in an attempt to pull her closer into his embrace. She felt confused, unsure of his intent, but she allowed her cheek to rest against his shoulder as his arms encircled her. She swayed to the music, thinking about this night, grateful she'd had the opportunity to attend her senior prom. It was a memory that would stay with her forever.

The song ended and Bree stepped back, silently forcing Chuck to drop his arms. He watched her for a moment, disappointed that she was in such a hurry to step away. He was thankful, though, that she was with him. Bree was unaware of the admiring glances cast her way by other boys, and equally unaware of the envious glances from some of the girls. But Chuck had seen the appreciative looks, and he was proud to be seen with Bree.

"Let's go get our picture taken. That way we'll always have something to remind us about tonight."

Bree smiled, amused that Chuck's thoughts were the same as her own. She took his hand and allowed him to lead her through the throng of young people crowding the dance floor.

A short line of couples waited their turn in front of the photographer. Bree and Chuck stood chatting about their plans for the future.

"I'm going to go work on a ranch with my uncle this summer. After that, I'm going to enlist in the military."

"The military!" Bree was surprised. She didn't know Chuck very well, but he didn't seem the type to subject himself to the rigid discipline of the military. "The Army?"

"No, the Air Force."

"Wow! I'm surprised!"

"Why? Don't I look like a soldier?" Chuck grinned down at Bree.

Bree answered his smile with one of her own and teasingly said, "No, you always seem to be on the verge of pulling some kind of joke or trick . . . and I just can't see you getting serious enough to be in the military."

Chuck looked pensive for a moment, apparently thinking about Bree's words. "You're right. I do like to have fun . . . a lot of fun!" He laughed out loud. "But there's just something about the military that intrigues me. I want to travel and see the world. And the Air Force seems like the way to go."

"I think that's great!" Bree felt a surprising surge of envy. She loved her brother and sister and would never want to leave them behind, but hearing about Chuck's plans for the future, imagining the adventures that awaited him, caused Bree to realize anew the limitations on her own future. A pang of sadness ached deep inside.

"Next." The photographer called Chuck and Bree to move forward.

Bree smiled into the camera with Chuck holding her hands. Later Bree would look at the photo and remember the confusing surge of envy and remorse she had felt at that moment.

Chapter 4

The next week passed by in a blur as Bree prepared to graduate and Brock's and Shari's elementary classes wound down. The day after Bree's graduation found her taking a break at the fast-food drive-in, perusing the help wanted ads in the *Idaho Statesman*. There wasn't much available, but she wasn't picky. She needed to find something full-time, and she needed to find it quickly.

Shaking out the paper, Bree set it down so that she could respond to the bell at the drive-up window. She efficiently took the orders and mindlessly set about filling the requests. With a smile of friendliness, she assisted Chuck, who was grilling the hamburgers and frying the frozen potatoes. After the food had been processed, Bree wiped down the counters and settled in once again to look at the ads. The restaurant was slow, and her manager had actually handed her the paper, knowing how desperate Bree was for full-time work.

"I'm sorry I can't offer you more hours here, Bree."

"I understand, Mel. It's okay."

"No, it's not okay, darn it. I want to help you. We just don't need another full-time person right now." Mel smiled, but regret was in her blue eyes. "I'm sorry I had to take you off the grill. I know you enjoy cooking, but I needed someone experienced to run the window tonight."

"It's okay, Mel. You don't have to keep apologizing."

"I sure hope you find something you like. If you had your choice, what would you like to do?"

Thinking for a moment, Bree smiled and answered, "Like you said, I love to cook. I always have. My mom couldn't figure out where I got it. I think it would be great if I could cook full-time."

Mel smiled at Bree. She seemed about to say something when they were interrupted by a small cough. They both turned and looked at Chuck standing awkwardly behind them. Ever since the night of the prom when Bree had rebuffed his attempt to kiss her at the conclusion of their date, he had been shy and distant.

"What is it, Chuck?" asked Mel, a smile of tolerance on her face.

"I don't mean to interrupt." He paused, evidently uncertain whether or not to continue. "I didn't eavesdrop on purpose, Bree, but I couldn't help but hear what you said about liking to cook."

Bree smiled gently. "Cooking is something I've enjoyed doing since I was a little girl."

Chuck rushed on with more confidence. "I know of a job you might be able to get!" His returning friendliness was welcome.

Bree looked at him questioningly. She had forgiven his fumbling advance on prom night, and had in fact sent him a note thanking him for a lovely time. She had felt bad that he had taken her rebuff so hard. She smiled warmly, trying to reestablish the rapport that had led to a simple but pleasant friendship.

"Yeah, my uncle works on a ranch up in the mountains, and he came to visit last weekend. He was complaining that their cook quit and that the boss has to fill in. He said that the boss's wife sometimes cooks for them, and it isn't too bad when she does, but when Steve cooks all they get is burned potatoes and tough chops."

Mel and Bree laughed. Bree's interested gaze encouraged Chuck to continue.

"Well, the ranch is owned by a man named Steve Sheridan. It's way out in the boonies . . . I mean, really high in the mountains, up north past Sun Valley. Uncle Ben said that it's great, which is why I'm excited to work with him this summer." Chuck looked sheepishly at Mel. "Sorry, Mel. I didn't mean to drop it on you like this, but I'll be quitting in a couple of weeks." Chuck turned back to Bree. "Uncle Ben is the foreman, so that's how he knows about the cook job."

"Do you have his phone number?"

"Yeah, and I can give you directions to the ranch, too."

Later that day, Bree stopped on her way home to use a pay phone. The call was long distance, but she sacrificed the change, hoping it would be worth it. Unfortunately, Ben Laird wasn't home.

After hanging up, Bree slowly started walking in the direction of her apartment. She desperately wanted this job. While Chuck had been telling her about it, something in her had sparked. She didn't know what the feeling was, but she knew that she wanted to find out everything she could.

Later that night, she couldn't rid herself of wondrous daydreams. She pictured herself and the children happily living in the mountains with plenty of money and plenty of food. As she lay sleeplessly, tossing and turning, Bree had an idea. She knew it was mad, and she tried to talk herself out of it. But when morning dawned, she jumped up and made a quick phone call to Melanie Russell. Then, after setting out a simple breakfast of cold cereal on the table, she woke Brock and Shari. It was Friday, their last day of school for the year, but she was going to keep them home. She didn't tell them of her plans until they were dressed and sitting at the small table eating their cereal.

"I have an announcement."

The two children looked up, cereal forgotten.

"We're going on a little trip today."

Brock's eyes widened, and his mouth fell open.

Shari said, "What about school?"

"You won't be going today."

"How come?"

Smiling at their eager questions, Bree continued, "We're going for a drive." Bree didn't wait for any response as she continued, "I found out about a job that I want to try and get. It's on a ranch up in the mountains, and it sounds great."

"In the mountains!" Brock and Shari spoke at the same time, their eyes sparkling with interest. "What would you be doing?" Shari asked after shushing Brock.

"The ranch needs a cook."

"You're the best cook in the whole world, Bree!" Brock grinned with excitement as Shari clapped her hands.

"You guys think this sounds like something we might want to do?"

Bree smiled as the children wrapped their arms around her waist and shouted their excitement.

Later, after cleaning away their breakfast dishes, Shari asked, "How're we gonna get there, Bree?"

Bree wasn't surprised that Shari, always the practical one, had asked the question. "I called Mel this morning, and she told me that I could borrow her son's pickup. He's out of town for a few days, and it's just sitting at her house. She told me that it's really her truck since she paid for it and the title is in her name, so she doesn't feel bad about lending it to someone while he's away."

"A pickup! And a ranch!" Brock shouted, galloping around the room. "We're gonna be ranchers. And I'm gonna ride me a horse and rope me a cow!"

Shari and Bree laughed at his antics. They eagerly grabbed light jackets and headed for the door. Four hours later, they were silent as the truck crested the top of a magnificent peak, awed and over-whelmed by the vista that spread out before them in panoramic splendor. They had been living in Idaho for almost a year, having moved there from Arizona with their parents. Boise was a nice city, and they had been impressed the first time the sun rose over the snowcapped peaks behind the city. But they had never taken the time to drive up into the surrounding mountains. And after their parents were killed, the opportunity just wasn't there.

The drive into the heart of Idaho's magnificent Sawtooth Mountain Range had Bree, Shari, and Brock all staring out the windows of the vehicle in wonder. They had never seen anything so beautiful. Bree found it inspirational.

The closer they got to their destination, the more Bree felt at home. She couldn't understand it, but she knew the feeling was real, and it was something she longed to retain.

As they followed the winding road down into the mountain valley, she knew that she would remember this day forever. In the distance she could see the layout of the ranch, looking like a minia-ture play set. It was exactly as Chuck had described. The velvety green pastures and the richly furrowed fields, newly planted with alfalfa, spread out before them. The fields filled the space between the moun-tain meadow through which they were driving and the buildings of the homestead nestled against the foot of the mountains on the other side of the valley. There were well-kept fences marking the boundaries of the paddocks where cattle idly meandered. Majestic granite peaks, many of them still wearing their winter crown of silvery snow, surrounded the entire valley.

Slowly, Bree approached the main cluster of buildings. Soon, houses with fenced yards dotted the road. Cottonwood and poplar trees shaded and separated the yards, offering their occupants a sense of privacy. The lane led to the main ranch house after leading past a huge barn and several other large buildings. Beyond the main ranch compound were heavily forested foothills. The homestead had been built up against the base of the mountains, with the trees and the ancient granite monoliths protecting and sheltering the ranch buildings.

Pulling to a stop in front of the wide verandah of the bleached pine homestead, Bree sat for a moment to gather her courage, but suddenly she felt foolish. She had wagered everything to come here unannounced. What if no one was home? And what if the job had already been filled? Bree felt her stomach tighten at the thought. Embarrassment for her impulsive gesture stained her cheeks with pink.

"Come on, Bree. Are we gonna go talk to 'em or not?"

Glancing at Brock, who showed none of the shyness or hesitancy that was gripping her, Bree said, "Yep. Let's go."

The three siblings clambered out of the truck and slowly climbed the wide steps. Bree took a deep breath and said to herself, "Here goes nothing." Tentatively, she rapped on the polished planks of the beautifully carved door.

Chapter 5

The timid knocking at the front door summoned Steve Sheridan, owner of the ranch and the only remaining descendant of the Sheridan clan who had settled the homestead over a hundred years ago. Opening the heavy front door, he was surprised to see three children standing on the verandah. He quickly examined each young face before stopping to gaze at the oldest girl.

"I'm sorry to just drop in on you like this, Mr. Sheridan. Oh, I assume you are Steve Sheridan?"

Touched by her quiet confusion, Steve smiled reassuringly. He nodded at her hesitant question, encouraging her to continue. A bright smile broke across her face, "Oh, good."

Waiting patiently for her to continue, Steve watched the play of emotions flitting across her expressive face. He grinned at the two children standing slightly behind her. The youngest, a boy who appeared to be about six years old, had sparkling brown eyes and a pug nose generously sprinkled with freckles the same shade as his ginger hair. The girl, maybe a year older than her brother, was slender and graceful. Her dark blue eyes and the cap of deep auburn curls were a reflection of the older girl.

Shifting his gaze back to Bree, he held out a hand and said, "I'm Steve Sheridan. What can I do for you?"

Bree grinned in response to Steve's firm handshake. A dimple appeared in her right cheek as her smile deepened. She said, "I'm Gabrielle Nelson, but most people call me Bree. This is my brother and sister, Brock and Shari."

Brock and Shari looked impressed when Steve solemnly shook their hands and welcomed them to the ranch. Brock drew himself up, his slight shoulders stiffening with pride, his small hand almost disappearing in Steve's bearlike paw. Steve's eyes twinkled with merriment when he gently squeezed the small hand.

He shifted his eyes back to Bree's face, listening intently. She continued, "I heard from a friend that you were in need of a ranch cook." Seeing the puzzlement that crossed his face, Bree hurried on, "I work with Chuck Laird. He said his uncle is your foreman. I know I should have called first. I just wanted the job so badly I didn't even think. We just hopped in the truck and came. I hope the job is still open."

Sudden tears filled her wide eyes, giving them the shimmer of a deep pool of clear water, ruffled slightly by a summer breeze. "Is the job still open?"

Embarrassed by the sudden and unexpected show of emotion, Bree quickly blinked away the moisture and continued to silently face the tall man before her. His friendly, sympathetic face instantly reassured her, and she felt the return of her smile tugging at her lips.

Looking concerned, Steve said, "Yes, I do still need a ranch cook. I was just surprised. You seem so young . . ."

Blushing, Bree said, "Well, I'm eighteen, but I really do know how to cook."

Before Steve could answer, Shari piped up, her voice girlish and eager. "She really is a good cook, mister. She cooks for us all the time."

"And she makes the best cookies!" Brock contributed, his smile framing the space where his two front teeth were missing.

"Well, with that testimonial, how can I not give you a chance?" Steve grinned and stepped back, holding the door wide open. "Come on in. We'll go to the kitchen and talk some more. I want you to meet my wife, and since you two seem to like cookies so much, you might enjoy the fresh batch of chocolate chip cookies that Sarah just took out of the oven."

Steve turned to lead the Nelson family into the house. He started with surprised pleasure when he felt a small hand slip into his, then glanced down into the trustful, blue-eyed gaze of Shari Nelson. "Sarah, we've got company!" he shouted, escorting his visitors deeper into the house.

A tall, blond woman, her hair pulled back with a white band, greeted them with a smile. Her finely sculpted face was strong, yet feminine.

Steve introduced their guests. "Sarah, this is Bree Nelson and her brother and sister, Brock and Shari. Bree, kids, this is my wife, Sarah."

Sarah's sparkling brown eyes added warmth to her greeting. "It's so nice to meet you. Kids, would you like a cookie? I just took a batch out of the oven."

"Yes, please." Their polite answer made Sarah smile even more warmly as she guided them to a place at the large, round table set in the middle of the spacious kitchen. After settling them with a plate of delicious-smelling cookies and large glasses of fresh, cold milk, Sarah joined Bree and Steve, who were watching from a short distance away.

Wiping her hands on a tea towel, Sarah smiled at Bree and asked, "So, Bree, what brings you out this way?"

"She's here about the cook job."

Sarah's eyebrows rose in surprise. "But she looks so . . ."

Steve laughed, finishing her sentence, "Young? I know, I said the same thing. But Brock and Shari assure me she's a great cook."

Bree shyly interrupted, "I just graduated from high school, but I've had a lot of experience cooking. My mom wasn't too great in the kitchen, so I've been cooking for our family since I was about twelve. I haven't had too many complaints."

Sarah smiled and glanced quickly at Steve. "Well then, I think you deserve a chance. I've already got lunch going, but you can help me serve and clean up. Then, if you can hang around for a while, I'll let you handle supper."

"That sounds great." Bree's excitement brought a flush of color to her cheeks.

Steve suddenly looked concerned. "I don't like the idea of you driving out of here at night. If you stay and fix supper, what are the chances you can stay overnight?"

Sarah instantly agreed with her husband. "We have plenty of room here at the main house, Bree. You and the children are welcome to stay with us tonight. That way you can try your hand at breakfast, too."

Bree, bereft of words, silently nodded in agreement, her bright smile and shining eyes expressing her gratitude. She watched while her little brother and sister greedily gobbled the last of the hot, home-made cookies and drained their milk glasses. They seemed more safe and secure than she had seen them in months.

Later, she and Sarah worked side by side in the large, well-accom-modated kitchen of the cookhouse. Lunch was almost ready, and Bree could hear the laughing voices and boisterous banter of men filling the room next door. She felt a flutter of nerves at the thought of meeting so many new people.

Sarah had already told her about the ranch hands. Four of them were married men who lived with their wives in the small houses she had passed earlier. They varied in age, and three of the wives worked in Sun Valley, twenty miles south of the ranch. The fourth wife taught school for the handful of youngsters who lived on the ranch. There were eight other children, ranging in ages from three to twelve. The three year old did not attend school, but rode into town with his mom, where he was dropped off at a day-care provider. If Bree were given the job, Brock and Shari would go to school on the ranch with the other children.

Sarah had then explained that there were eight additional ranch hands, all single. She spoke of the men with affection in her voice. "We're more of a family than employer and employees out here. Some of our workers are second and third generation. In fact, Thomas, our oldest ranch hand, and his son Michael, are fourth and fifth genera-tion. Thomas's great-grandparents settled here with Steve's ancestors, and their family has been represented every generation since."

Bree smilingly acknowledged Sarah's information, swallowing her envy. She hungered for the sense of family that these people repre-sented, something she had missed since her parents' passing. She still, at times, felt a poignant longing to be a part of a well-established heritage like the one enjoyed by Steve and Sarah Sheridan and their employees.

Just then, Bree and Sarah heard a loud and boisterous voice bellow, "Well, what have we got here? Howdy do there, little pardner and little miss!"

Sarah smiled at Bree and laughingly said, "I think it's time for introductions. That's Jonathan Smith. He's one of our married hands. He and the other married men eat lunch with us, but they usually have breakfast and dinner at home. There are times, however, when we all get together for a great big feast." Seeing a look of overwhelmed consternation dawning on Bree's face, Sarah laughingly reassured her, "But don't worry. When we have those big shindigs, everyone pitches in and helps with the cooking and cleaning." Laying a motherly hand on Bree's shoulder, Sarah asked, "Are you ready to meet this motley crew that you may be cooking for?"

Smiling, Bree wiped her hands on a dishcloth and followed Sarah out into the large, open dining room. She felt her stomach twist with nervousness and licked her dry lips, wishing for a drink of cold water to help soothe her nerves. But when she walked through the swinging doors that separated the kitchen from the dining hall, Bree smiled at the sight of Brock and Shari. They were talking animatedly to a gruff-looking, middle-aged man. An older ranch hand was nearby, watching them with a look of kind tolerance in his eyes. A few other men were loitering around the room, casually watching the children.

"Hey, Jonathan, I see you've already met our young guests."

"Hey, Sarah. We sure have. Where'd these two calves come from?"

"We come from Boise," Brock piped up before Sarah could answer.

"Boise! Well hot dang, lil' pardner. Whatcha come all this way fer? You wanting to be a cowpoke?"

Before Brock could respond, Sarah stepped in and said, "They came with their older sister here." Bree felt herself blush when she suddenly became the center of attention. Several sets of eyes looked on with interest when they rested on the petite redhead standing quietly next to Sarah. "Gentlemen, this is Bree Nelson. She's come looking for work and is going to help me out with lunch and dinner."

Jonathan Smith was the first to reach Bree. He strode her way, arm outstretched. "Welcome to the ranch, miss. Hope you like us and want to stay. We sure could use somethin' purty to look at ever' now and then. I get tired of all these ugly mugs I have to look at day in and day out."

"Welcome Bree," a second man said as he held out his hand. "I'm Ben Laird. Hope you have a good experience here and that things work out."

Bree brightened, transferring her amused glance from Jonathan to the sculpted, brown face of the man standing in front of her. "Ben, I've been looking forward to meeting you and saying thank you."

Ben looked puzzled, glancing questioningly at Sarah. Sarah shrugged her shoulders and shook her head. He looked back at Bree and said, "Why?"

"You're the reason I'm here." Bree laughed out loud at the dumbfounded expression on Ben's face. She hastened to explain, "I work with your nephew Chuck. He's the one who told me about this job. Evidently you visited his family a few days ago and mentioned that the Sheridans needed a new cook. He and his mom gave us directions here."

"My word." Ben removed his tan Stetson and ran a hand through his ruffled hair. "Can you beat that? I'll have to tell Chuck thanks for sending you our way."

"Maybe you should wait until you've tasted my cooking first!"

Laughing, Ben tipped his hat to Bree and stepped out of the way so the other ranch hands could meet her. They were all friendly, and Bree felt her nervousness melt away. She watched the men tease and interact with Brock and Shari, and she felt an intense feeling of longing tugging at her heart. Oh how she wanted this job!

Two men stepped up to Bree. The older of the two, a man about forty years old, removed his hat and smiled at Bree. "Hi, Bree. I'm Lex Larsen. My wife, Tina, will be excited to meet you. And this," he gestured toward the young man standing next to him, "is Michael Reilly."

Bree transferred her gaze to the handsome face of the shy young man standing next to Lex. He looked to be in his early to midtwenties. He wasn't very tall, barely 5'10", and he was lean. But he looked strong and healthy and very fit. Bree felt her pulse quicken with awareness as she said, "Hi, Michael."

He smiled at her and nodded, murmuring a quiet greeting. Behind the reserved demeanor, Bree could see a spark of interest light up the dark, blue-gray eyes that met her gaze.

Bree smiled at him, liking him at once. Before she could say anything else, however, she felt a firm hand gently touch her shoulder. With a smile in her eyes, she turned to meet the last of the cowboys. She found herself staring into the sage eyes of an aged man. His shoulders were stooped, his sparse hair gray and wiry. His face was deeply tanned, with sharply imbedded creases cutting through the skin around his eyes and mouth. He was gnarled and wrinkled and appeared to be carrying the weight of the world on his weary shoulders. But his grip when he shook Bree's hand was surprisingly strong. The man's entire being exuded tenderness. It was in his handshake, in his smile, and as Bree looked into the wise, old eyes, she found herself gazing at the kindly soul of a friend.

"I'm right pleased to meet you, Bree. My name's Thomas Reilly."

Thomas smiled at Bree's sudden glance toward the lean, wiry young man who had stepped back but still stood near. "My youngest son," he offered by way of explanation. "I think you're gonna do just fine. And I hope you can stay. I can tell already that you and those youngsters belong here."

"Thank you, Thomas. I feel like we belong here too. I just hope after all of you sample my cooking that Sarah and Steve think so too."

Responding to Sarah's quiet reminder, Bree nodded a farewell to Thomas and returned to the kitchen. She was eager and anxious for lunch to be over so that she could start supper. She was determined to make a favorable impression.

A few minutes later, she stood back and watched the men hungrily consume the well-prepared fare served to them. Brock and Shari were at the long table, sitting amongst the men and happily gorging themselves on the hearty beef stew and biscuits that Sarah had prepared. Bree felt her heart turn over, watching them eat so hungrily. They hadn't had a substantial meal like this in so long.

Sarah saw the sadness in Bree's face as she, too, watched the children. "They sure seem to have good appetites."

Bree nodded, a thick lump in her throat preventing her from talking.

The swinging door behind them opened, and Steve Sheridan sauntered over and joined his wife and Bree, who stood behind the serving table. "Everyone seems to be enjoying the stew."

"You ready to eat, hon?" Sarah asked, ladling a generous serving of the savory concoction into a bowl and handing it to Steve.

"You better believe it! That smells great." The happy laughter and cheerful voices of Brock and Shari caught Steve's attention. "Would you look at those two! They're eating like they haven't seen food in days."

Steve and Sarah's attention was diverted by the small whimpering sound that escaped Bree's trembling lips. In shock they looked down into her tear-filled eyes. Bree gasped, her hands flying up to cover her face. Suddenly she turned and ran from the dining room. Steve and Sarah looked at each other, dismay and confusion evident on their faces. Setting down his brimming bowl of stew, Steve grasped Sarah by the hand and pulled her after him, following Bree into the solitude of the deserted kitchen.

They found her sitting on the floor, her shoulders shaking with sobs. "Bree, honey, what's the matter?" Sarah sank down onto her knees next to the distraught girl and put a comforting arm around the slender shoulders.

Bree continued to cry, though she tried to stem the flow of tears. Sarah, observing her struggle, consoled her by saying, "Hush, it's okay. You go ahead and cry." Bree turned and found herself embraced in the tender arms of the older woman. She buried her face in Sarah's shoulder and cried the tears of a lifetime. Finally she drew in a tremulous breath and raised her head. Her face was etched with grief, and her eyes were shimmering with tears.

Steve handed her a damp cloth, and she wiped her cheeks. Sarah held on to Bree's left hand and softly said, "Bree, honey, why don't you tell us what's wrong."

Her gentle encouragement broke the dam of Bree's pride, and with one final, shuddering sob, the whole sad tale poured forth. She told them of her parents' accident and how she and the two children had struggled ever since. She told them of trying to keep food on the table. Finally she finished by saying, "Just seeing them sitting out there, eating like that, knowing that they can have as much as they want, knowing that at least for today they won't be hungry . . ." Bree paused and then continued, "It hurts so much to think that tomorrow, they may be hungry again."

As Bree fell silent, Sarah and Steve both started to speak, "That won't happen . . ."

With a small laugh born of sadness and empathy for Bree and her family, Sarah said, "Go ahead, Steve."

Nodding, Steve said, "Don't you worry, Bree. You and the kids won't have to worry about going hungry. You've got the job."

"But you don't even know if I can cook." Hopeful confusion flitted across Bree's face.

"That's okay. I have an instinct when it comes to hiring people. I have every confidence that you'll do fine. Sarah will go over the schedule with you, when meals are served and where everything is stored. She'll show you how we menu everything and how to get supplies ordered." Reaching over, Steve took Bree by the right hand and gently squeezed her fingers, "You're home, Bree. You and the kids are home."

Chapter 6

The weathered boards of the sturdy corral supported the considerable weight of the large man leaning against its firm support. Steve Sheridan removed his battered Stetson and wiped a gloved hand across his perspiring brow. He straightened and turned to lean against the shoulder-high post of the corral fencing. As he did so, he shaded his eyes with his large, calloused hand and looked out across the vista spread before him. No matter how many times he paused in his work to look at the countryside, the beauty and grandeur of his holdings never failed to stir his senses.

Acres of golden-green pastures stretched before him, undulating in waves from the forces of nature stirring the long, lush grass. He sighed as the same gentle breeze cooled his brow, and with sudden determination, he slapped his hat back on his head and pulled the brim low over his forehead, shielding his eyes from the brightness of the early summer sun. He grimaced, thinking about the weeks of hard labor facing him and his ranch hands. Summer was just beginning, and it was always a busy time of the year. Steve knew how quickly the hot, summer weeks would fly, followed by the busy months of autumn, during which they would prepare the ranch for the long, cold stretch of winter.

A sense of excitement filled him as he thought of the fall roundup. Sure, it was hard, backbreaking work, but there was nowhere else on earth that a man could feel so free and so close to the land. The roundup heralded a return to the old days when a cowboy was unhindered by the intrusion of modern-day amenities and labor-saving devices. It was a time when a man could be tested, by nature and by himself, and Steve looked forward to the challenge of the land and the animals that were his life.

His family had homesteaded the Idaho wilderness over a hundred years ago, and Steve was proud of his heritage. He had inherited the ranch five years earlier. He had been thirty-three years old when his father had contracted pneumonia one harsh winter. His illness and resulting death had been a shock to everyone who knew Lucas Sheridan. When the sickness had progressed, toppling the strong head of the ranch, his family and friends had been devastated. Steve had then picked up the reins, however, having been groomed from boyhood for the day when the ranch would be his.

This lush, green valley, surrounded by towering ridges of formidable mountains and accessible only by narrow, winding gravel roads, was his domain, and he ruled it wisely. He knew and respected the forces of nature, and he worked the land in a way that enhanced and preserved its natural beauty and abundance while incorporating the knowledge and wisdom of man. His methods yielded success, and he was proud of the accomplishments of Sheridans' ranch.

But his pride was held in check. Steve knew that his success was dependent upon the varying and unpredictable forces of nature, and he worked hard to maintain a balance between his will and that of the land. He had earned the respect of his ranch hands by working alongside them, sweating and aching as they toiled through the hard labors of ranch work. He put in long hours on horseback, guiding the days' labors, and long after the men had retired to their quarters, Steve could be found at his desk, working long into the night.

He and Sarah worked side by side to keep the ranch going, even during difficult economic times. He smiled, thinking about his wife. She was so lovely. They had grown up together, Sarah being the daughter of his father's ranch foreman. They had always been close, and Sarah had been his constant companion when they were children. She could ride with the best of them, and she had never been afraid of the daring escapades that he had led. His smile broadened when he remembered the gray hairs and worried frowns of their mothers.

When they had entered their teenage years, he had suddenly started noticing the changes in his best friend. Looking at the bright sun, he realized that it had been on a day much like this one, only later in the year, with autumn painting the mountainside with its warm palette of color.

They had been sent to the small apple orchard that bordered the western boundaries of the ranch. They were supposed to start picking the ripe, red globes that hung heavy on the trees. After they had worked hard for some time, Sarah had started playing around. She began to challenge him that she could climb higher in the trees than he could, and without waiting, she had begun clambering high into the spreading branches. He had stood below her, taunting and laughing, but had fallen silent as he had watched her disappear into the cover of dense leaves. He had been confused by the strange, new feelings coursing through him. Sarah was his best friend, his buddy. But all of a sudden, he was aware of her feminine beauty.

Suddenly, Sarah had squealed, and the rustle and crash of leaves and limbs had heralded her unexpected, unplanned descent. Realizing that she was falling, Steve had stepped forward, his arms outstretched to break her fall.

The impetus of her fall, however, was too forceful, and Steve was knocked off his feet when Sarah's legs caught him on the shoulder. Steve had hit the ground first, with Sarah landing next to him, her arms flung out and her eyes tightly closed. She had merely nodded at Steve's frantic questions, reassuring him that she was okay. They had lain there, winded and shocked for several minutes. Steve realized that his labored breathing matched her broken gasps, but as the panic from the fall faded, Steve had become aware of another reason for his quickened breathing.

Sarah lay next to him, her golden hair fanned out, framing her lovely face like a shining halo. Her eyes were wide, with a startled expression in their warm, brown depths, and her lips were parted.

They were both caught in the grips of a sudden, mutual awareness. Steve knew that he should move, but he just couldn't bring himself to do so. He had started to lower his head when a thudding clamor filled his ears. At first he had thought it was his own heartbeat sounding in his ears, but then he had felt the vibration of the ground and recognized the sound of approaching horses.

Sarah had recognized the sound at the same time and they sprang apart, cheeks flushed and reddened. They had both been secretly glad of the interruption.

But things had never been quite the same after that. By the time another year had passed, their friendship had developed into love. At first they had been shy with each other, awkward and unsure of their shared feelings. Steve found himself inventing reasons to invite Sarah along on isolated rides, enjoying the feeling of having her nearby. Sarah had suddenly started taking pains with her appearance, wearing perfume and experimenting with makeup. Her returned interest was obvious, and one day, as they wandered through the deserted fields, leading their horses by the reins, Steve had known that he couldn't wait any longer.

He had reached for Sarah's hand, taking the trailing rope from her slack fingers. After tethering the reins of their horses to a nearby tree, he had led Sarah by the hand to a large outcropping of rock. The soft carpet of pasture grass was just turning the golden brown of autumn, and the air was scented with the sweet aroma of fall as he had turned to lean against a large boulder. He pulled Sarah into his arms and looked into her lovely, fresh face, her eyes mirroring his love. Their kiss held the promise of a lifetime, and a year later, they had been married at the tender age of eighteen.

Steve shook his head as he thought of the twenty years that had passed since then. They had been good years, and he and Sarah had continued to grow closer in their love and mutual respect. Their happiness had been tempered with trials, though, one of which was that they had never been able to have children.

During the weeks since hiring Bree, he had become attached to the three Nelson siblings. They seemed to fill the void in his and Sarah's lives. They fit in with the rest of their ranch family so well, and he was pleased that he and Sarah could offer the Nelson family a sense of security. He smiled, thinking about Brock and Shari. They were bright, precocious children, and he had seen them blossom with the freedom and security that their new life gave them.

With a gentle smile and a sense of fulfillment, Steve took one last look around, enjoying the sights and sounds surrounding him. He then turned to the job at hand, mounted his horse, and continued riding the perimeter of the fence, eager for that day's labors to come to an end. He had much to return home to at the end of the day, and he felt himself a lucky man.

Chapter 7

Thomas and Michael Reilly watched the two children riding around the perimeter of the fenced corral. Their mounts were two of the smallest, gentlest mares in the Sheridan remuda of equine stock. Brock and Shari both had large smiles on their bright, eager faces as they independently maneuvered around the enclosed arena.

"Looky there, Mike. See how that little girl rides that pony? She's a natural."

Michael grinned at his father's enthusiasm. "The boy's doin' pretty good himself."

"He sure is," Thomas agreed. He pushed his sweat-stained Stetson to the back of his head and squinted into the bright afternoon sun. "You know, it sure is good having these youngsters here." Thomas paused before continuing, "Bree too."

Michael fell silent, contemplating his father's words. Thomas cast a teasing glance at his son's averted face, noting the stain of embarrassment flushing his cheeks. He was going to say something more, but decided to spare the boy. Michael was shy and quiet, like his mother had been. Thomas appreciated the boy's sensitive nature, and he didn't want to say anything that would make him feel more uncomfortable.

"Thomas! Michael! Watch me!"

Thomas's reverie was broken by the high-pitched, excited squeal coming from the girl riding in the corral. He transferred his watchful gaze back to the children, then stood upright, a sudden tenseness lifting his stooped shoulders. "You be careful, missy. You better slow that mare down a bit."

Shari was riding out ahead of her brother and urging her mare into a faster pace than Thomas felt she was ready for. "Shari! Do as I say. Keep that horse to a walk."

Shari glanced over her shoulder at the old man who had become such a good friend. She was flushed from the thrill of the horseback ride and found herself wanting to go faster. But Bree had taught them to mind, and when she heard the firm resolution in Thomas's voice, she automatically began to respond.

It was too late, however. The steady, gray-toned mare had felt her rider's cues, and before Shari could recant the command, the horse began trotting. Shari felt herself bouncing in the saddle, coming down hard and losing control of her mount. "Thomas!" Her voice was filled with uncertainty as the horse began to pick up its pace.

Michael vaulted over the corral fence, Thomas right behind him, making a slower climb. Before either man could reach her, Shari lost her knee grip on the horse, her feet flying out of the stirrups, and as she flailed her arms to gain her balance, she toppled sideways off the saddle.

She landed with a thump on the loose dirt of the corral floor and lay there, winded, in a cloud of dust. The mare trotted a few feet away before coming to a stop, its head down, sniffing the ground, its reins trailing in the dirt.

As soon as Shari gulped in a full breath and realized what had happened, she began to cry. Michael reached her just as the first tear appeared. He dropped to his knees and put his arms around her. She cried on his shoulder for a moment, and then raised a tearstained face to Thomas, who was bending over her. He held out his arms, and she went to him willingly.

The older man cradled her in his embrace for a couple of minutes while Michael caught her pony's reins. Brock, still mounted, was slowly walking his horse over to his sister, his freckled face looking worried. "Is Shari okay, Thomas?"

"She's just fine, little buddy. In fact," Thomas turned toward Michael, "she's so fine, she's gonna get right back in that saddle."

Shari tightened her arms around Thomas's neck. "No! I don't want to!"

"I know you don't want to, sweetheart, but you're gonna do it anyway."

"No, please don't make me!" Shari's voice was more insistent, her tears forgotten as she struggled in Thomas's arms.

"Now, sweetheart, you listen to ol' Thomas. You were having fun riding that pony just a minute ago, weren't you?"

Shari nodded her head, unwilling to admit out loud just how much fun she had been having. She buried her face against the leathery curve of Thomas' neck. He felt her warm breath against his skin as she whispered, "But I fell off. I don't want to fall off again."

Thomas grinned at Michael, who stood a few feet away holding Shari's mount, waiting to help her back in the saddle. He grinned back at his father and pulled on the brim of his hat, remembering the first time he had fallen from the back of a horse. It was a frightening sensation, and he knew that Shari was probably sore. But he also understood Thomas's urging for Shari to get back in the saddle again. The old advice to get right back on after you fall off was still pertinent. Michael listened as his father reasoned with the frightened little girl.

Brock, also watching the scene, said, "C'mon, Shari. Bree will be so proud of you."

Shari lifted her head and looked at her brother. He was right. She nodded her head. "Okay, I'll do it."

"That's my girl," Thomas said as he patted her on the back reassuringly. He set her on her feet, and she walked slowly over to Michael, who reached down, his hands cupped in order to give her a boost into the stirrup. Right from the start, Thomas had taught the children how to properly mount their horse, and Michael wanted to reinforce his father's teachings.

Seconds later, Shari sat high in the saddle, her face pale but determined. "Would you lead her for me, Michael? Please?"

Michael glanced quickly at Thomas, who nodded his head. "Sure thing, Shari. But just for a few feet. Then you need to take the reins."

Less than a minute later, Shari said, "Okay, Michael. I'm ready to take the reins now."

Michael looked at her, his smile reaching into the depths of his blue eyes. Thomas stood back, watching proudly as his son handed the reins to Shari. Both men continued to watch the children for several minutes. "That little girl sure has a lot of courage," Thomas commented.

Michael nodded his agreement. "I think it runs in the family. They've been through a lot, but look at how great they've handled everything."

Before Thomas could agree, they were hailed by a welcome voice. "Hey, look at you two!" Bree joined Thomas and Michael at the fence railing, leaning into the treated timbers on the other side of the corral. Her face was wreathed in a huge smile, her dark blue eyes sparkling with pleasure at the sight of her brother and sister riding around the corral.

Michael glanced at her before lowering his eyes shyly. "Hey, Bree. They're doin' real good."

"I can see that. They've had great teachers!" Bree's smile was meant for both men.

"When are you gonna let me show you the ropes, Bree? You can't live on a ranch and not know how to ride!" Thomas smiled gently at the young woman he had come to regard as a granddaughter.

"I know, Thomas. I need to learn. I just . . ."

"Now, no excuses. If those two youngsters can learn, so can you!"

Bree glanced at Thomas, her soft smile a sign of acquiescence. "I know. One day soon, okay?"

"Okay, honey. When you're ready."

"I can help you too, Bree."

Bree looked at Michael, surprise widening her eyes. He was usually so shy, but as she watched him, he raised his eyes to hers, and Bree caught her breath.

He had such beautiful eyes. They were the color of deep ocean waters, a mixture of blue and gray with a shadow of green. Bree looked into those eyes and said, "I'd like that."

Thomas, watching the exchange, hid a smile behind the hand he raised to his mouth. Putting two fingers between his lips, he emitted a soft but piercing whistle. The horses bearing the two children responded immediately and headed toward him.

"Time to put these two ponies in for the night, younguns," Thomas informed them.

Shari and Brock dismounted with help from Michael. Thomas led the two children and their horses into the barn. He was teaching the children not only how to ride but how to care for their mounts before and after the ride.

Bree watched them disappear, gratitude evident on her features. "I just love your dad. He is so great!"

Michael nodded his head in agreement. "That he is. He's had a rough time of it, though."

Bree looked at him surprised. "In what way?"

Michael looked slightly uncomfortable. He liked Bree. In fact, he liked her a lot. But he wasn't sure how much of his family's dirty laundry he should air. He glanced at her, then said, "Well, I had two brothers, Tom and Carl. Tom was killed in the Vietnam War. Then a few years later, my mom and Carl were killed in a car accident. That was really hard on Dad."

"I'm so sorry. That must have been hard on you, too."

"Yeah." Michael removed his hat and ran his fingers through his thick, dark blond hair. "It was, but I don't remember that much. I was so little. Tom and Carl were both almost grown when Mom had me. I guess I was a surprise package."

Bree smiled at Michael's shy confession. She put a friendly hand on his forearm. "I'd really like to start on those riding lessons. Do you think we could start tomorrow?"

Michael looked at her, his face brightening as he pushed aside the sadness he always felt when he talked about his mom and brothers. He focused on Bree's eager face and smiled down into her blue eyes. "You bet. I'll make arrangements with Dad and see what time he can let me go."

Bree smiled, a dimple appearing in her cheek. "I'll be looking forward to it."

Michael grinned shyly. "Me too."

Chapter 8

"Hey, Bree, how's it going?"

"Oh, hi, Sarah. Things are great!" Bree smiled at the tall, blond woman who had entered the cookhouse kitchen.

"I just came to tell you that we're going to have a new ranch hand starting today. He'll be here for lunch."

"Great. There'll be plenty of food."

"I think you may know him."

Bree looked at Sarah, puzzled. "How in the world would I know him?"

Sarah laughed and said, "Well, I think we have him to thank for your being here!"

Realization dawned in Bree's eyes, and her smiled broadened. "You mean Chuck Laird?"

Sarah nodded, confirming Bree's statement. "Yes, Ben's nephew Chuck is coming to work with us this summer."

"I remember him telling me that he hoped he'd be able to work here this summer. I just forgot. It'll be great to see him!"

"Anything I can do to help?" Sarah asked.

Bree glanced at the woman who had become such a good friend to her. "No, but thank you, Sarah. I'm just finishing up the dishes from breakfast, and I've got the stuff to throw a casserole together for lunch."

Sarah smiled at Bree. She and Steve often spoke of how lucky they were to have had her, Brock, and Shari come into their lives. Bree was a marvel in the kitchen, and for someone so young, she handled the responsibilities like a pro. Sarah knew that whatever leftovers were being used for today's casserole, the result would be hearty, filling, and savory. "If you need anything, let me know."

"I will, thank you." Bree's words held so much more meaning than a simple expression of gratitude for Sarah's offer of assistance. Sarah and Steve had given Bree the opportunity to provide a decent life for her young brother and sister. They had become almost like surrogate parents, and Bree knew that she would be indebted to them forever.

Bree soon turned back to her tasks. Two hours later, the kitchen emanated the mouthwatering aromas coming from the oven, where Bree's casserole bubbled toward perfection and a large tray of home-made rolls baked to a toasty brown.

Bree was wiping the counters preparatory to setting out the food and dishes to be carried into the dining room when the swinging door from the dining hall opened. She glanced up and smiled at the tall man who seemed to fill the kitchen with his presence.

"Hi, Bree. Something smells wonderful."

Grinning at Ben Laird, the ranch foreman, Bree answered, "Thanks, Ben."

Ben smiled at her, his brown eyes reflecting his admiration for the petite redhead. "I just wanted to tell you that my nephew Chuck came today. He's out riding the fences with Michael right now, but he'll be in for lunch with the rest of the guys."

"I know. Sarah came in earlier to tell me. I'm anxious to see him."

"He's excited to see you too. In fact, on our drive here from Boise this morning, that's all he could talk about."

"Really?" Bree looked at him quizzically.

"Yeah, he said that you two used to have some fun times working together."

"I suppose we did." Bree's answer was vague. So many wonderful things had happened to her over the past few weeks that the life she had lived in Boise seemed so far away, a distant part of her memory. Chuck Laird was a part of that dimness, but she didn't tell Ben that. She didn't want it getting back to Chuck that she had forgotten about him.

"How are your riding lessons coming?"

Bree raised her eyebrows at Ben's question, pulling her thoughts back to the present. "They're going well, thank you. Michael's a good teacher."

"I imagine he is. He grew up here and has probably been riding since before he could walk."

Bree smiled at the foreman as she bustled past him, anxious to set things out for lunch.

Ben watched her, seeming amused by her busy preoccupation with the upcoming meal. "Have you had any trouble with his temper flaring up?"

Ben's question stopped Bree in her tracks. She slowly turned and looked at him, pushing a stray curl away from her face. "What?"

"Michael. Has he been patient with you?"

"Of course he has. I don't know what you're trying to say."

Ben looked sheepish. "I'm sorry, Bree. I don't mean to imply anything. It's just that Michael used to have some difficulty holding on to his temper. He'd get impatient with the horses and sometimes get a little rough with them."

"Michael?" Bree's voice was filled with disbelief.

"I know, it seems a little odd for Michael. He's so shy and quiet. I guess I shouldn't worry. That was a long time ago that he had those problems, before I even came to work here. He seems to have outgrown all of that."

Bree slowly turned away from Ben, her posture rigid. "He's been perfectly patient with me and with the horses. I don't think you have anything to worry about."

Ben recognized that he had somehow offended Bree. "I'm sorry, Bree. I didn't mean to upset you. I'm sure Michael is doing fine. He's a good man. Please don't worry about what I said."

Bree nodded, her back still toward Ben. The tall foreman sighed deeply, putting his hat back on his head. "The men will be here soon, and they'll be wanting that great-smelling food you've got cooking there. I better go and let you get back to your work."

Taking a deep breath, Bree turned to Ben with a warm, forgiving smile. "Thanks, Ben. I do need to get the food on the table."

Ben started to walk away, and Bree called out to him, "Ben."

"Yes, Bree?"

"Please don't worry. Michael is a wonderful teacher. I appreciate your concern, but there's really nothing for you to worry about."

"I know, Bree. I don't know why I commented. Maybe one of these days you and I could go riding. I'd like to see what Michael's been teaching you."

"Sure, that would be fun. I think Michael would enjoy it too. Maybe we could have Chuck go along. And Brock and Shari. It would be fun."

Ben nodded in agreement and grinned. Bree watched him leave and turned back to her lunch preparations, a smile on her face.

Chapter 9

Two days later Bree was in the barn, taking a break between lunch and dinner preparations. She was rubbing the saddle she had been given with a soft, conditioning saddle soap. She loved the smell of leather and the warm essence of the barn. The air not only felt warm and friendly, it smelled comforting and homey. Bree loved being around the horses, and she was getting more comfortable being on one. The height frightened her, but she knew that with time, she would overcome the discomfort she felt every time she mounted.

The barn was quiet except for the rustling and the stamping hooves of the few horses remaining in their stalls. Bree was humming to herself when the sound of footsteps intruded on her serene isolation. She dropped her cloth and walked through the door of the tack room, pausing on the other side of the door and squinting to see through the shadowy gloom of the barn's interior. She waited for a moment before turning back toward the tack room.

She screamed when she bumped into someone standing right behind her. His hands reached out and grasped her shoulders as she slumped, and the pounding of her heart quieted as she recognized him.

"Chuck, I swear if you sneak up behind me like that again, I'm going to hit you!"

Chuck Laird flashed his toothy grin. "I couldn't resist it, Bree. You were so deep in thought!"

"I don't remember you being such a prankster when we worked together at Mel's."

Chuck grinned sheepishly. "That's because Mel was a tyrant and she wouldn't have let me pull any pranks on you or anyone else!"

Bree grinned at him, her momentary irritation fading. "You're one hundred percent correct about that! Maybe I should call her and tell her what a sneak you've turned into. Just what are you doing here, anyway?"

"Uncle Ben asked me to ride in and tell you that we've run into some problems and that most of the men are going to be held up."

"In other words, you're going to be late for supper."

"Yep, I think that's what he means."

Bree was mentally adjusting her plans for starting the evening meal. "That shouldn't be a problem. We probably should let Mary Smith and Tina Larsen know too. And the other wives of the married men."

"I've already done that. Some of them weren't home yet, so I left 'em a note."

"With what?"

"With this." Chuck pulled a small notepad and pencil from his back pocket. "I noticed that Uncle Ben, Steve, and a couple of the other men always have this stuff with them, so I figured it must be a good idea. Kind of like a Boy Scout . . . always prepared."

Bree pursed her lips and raised her eyebrows. Nodding, she admitted, "Sounds like a pretty good habit to have." She punched Chuck in the arm.

"Hey, what was that for?"

"For the next time you give in to *your* habit . . . the one that isn't so nice!"

"You mean when I try to sneak up on you?" As Bree turned away from him to head back into the tack room, Chuck reached for her and goosed her in the ribs, "You mean like this?"

Bree jumped and squealed while Chuck continued trying to tickle her ribs. "Knock it off, Chuck."

He followed her into the tack room, his face alight with humor, tightening his hold on her rib cage, digging his fingers gently into her sides.

"Stop it, Chuck. I mean it!" Bree was serious, but he continued to tickle her mercilessly, and her words were lost in peals of helpless laughter. Tears streamed from her eyes while Chuck spun her around, catching her to him. Bree's giggles died away when she felt Chuck's arms slide around her waist, pulling her up against his chest.

"Chuck, don't. Please."

"Aw, c'mon Bree. I know you like me. And I like you. Just one little kiss! You wouldn't kiss me the night of prom. I think it's time you made that up to me."

"No. I'm serious, Chuck."

Chuck's eyes took on a confident gaze. Since coming to the ranch, a new spirit of machismo had erased the boyish awkwardness that had accompanied his advances the night of the prom. "I've wanted to kiss you for so long, Bree. Just one."

Despite Bree's struggles, she found her lips captured by Chuck's. His hands held her tight, but she was able to tear her mouth away from his. Her hands pushed against his chest and she said, her voice rising in anger, "I said let me go!"

The vehemence in her voice finally convinced Chuck, and he dropped his arms, his fingers trailing down her sides as she whirled backward out of his reach.

"Don't ever do that again." Bree was scrubbing at her mouth, trying to rub away the taste of his kiss.

Chuck looked downcast. He stared at Bree's flushed face and, finally deciding she was serious, said, "I'm sorry, Bree. I just thought . . ."

"I told you I didn't want you to kiss me! And I meant it." Bree felt like crying. She had never been kissed before, and she felt like Chuck had taken something very precious away from her. She had always dreamed of her first kiss being romantic and tender, a mutual desire between her and a special boyfriend. Lately, that heretofore-unknown boyfriend had taken on the handsome face of a young man with dark blond hair and eyes the color of the ocean.

Chuck flushed and reached out a hand toward Bree. "I'm sorry Bree. I'm not very good with girls, and I just thought . . ." Chuck dropped his head and hung his hands at his side, his remorse evident on his face. "I just thought you were teasing. I mean, we were having fun, and you were laughing."

Bree felt some of the anger and fear subside. "I was laughing because you were tickling me. I hate being tickled! Laughing about it is out of my control. It just happens. So please," Bree spoke firmly, "don't tickle me ever again, and don't kiss me unless I tell you it's okay."

"You mean," Chuck's eyes lit up at Bree's words, "you might want me to kiss you again? I mean, someday?"

Bree stared at Chuck, shaking her head. She was still mad at him, but her forgiving nature softened her ire. "You really are incorrigible. Now get out of here. I need to finish cleaning my saddle so I can go get supper started."

"Okay, I'm leaving. One of these days you should let me give you a riding lesson. Why should Michael have all the fun?"

Bree looked at Chuck, squinting her eyes and tilting her head. "Michael gets to have all the fun because I want him to!"

"Lucky jerk."

Bree smiled resignedly as Chuck left her alone, the isolation of the barn once again surrounding her with its peaceful silence.

Chapter 10

Bree left the confines of the kitchen, the counters and floors sparkly clean and a roast slow cooking in the oven. She could hardly believe the richness of her life. The children were thriving amidst the acceptance and friendship they had found among the ranch families. The other children had immediately embraced Brock and Shari, and their laughter could be heard at any hour of the day ringing through the clear mountain air.

Bree felt her heart swell with gratitude as she thought of her employers. Steve and Sarah Sheridan had been so wonderful. She loved them both so much. Sarah had taken her under her wing, teaching the girl all that she needed to know in order to run the kitchen economically.

Bree deeply appreciated them and welcomed their supportive and positive influence, but at the same time she often felt the loneliness of missing her own parents. She had noticed that sometimes Seth and Vicki Nelson's image seemed to be fading in her memory, and she knew that it was probably even more difficult for Brock and Shari to remember their mother and father. She had recently started telling the children stories of their parents, and she had placed a family portrait on the mantel of the fireplace in their house. She was determined to keep the memory of their parents' love alive for her brother and sister, as well as for herself.

Bree sighed and blinked away her momentary sadness. She tried to believe that they weren't really gone, that they were still close in spirit, and she hoped they knew that she and the children were safe and happy with their new life on the ranch.

Bree had quickly become friends with the wives of the married hands, especially Tina Larsen and Mary Smith. Right from the beginning, she had also felt a special friendship with Thomas Reilly. He was so kind, and she had been drawn to him instantly—just as she was drawn to his son Michael. Bree blushed slightly, her thoughts wandering to her developing friendship with the young cowboy. He made her feel special, and just thinking about him brought a smile to her lips.

"What's put that pretty smile on your face, young lady?"

Bree looked up, surprised and pleased to see Thomas himself coming toward her. She held out her hand to him, and he took it, giving her fingers a friendly squeeze.

"I was just thinking about how wonderfully happy I am, living and working here on the ranch. It still seems like a dream."

"Well, darlin', it's no dream." Thomas lifted his eyes to gaze at the mountains and the sky and the openness surrounding them. "This is as real as it gets!"

Bree squeezed his fingers before withdrawing her hand from his and said, "Let's go for a walk. Do you have the time?"

"I always have time for you and them younguns, darlin'."

Bree trusted the truth behind his loving words. He had taken them in from the beginning, treating them like his own, and Bree couldn't love him more. She smiled at Thomas as they headed toward the back of the barn, heading for one of the many footpaths that led up into the mountains.

Bree knew that the mountains rising majestically behind the homestead extended far north, into the panhandle of Idaho. She also knew that the ranch sat at the gateway to the "Frank Church Wilderness Area," known for its inaccessibility and rugged wildness. She loved the mountains, but she had also learned to respect them.

As Thomas led her along a narrow trail that meandered through the trees directly behind the homestead, Bree breathed in the warm scent of pine and mountain heather. The dappled shadows shielding them from the summer sun had a cooling effect and were a welcome relief from the intensity of the sun's rays.

They were silent, lost in their own personal thoughts, when Thomas turned to Bree and touched her arm with a trembling hand.

His dry, work-roughened skin felt leathery and cool against the softness of her arm. With surprise in her eyes, Bree turned to face him. Thomas's eyes reflected the shadows of the towering trees, and Bree knew that he was struggling with some deep, inner emotion. With a quivering voice he stated firmly, "Bree, I just wanted to tell you how much you and the kids have come to mean to me."

In spite of the shadows of twilight, Bree detected a hint of moisture in his faded blue eyes, and she remained silent as he started speaking.

His story was one of sorrow and heartache. He told her of his family, a wife and three sons, who had been the light of his life. "We've lived on Sheridans' ranch for as long as I can remember. My dad was a small boy when my great-grandparents settled here along with Steve Sheridan's ancestors. I met my wife, Linda, at a harvest dance held in town."

Thomas had to pause for a moment as he fought a surge of tenderness. "She was the prettiest thing I'd ever seen."

Bree smiled at him as he relived that first meeting. "We fell in love right away. I never dreamed someone so fine could love an arrogant young whippersnapper like me, but she did. We got married right before Christmas that year."

Thomas's story continued as he told her how the years had passed happily. Their first two boys came in quick succession, with Michael surprising them in their later years. All were a source of joy for both Thomas and Linda.

"All three boys were as tied to the land as we were. They wanted to stay here forever." Thomas paused, taking a deep breath before he could continue.

"Then Uncle Sam stepped in, his hand of authority changing the directions of our lives forever. Tom, my eldest, was drafted in 1972 and sent to Vietnam." Thomas had a hard time continuing. He told Bree how Tom's service had been brief and tragic. He was killed within a month of his arrival in the jungles of Southeast Asia.

"Carl was also called up. His life was spared, but he was never the same. None of us were." Thomas rubbed a hand across his eyes, brushing away the moisture. "My Linda became as silent as Tom's grave."

Bree felt her heart thud. She put her arms around Thomas and watched him closely. His breath was a dry whisper as he said, "She lost her joy for life the day she lost Tom."

Thomas fell into silence just as the shadows around them began to emerge. Bree respected his quiet, and she walked by his side, offering her support, lost in her own thoughts of life and loss.

Finally, Thomas turned to her with a sad but tender smile. "We better be heading back. It's getting late, and I know you're probably needing to get supper on the table."

Bree acknowledged his remarks with a smile of her own, knowing that her old friend was more anxious to leave the painful memories behind than he was to return for supper. "Yes, those cowhands come in hungry and impatient for their food. I better not keep them waiting. They might try to lynch me if they knew supper was late because I was out gallivanting in the mountains with the handsomest man on the ranch!"

Chapter 11

Bree and Thomas reentered the ranch yard unaware of the man standing in the shadows of the outbuildings. He watched as Bree gave Thomas a quick hug and then turned and ran toward the cookhouse. The hidden figure felt jealousy twist his stomach into knots as Thomas and Bree disappeared from view.

Bree was so beautiful. He felt like he had been in love with her forever. It wasn't just her auburn hair or the unbelievable depths of her dark blue eyes. It was so much more than that. He loved her for the goodness and the kindness that shone out of those beautiful eyes. He loved the softness of her touch and the good humor that made the dimple in her cheek appear.

One day soon, he would tell her. He would proclaim his love to her and she would tell him that she felt the same. He thought maybe she already did. But if she didn't love him now, she soon would. Thoughts of loving Bree for the rest of his life filled his head with visions, and as he reset his hat on his head, the man strode toward the tack room. It was time to unsaddle his horse. Bree would be calling them all in to supper soon.

A smile carved his face with joy at the thought of seeing her up close, near enough to smell her perfume, to gaze into her eyes, and to be warmed by the loving grace of her smile.

Chapter 12

The cookhouse was bustling with the scurrying figures of men, women, and children working together to complete the preparations for that night's fiesta. Bree was excited. Sarah had approached her the week before with the idea of holding a party for all the ranch employees and their families.

"Everyone has been working so hard this summer, and except for that impromptu potluck dinner we had last month, we haven't had a real shindig since you and the kids have been here."

Bree had greeted Sarah's idea with enthusiasm, and she spent the next week planning the meal for the big night. Steve and the men had worked on stringing lights outside and then clearing a large section of the ranch compound for outside dining and dancing.

Ben had contacted a group of musicians from Sun Valley, and Bree was excited to learn some of the steps for western-style dancing. She knew that Brock and Shari were beside themselves with anticipation, and she loved the sound of their laughter as they played with the other children.

"Okay, Bree, we've got all the tables outside. How's the food coming?"

"It's all ready to go. We just have to set it out and ring the dinner bell."

"Do you know how proud I am of you, Bree?" Steve looked at her gratefully.

Bree felt herself blush with pleasure. She shook her head, but her smile grew when Steve continued, "You and the kids are wonderful. I'm sure happy you came searching for a job last spring."

"Me too!" Sarah walked up beside her husband and slid an arm through the crook of his elbow. "The troops are getting restless, hon. I think we need to get this food out there or we're going to have a mutiny on our hands!"

Bree laughed out loud and joined the throng of helping hands as platters of steaming, appetite-teasing food were carried outside. The party had taken on a Mexican theme, and the aroma of chilies, cheese, and spices enveloped the crowd with mouthwatering intensity.

Half an hour later, the platters and dishes were empty, chairs were pushed back, and groans of happy satisfaction could be heard among the adults. The children had already left the tables in pursuit of the games and activities planned for them.

Bree rose to begin clearing the tables, but Michael put a restraining hand on her arm. "Sit, Bree. Me and the other single guys are gonna take care of the cleanup tonight. You and the other ladies have earned the right to sit and relax."

Bree looked at him in surprise. "Really?"

"Uh-huh!"

Sarah and the other wives were staring at him, their mouths hanging open in surprise. "What's gotten into you guys?"

Michael laughed but didn't answer her as the other men joined him in clearing the table. With surprising speed and efficiency, the tables were cleared, the dishes were washed, and the men returned, rowdy and recovered from the lethargy that had claimed them directly after the meal.

"I think it's time to get them fiddles fired up. What do you say?" Steve put his arm around Sarah, hugging her close to his side. "My toes are practically tapping, and there's not even any music playing!"

"I say you're right!" Sarah laughed when Steve took her hand and spun her around, twirling her under his raised arm.

Bree laughed at her friends before saying, "I'll be right back. I need to check on the dessert. I think I'll set it out on the tables so folks can have it whenever they're ready."

She turned and left, oblivious to the single set of narrowed eyes that followed her departure.

She breathed a happy sigh as she entered the cookhouse, her practiced eye scrutinizing the kitchen and admiring the freshly scrubbed counters. Then she gasped, her gaze catching a spot of color glowing brightly against the dark, wood-grained counters.

It was a rose. A single, long-stemmed, pink rose.

Bree walked over and picked it up, her eyes glowing. She held the soft petals to her face and breathed the sweet, subtle perfume. A small piece of satiny ribbon was tied around the stem, attaching a card. The card had her name on it but nothing else.

Bree felt her lips curve upward, her smile reflecting the joy in her eyes. *It has to be from Michael.*

With regret, Bree set the rose aside and hurried through her self-appointed task of setting out the trays of brownies and cookies, sliced pie and cake, along with paper plates, napkins, and plastic forks. She finished quickly, anxious to find Michael to thank him for the rose.

Holding the bloom gently in her hands, Bree rejoined the noisy crowd gathered under the canopy of lights strung across the ranch compound. The sun was setting in the west, and the soft cloak of darkness beginning to envelop the valley was dispelled by the twinkling lights and the lively music coming from the small ensemble playing from the raised platform erected as a bandstand.

Sarah saw Bree coming toward her and exclaimed, "Bree, what have you got there?"

"Isn't it beautiful! I found it in the kitchen. It has a card, so I know it's for me, but it doesn't say who left it." Bree sounded young and in love. Her joyful shyness made Sarah smile.

"Let me see." Sarah held out her hand, and Bree handed her the flower. Sarah smelled the bloom, admiring the sweet scent. She fingered the card and murmured, "Hmm . . . I don't recognize the handwriting. It looks like it's just a piece of notebook paper that's been trimmed. It's neatly done, but I can't tell who it's from either."

"I hadn't noticed that," Bree murmured, her pleasure in the unexpected gift fading. She glanced quickly over her shoulder and saw Chuck standing a few feet away. He was talking to one of the other cowboys, his hands in his back pocket. Bree remembered that Chuck had told her that he was going to start carrying a pencil and notepad around. At the time she had wondered if it was merely hero worship or a pretentious attempt at identifying himself with the ranch foreman and the ranch owner. *Could the flower be from Chuck?*

Just then, Michael came up to Bree and asked, "What have you got there, Bree?"

Bree smiled at him, her eyes not quite focusing on his face, her thoughts still wondering if Chuck could have left her the rose.

"Bree?"

Bree suddenly realized that Michael was talking to her. She looked him in the eye, clearing her mind of the troubling questions about Chuck. "Oh, it's a rose. Someone left it for me in the kitchen." She studied Michael's face, looking for a hint indicating that he knew about the flower, and was, in fact, the person who had left it for her. But his face was inscrutable, his eyes on the flower resting in Bree's hands.

"It's beautiful."

"Yes, it is. I wish I knew who gave it to me so I could thank them properly!"

Michael grinned. "Why don't you thank me, and then when you find out, I can pass on your message."

Bree recognized the teasing light in his eyes, and she laughed out loud. Before she could answer, though, Michael took the flower out of her hand and laid it on a nearby table. "Let's just leave it there for a few minutes. Come dance with me."

A soft, lilting waltz was playing, and Bree went into Michael's outstretched arms willingly. She felt dizzy and breathless with romance. The music and the lights blended and spun into a kaleido-scope of sensation, and Michael's arms were so strong and steady holding her close. She loved the scent of his aftershave blending with the heady aroma of the warm mountain air. She felt as though she belonged in his arms, as if she could stay there forever.

They danced through several songs, conscious of the other's near-ness and the joy they found in their shared company. When the music changed, however, Michael felt a firm hand on his shoulder. "Excuse me, son. I'd like to cut in."

Michael smilingly turned Bree over to his father. Thomas took Bree's hand and led her through the movements of a slow two-step. Bree enjoyed the dance and thanked her old friend as she was handed over to Ben Laird.

"Are you having fun, Bree?"

Bree's smile sparkled as she gazed up at the tall foreman. His arms held her loosely, but she felt the strength of his muscles under her hands. "I'm having a great time, Ben. Thank you for your help tonight."

"You know it's my pleasure. That's what is so great about working for Sheridans. Everyone here works hard, but we do it together so that we can play hard, too."

Bree danced through two songs with Ben, enjoying his easy companionship and laughing at his jokes. She enjoyed his uncomplicated friendship and found his booming laughter and sharp wit entertaining.

"Bree, I was thinking—we have yet to go on that horseback ride together."

Bree thought back to the foreman's invitation issued earlier that summer. Back then she had been hesitant to accept, unsure of her place in the structure of the ranch family, and confused about her growing friendship with Michael. But after dancing with Ben, she realized that the friendship he offered was simple and straightforward. She smiled back at him, "Well, then, I think we should do something to remedy that!"

"Really?"

"Sure. I've gotten a lot more comfortable on horseback, and I think it would be fun."

Ben's answering smile was heartwarming, and Bree was glad she had agreed to the outing.

"Let's do it tomorrow then. We're going to be heading into fall roundup season soon. I'll be too busy once we start, so we should go as soon as possible."

Bree nodded in agreement to Ben's suggestion and smiled at him over her shoulder as she was handed over to another dance partner.

Bree found herself dancing with a different partner nearly every time the music changed. She didn't mind, though. The men were all courteous and friendly, and she was having the time of her life. She frequently heard the laughter of children, recognizing the voices of her little brother and sister, and she relaxed knowing that they were enjoying themselves as much as she was. She occasionally searched the crowd for Michael, wanting desperately to dance with him again, but wasn't able to see him. She assumed that he was dancing with someone else or had gone inside for some dessert.

The evening passed in a blur, and finally Bree had to remove herself from the dance floor. She was flushed with exertion, her cheeks glowing with healthy vigor. She wandered away from the lighted canopy, the music fading softly into the night. She meandered around the perimeter of the ranch compound, enjoying the cooling night air. Suddenly, she remembered her rose. *I probably should put it in some water!*

Turning back toward the music and the dancing, Bree made her way through the throng, exchanging a few words with some of her friends. She approached the table where Michael had laid the flower, but the bloom wasn't there.

Consternation wrinkled her brow. *Maybe someone already took it inside for me and put it in water.* Smiling, Bree realized that would be the kind of thoughtful gesture Sarah would do. She turned and headed for the dining hall. She entered the doors, silently taking note that the desserts were almost depleted. At that time, however, the room was empty, and her steps echoed on the wooden floor as she made her way to the kitchen, the glow of its lights shining above and below the loosely hung, swinging doors.

She pushed through the doors, startled to find the room suddenly plunged into total darkness. "Who's there?" Bree called out, her voice breathless from apprehension.

Just then, the opening of the door on the far side of the kitchen broke the blackness. Bree blinked furiously, trying to make out the shape silhouetted against the rectangle of gray. The figure paused momentarily but was swallowed up in the inky gloom when the door slammed shut.

Chapter 13

The man let the black of night cover his retreat from the cookhouse. He had heard the fear in Bree's voice when he had turned out the lights, and the memory of the quivering tones made him smile, a wicked thought entering his mind. *Maybe this could be a new game!*

Suddenly, he stopped, his heart hammering with a surge of anger and his lips curving into a frown. *She deserves it!* The sight of Bree cradling the rose earlier that evening had filled him with longing. He had left the rose for her, knowing that she would find it in the kitchen. He had hoped that she would think of him, at least wonder if he could have been the bearer of gifts. But no! Her suspicions had immediately been drawn to others.

When she had laid it on the table, seemingly forgotten, the sweetness of his longing had faded only to be replaced by resentment and anger. He had watched her dancing throughout the night. Sure, she had danced with him, teasing and flirting, but it hadn't meant anything to her. He could tell. She had sparkled at all the men she'd danced with. *A regular belle of the ball!* he thought sarcastically.

Impulsively he had stalked toward the table. If she didn't want the flower, fine. He'd show her!

But it was gone. He'd looked up, and his eyes had been drawn to Sarah, who was walking toward the cookhouse. She'd turned toward someone who called out her name and he'd seen the rose held gently in her hands.

He had followed her into the cookhouse on the pretense of helping himself to some dessert. He and Sarah had even visited for a

few minutes, the tall, blond woman laughingly telling him about
Bree's excitement over her unexpected gift.

Sarah's words had fueled his ire, and after she left, when he'd been
alone in the cookhouse, he had gone into the kitchen. By the time he
had reached the counter, all rational thought was gone. With great
force, he had hurled the vase to the floor, the fine crystal shattering
into a shower of glistening shards. He'd snatched the rose off the floor
where it lay among the debris and had twisted the stem until it broke
in several places. Soft petals came loose and drifted down, and he'd
stared at the dark pink blooms, fragmented and forlorn, lying on the
floor. His anger left as suddenly as it had come, and he began to
pluck the remaining petals, his fingers shaking as he watched them
drift.

The last splash of color had barely touched the floor when he'd
heard the soft tread of feet that he'd recognized as Bree's. He'd quickly
turned on his heel and headed for the door. It was only at the last
moment that he had thought to flick the light switch, plunging the
room into darkness just as Bree came through the doors on the opposite side of the room. He'd paused, then had reluctantly turned and
run around the cookhouse.

As he rejoined the throng, dancing under the lighted canopy, he
knew he was going to continue the game he had started with Bree
that night. She was going to turn to him one way or another—either
out of love or out of fear.

Chapter 14

Bree stood in the kitchen doorway, her heart pounding and sweat breaking out on her forehead. With a trembling hand, she searched the wall for the light switch. Flicking it, she blinked in the bright glare. Desperately, her eyes scanned the room, but it was empty.

She moved into the room, her eyes wide and a frown of dismay marring the happiness she had felt earlier. Lying on the floor was the shattered remains of a glass vase. The shards rested in a puddle of water, and lying among the debris was the stem of her rose. It was broken in several places, bent at odd angles, twisted and destroyed. The end of the stem was bare, the petals scattered on the floor.

Bree dropped to her knees and reached for the fragile, broken flower, tears pooling in her blue eyes. She gently picked up a lone petal and held it to her cheek as she cried. Her eyes were fastened on the door. *Who had been in here? Did they do this on purpose? Or was it an accident?*

Just as she was choking back the sobs, the door from the dining hall swung inward and the loud laughter of several people intruded on Bree's miserable musings.

"Hey, Bree. Got any more of that apple pie?"

"Yeah . . . these gluttons ate all of it." Several of the ranch hands walked in, laughing with one another, oblivious to her grief.

"Me and Shari didn't get any of your pie, Bree." Brock was the first to notice Bree's slumped figure. He ran to her, his voice full of worry. "Bree, what's the matter?" He dropped to his knees next to Bree and was followed closely by Shari, whose voice quivered, "Bree, you okay?"

Bree gulped before turning to look at her sister and brother. "I'm fine, kiddos."

"What's that?" Brock pointed at the broken glass and the ruined flower.

"It's a flower."

"Did somebody hurt it?"

Bree smiled wanly at Brock's innocent question. "Yeah, it's been hurt. But I don't know how."

"Bree?"

Bree glanced up at the men, whose laughter had been stilled at the sight of the young woman sitting on the floor. Ben and Michael were standing behind the children, their eyes dark with concern. Bree was watching Michael even though Ben was speaking to her.

"What happened here?"

"I don't know." Bree shook her head, unwilling to voice her fear in front of the children. Standing with resolution, she pulled Brock and Shari to their feet. "Let me get these two some apple pie and then we can talk."

Bree quickly dished up several slices of the savory apple pie and then shepherded the children into the other room. Steve, Sarah, Thomas, and Chuck were standing by the nearly depleted tables, munching on a few remaining cookies. They watched as Bree settled Brock and Shari at one of the tables with their pie.

Sarah noticed the shadows around Bree's eyes and asked, "Bree, honey, is everything okay?"

Bree's voice was quivering when she answered, "It will be. Something happened out in the kitchen. I can't explain it." Looking down at the kids, she murmured, "Not just yet, anyway."

Sarah caught her meaning and nodded. "Let's go into the kitchen. I can help with dishing up some more desserts. This crowd's appetite seems insatiable."

Bree turned, leaving Brock and Shari happily consuming their treat. Sarah, Steve, Thomas, and Chuck followed her into the kitchen. Just as they came through the door, Sarah said, "Did you see that I put your rose in a vase with water. It's so beautiful I didn't want it to die . . ."

Her voice trailed off as she stared at the shimmering pool of water and fragmented glass. The deep pink petals surrounding the crushed stem looked like large droplets of blood as they lay scattered in the midst of the destruction.

"What happened? Oh, honey . . ."

Bree was shaking her head as she stared at the remnants of her flower. "I don't know. Just as I was coming into the kitchen, the lights went out and someone left through that door." She pointed on the far side of the room. "I don't know who it was. Or if they did this." Bree dropped her hand. "If they did, I don't understand . . . why?"

Sarah put her arm around Bree's shoulder as Michael spoke up, "Did you ever find out who gave you the flower?"

Before Bree could say anything, Chuck spoke up, his voice surprisingly bitter. "You mean it wasn't you, Reilly?"

Michael stiffened his shoulders, turning to face Chuck. "What's that supposed to mean?"

"I think I spoke pretty clear, Reilly. You're the only one around here who would be givin' Bree flowers." Jealousy gave Chuck's words a sharp, bitter edge. The corners of his mouth turned up in a cynical grin. "Or did someone else give it to her, and maybe you didn't like the idea. And you did that." Chuck thrust his chin forward, the motion aggressive and decisive. "We all know about that temper of yours, Reilly."

"Chuck, back off." Ben Laird's voice was stern as he warned his nephew.

"No! I won't back off. Reilly here's gotten too smart for his own good. He thinks he's so special jus' cuz Bree seems to like him best."

"You better be ready to put your fists where your words are, Laird." Michael's jaw was tight with anger, and his hands were clenched at his sides. "How do we know it wasn't you? We all know how you've been chasing Bree and how she's had to fight you off at every turn."

Chuck's eyes took on an ugly glint as he shouted, "That ain't true! Yeah, I kissed her, but if you ask me, she liked it!"

Chuck and Michael seemed unaware of the other people in the room. Bree stood in shock, her face white and drawn. Sarah grasped Bree's hand, pulling her close to her side. Steve was poised, ready to interrupt the verbal sparring of the two young men, when Thomas stepped forward and put a restraining hand on Michael's shoulder. "Son, back down."

Michael shook off Thomas's hand, ignoring the advice. With a suddenness that took the entire group by surprise, Michael struck, his fist flying up to connect with Chuck's nose. Blood poured out of the younger man's nostrils, but he didn't back down. He started swinging and landed a powerful punch on Michael's jaw before Steve and Ben stepped in.

Steve restrained Michael, his arms locked behind him by strong, determined hands. Chuck struggled against his uncle's hold, his face red and sweating. Both young men were gasping for breath, annoyed and frustrated at not being able to complete their battle.

"Michael, stop it!" Thomas's shout went unheeded.

Michael and Chuck were shouting at each other, their venomous words surprising the young woman standing on the side of the fray, watching in horror. Michael finally freed one of his hands and lunged forward, grabbing Chuck's shirtfront and ripping the fabric. "Stay away from Bree! You hear me? You stay away from her!"

Chuck shouted back, but their shouts suddenly died when Bree's voice cried out, "Stop it! Both of you! Stop it now! And you both stay away from me!" She spun on her heels and ran outside, tears streaking down her cheeks.

It was horrible enough that the flower had been destroyed, but to see Michael and Chuck turn on each other as they had seemed like a personal attack on her. Chuck's behavior didn't bother her as much as Michael's. She was stunned, revolted. And she was terrified.

Where did that anger come from? Was he really such a violent man? She thought she knew him. She thought she might even be falling in love with him! Bree brought a hand to her lips as a cry of sheer despair choked her. She stopped and leaned against a tree, shaking with sobs. Michael was so gentle with her. Had she misjudged him? How could he be so jealous?

The overhead stars twinkled in the crisp mountain air and the distant strains of music mocked Bree's questions. Did she really know him? Most of all, did she love him?

Chapter 15

Steve wasted no time lecturing his two ranch hands. Chuck was subdued, his silence filled with resentment. Michael looked as though his own behavior had stupefied him. His eyes were glazed as he thought about the look on Bree's face and the terror in her voice. He wanted to go after her, but his father's aged hands, surprisingly firm, were holding him in place.

Thomas stared his son in the face and said, "Michael, I don't know what came over you, but you've got to keep a handle on that temper. I thought you'd already learned that!"

"I thought so too, Dad." Michael's voice reflected his anguish. "I need to go find Bree!"

"You stay away from her!" Chuck meant what he said, but his voice lacked force. He, too, regretted losing his temper, at least in front of Bree.

"Chuck, keep your mouth shut." Ben's voice was authoritative and caused his nephew to close his mouth. "We're leaving, and you're going to go straight to the bunkhouse. And you'll stay there until morning!"

Chuck nodded. He paled when Ben continued, "And tomorrow, you will find the time to apologize to Bree. After that, you're going to stay away from her. Do you hear me?"

"Yes, Uncle Ben." Chuck sounded like the boy he still was, and he turned without another word to follow Ben out of the room.

Sarah had stood by, silent and unhappy. She wanted to go after Bree, but felt the girl might need a few moments to herself. She watched Steve as he stepped back, leaving Michael to his father. Steve took Sarah's hand, and silently they, too, left the kitchen.

Entering the dining room, Sarah gasped. Brock and Shari were sitting at the table, turned toward the kitchen. They had heard the fight but had been too frightened to move. Sarah went and sat down between them, putting an arm around each child.

"Who was fighting, Sarah?" Shari leaned against her friend's side and hugged her tight.

"Just a couple of silly boys, sweetie. It's okay now."

"Is Bree okay?" Brock had apparently sensed that somehow his older sister was involved.

Sarah squeezed his shoulder. "Yeah. Bree's fine. She just needs some quiet time. She's kind of upset about losing her flower. In fact," Sarah stood up and smiled down at the youngsters, "she asked me to stay with you two." After looking down at her watch, she raised her eyebrows. "I didn't know it was so late." She turned to Steve and asked, "Isn't it about time we start sending folks home?"

"It sure is, hon. Why don't you take these two home and get them ready for bed? I'm sure Bree will be back soon to tuck them in. I'll go out and get things closed down."

Smiling at her husband, Sarah shuffled the tired children out the door. Steve followed her closely, but looked back over his shoulder toward the kitchen. He could hear the murmur of voices, and he smiled grimly. Michael was probably getting the reaming of his life.

Meanwhile, in the kitchen, Thomas's stern countenance softened in the face of his son's remorse. He put a gentle arm around the young man's shoulders and held him close for a minute. "I know you didn't mean to lose your temper, son, but it doesn't matter what happens—you need to keep it in check."

"I know." Michael bowed his head. "Chuck knows how much Bree means to me, and he's so jealous because she seems to care for me, too." His shoulders seemed to slump. "I don't know how she feels now, though. Not after that display."

Thomas patted Michael's shoulder. "Go to her, son. I don't think she meant it when she told you to stay away. That little girl does care for you."

"Now?"

"Yes, now. You don't want to leave her like this. She's hurting, and she needs to hear your apology tonight."

"You're right, Dad. Thanks."

Thomas watched the young man. His son was a good person. Thomas was confident Michael would come through this with a stronger determination to control his temper. Uttering a silent prayer for his son and for Bree, Thomas left the cookhouse and joined the men and women who were busy cleaning up after that night's party. Luckily, the majority of them were blissfully ignorant of the fight that had erupted in the kitchen. Thomas just hoped that the rumor mill wouldn't start running rampant with escalating stories of the violence.

Chapter 16

Michael wandered away from the noise and bustle of the ranch compound. He was sure Bree wouldn't have rejoined the throng. At least not yet. She'd been too upset. He'd hated the sight of her tears, knowing he had been the cause of her distress.

He still felt the muscles of his stomach tighten at the sight and sound of Chuck Laird's jealousy. And Michael had to admit to himself that he was jealous too. He knew how determinedly Chuck was pursuing Bree. Maybe tonight's little altercation would show the boy that he wasn't in the running for Bree's affection. Even as he thought that, Michael wondered if he was still in the running himself.

The quiet night calmed his nerves, and he stopped, suddenly sensing the presence of another person. He looked around, his eyes adjusting to the moonlit night, and he saw her.

She was sitting on the stoop of his father's house, watching him.

He hesitated only slightly before continuing his approach. He sat next to her on the top step, not touching her but his senses aware of her nearness.

Silence wrapped around them, and Michael found it difficult to utter the words he so desperately wanted to say. Finally he looked at her, his eyes beseeching. "I'm so sorry, Bree."

She looked at him, the emotion in her eyes masked by the night, but he saw the gentle nod of her head. "I know you are, Michael."

She sounded so distant that Michael gulped, wondering if he should continue. "I had no business getting so angry . . . and so possessive . . . tonight." In the face of Bree's stillness, he plunged on. "I don't know why I felt so jealous of Chuck. I let him provoke me . . ."

Michael echoed the words his father had used earlier that evening, "and I lost my temper. It's been a long time since I've gotten that angry. I'm sorry you were hurt tonight, Bree. I will never hurt you again—if you think you could give me a second chance."

The contriteness in Michael's voice penetrated the shell of Bree's hurt. She glanced at him and saw that he was looking away from her now, wringing his hands together as he waited for her reply. He heard her take a deep breath, and then he felt the soft touch of her hand slipping between his clasped hands, her fingers linking with his, joining her to him with the promise of forgiveness.

Chapter 17

The next day, Bree went to the kitchen early to start preparing for breakfast. When the door leading to the outside opened, she felt her cheeks flush with surprise when she saw Chuck Laird enter the room.

He stood several feet away from her, his hat in his hands, turning it awkwardly. His head was bent, and his shaggy hair was falling into his face. Finally, he looked up and Bree gasped at the sight. Bruises clustered around both eyes, and his nose looked sore and swollen. Instantly she felt sorry for him, and she approached him, holding out her hand in friendship.

He took her fingers and shyly squeezed. She gave him a sympathetic smile. "Oh, Chuck. This didn't have to happen."

"I know, Bree. I am so sorry. I've been such a creep lately, and I'm sorry. For everything."

Bree smiled again at her friend, then dropped his hand and stepped close to him, putting her arms around him in an impulsive hug. "I know you are, Chuck. Apology accepted."

Chuck dropped his hat on the floor and returned Bree's hug. "I don't want to lose your friendship, Bree."

"You haven't. What would I do without your teasing and your little pranks to keep me on my toes?"

Chuck stepped away from Bree and bent down to pick up his hat, the movement hiding his expression. When he straightened up, he grinned at her, a sheepish look on his face. He appeared to be humble and penitent, and Bree couldn't resist giving him a final hug.

"Thank you for forgiving me, Bree. It means the world to me that you're not going to hold this against me."

Bree reassured him once more before he turned and hurriedly left the kitchen. She sighed, grateful to have things settled between them, but weary of the constant need to defend herself from her friend.

Chapter 18

The crispness of the late September morning and the hint of oncoming winter added fuel to the feverish activity of the ranch. Cowboys hurried from one place to another, ensuring that the equipment and supplies needed for the fall cattle drive were in place. Bree felt the excitement and anticipation pushing her as she scurried around the kitchen. She knew that Brock and Shari were beside themselves at the idea of camping out with the cowboys. Bree had to admit to herself that she, too, was excited.

Steve had told her that traditionally, the fall roundup wasn't as elaborate as the one held in the spring. Generally, the cowboys took their bedrolls and packed food in their saddlebags for the days spent out on the mountain ranges. But Steve had broken that tradition a few years ago after he'd purchased the new, modernized chuckwagon. The men liked having cooked meals, and somehow, things seemed to run more smoothly when a cook went along to help prepare meals.

Bree was grateful that the Sheridans' ranch had established their own tradition relating to the fall roundup. She was especially thankful for Brock and Shari's sakes. They were so excited, and she loved the sight of their sparkling eyes and smiling faces.

She left the kitchen, securing the door behind her. The chuckwagon waiting out in the ranch yard was loaded and ready to go. Bree felt a surge of exhilaration as she approached the waiting wagon, which was hitched to Ben Laird's pickup. She peeked into the pickup bed to make sure all of her personal items had been stored. She'd taken special care to ensure she had extra clothes for her siblings as well as warm sleeping bags and foam pads. This would be their first experience camping, and even though she was eager to participate in a new adventure, she was overly conscientious, wanting to make sure they would have everything they could possibly need. She had received advice from Sarah, as well as from Thomas and Michael. They had all teasingly reassured her that she and the kids were going to be well prepared.

"Bree, are you ready to pull out?" Ben Laird's voice intruded on her musings.

"Yep, I think we're all set."

"Good. Let's go, then. The men are about ready to pull out. We should be able to reach the base camp well ahead of them and have everything set up by the time they pull in. Where's Sarah?"

"She had to run to the homestead. She'll be back any minute."

Bree tightened her hold on her heavily padded denim jacket, patting the pocket to make sure she still had her warm leather gloves. She felt her insides tighten with nervousness. She smiled at Ben, grateful for his assistance but wishing Michael had been assigned the task of accompanying Sarah and herself to the base camp. Bree's eyes took on a faraway dreaminess as she lost herself in pleasant thoughts of her relationship with Michael. He still hadn't kissed her yet, but they had come close. He had taken to holding her hand when they went for walks, and Bree felt her pulse quicken at the thought of spending time with him during the roundup. Her mind was filled with images of romantic walks under the wide-open, star-studded night skies when Ben gently nudged her with his elbow. "Hey, Bree, you still with me?"

Bree refocused her eyes on Ben's face and blushed, embarrassed that she had been caught daydreaming. She gave him a nervous smile and then turned as a movement caught her eye.

"Here comes Sarah now," Bree announced, grateful for the interruption. She glanced up and watched Sarah as she approached.

The two women were dressed similarly in sturdy, tight-fitting denim jeans, warm flannel shirts, heavy boots, and thick, woolen socks. Sarah wore a dark blue, down-filled parka, and her blond hair was pulled back in a tidy bun. The sleek hairstyle emphasized the grace and mature beauty of her features. She looked tall and graceful in her rugged, outdoorsy clothes, and Bree watched her in admiration as Sarah joined them.

Sarah was silently thinking that Bree had never looked lovelier. The young girl's wild, auburn curls were caught back in a ponytail with unruly tendrils escaping to dance around her delicate face. Sarah smiled warmly as she joined Bree and Ben.

Sarah glanced at Ben. He looked rugged and handsome, his closely shaven cheeks already showing the hint of a five o'clock shadow. His dark hair shone like ebony in the cool morning air, and his dark eyes glowed warmly in his face.

He winked, his face creased in teasing lines. "I swear, I gotta be the luckiest ol' cowhand in these here parts. I get to ride in the company of two of the prettiest ladies around." Pushing his wide-brimmed hat back on his head, jauntily angling it back, he continued, "Well, ladies, if you all are ready, let's move 'em on out."

Bree and Sarah both laughed and clambered into the cab of the truck, Bree sitting in the middle. Ben climbed in next to her and quickly had the truck in motion.

"I'm glad you're riding with us, Sarah. I really appreciate your offer to help set up the cook wagon."

"It's my pleasure, Bree." Sarah had volunteered to help their young cook, willingly sacrificing the time she could have spent with her husband on the long ride to camp. As they bounced down the rutted road leading to the far-reaching corners of the ranch, the three companions chatted amiably for the duration of the trip.

Bree enjoyed the drive and hoped that Brock and Shari were having fun too. After Sarah had offered to ride along with Bree and Ben, Steve had invited the youngsters to ride with him and Thomas. Most of the men were riding their horses to the site of the roundup, but Steve was driving his truck, his horses traveling comfortably behind it in their trailer. Brock and Shari had eagerly accepted his invitation, and Bree hoped they weren't trying the patience of the men with their endless chatter. She smiled, though, realizing that was a vain hope, especially considering the level of excitement that had catapulted them both out of bed that morning before dawn.

It took Ben almost an hour to drive to the clearing that would form the base camp. There was a large, open area that would serve as the central hub for camp, and the chuckwagon would sit on the outer edge of this area. Sturdy, weathered corrals would hold the extra horses, and as the cattle were herded together, they would be brought to the large patch of pasture bordering the circular camp area. Across the clearing, far enough away for a semblance of privacy, was an old, wooden privy.

A large, charcoal-blackened circle showed the remains of former camps, and Ben grimaced when he said, "I guess my first order of business will be to gather some firewood. These ol' cowpokes won't admit it, but they like the romance of a blazing campfire to keep them company at night. While you ladies get the chuckwagon set up, I'll see what I can do about gathering some wood."

Bree and Sarah companionably worked side by side as they prepared the small, compact chuckwagon for work. Its ovens and stoves were operated by propane, and it included an intricate network of cupboards and drawers that provided adequate storage for the supplies that would be used.

The fare during the roundup would be simple but hearty. Relying on staples such as flour, cornmeal, sugar, coffee, sourdough, powdered milk, and beans, Bree would be turning out meals of sourdough hotcakes and biscuits, chilis, stews, and lots of strong, hot, black coffee. There were also packets of hot cocoa for the children, as well as for Thomas, Michael, and Lex, who didn't drink coffee.

"How's it comin', ladies?"

Sarah smiled at Ben as he dumped his final armload of sap-heavy logs on the towering stack he had piled a few feet away from the fire circle. "I think we're all set to go. Any idea when the guys are gonna show up for lunch?"

"Well, it's already past noon. They should be here soon. What've you got planned?"

Bree answered his query. "We're just doing a cold lunch today since we weren't sure what time we'd be eating. We have sandwiches, chips, fruit, and brownies."

"Think anyone would mind if I dug in first?" Ben asked with a smile. Rubbing his taut stomach, he said, "I'm starved! Are you ladies willin' to satisfy the appetite of a hardworking cowboy?"

There was a look in his eye that made Bree uncomfortable, but she tried to shake off the unwelcome feeling, her nervousness making her laughter ring with a false brightness. "I'll set those sandwiches out now, and you can eat whenever you like."

Ben smiled at her and left with his plate of food. Bree shrugged away the sense of awkwardness that had accompanied Ben's teasing, flirtatious remarks. She liked and trusted him. Twice during the last month she had accompanied him on afternoon horseback rides. Bree had enjoyed his company on those rides across the mountain meadows. He had been funny and charming, his wit amusing and sharp. She liked Ben and knew that the feeling was mutual.

Soon, the small camp area rang with the laughter and rowdiness of the gathering cowboys. The horses in the nearby corral added to the din with their whinnying snorts and dust kicked up by stomping feet.

The rest of the day passed quickly, and it was with a sigh of relief that Bree climbed into her sleeping bag that night. It was her first experience sleeping under the stars and she found herself lying there for a while looking up at the incredible, heavenly display. She couldn't help but reflect on Brock and Shari. They loved the hustle, the dirt, and the noise, but mostly they seemed to be cherishing the loving companionship of the cowboys, the Sheridans, and their sister Bree.

They had eagerly crawled into their sleeping bags, stretched out beside Bree, exhausted but unwilling to admit how tired they were. Their excited chatter had faded within minutes, however. The moment their heads had touched their pillows, their eyes had drifted shut and they had fallen into a sound sleep.

A quiet voice sounded near Bree's ear, and she started with surprise. "Oh, Thomas, you startled me."

"Sorry, child. I was wondering if I could toss my bedroll out next to you and the younguns?"

"Sure. I'd like that," Bree answered. She had spread their sleeping bags near the outer edge of the clearing, preferring the quieter perimeter to the rustles and snores that surrounded the softly glowing fire.

Thomas took a moment to straighten his bedroll before he kicked off his boots and crawled under the covers with a groan. "My good-ness! I think these old bones of mine are tryin' to tell me they prefer their mattress back home."

Bree smiled in the darkness as Thomas settled in and the stillness of the night covered them like a cloak. The air was crisp and cool, and

Bree was grateful for the warmth of her down-filled sleeping bag. She turned on her side and gazed through the gloom at the indistinct form lying next to her, suddenly thankful for Thomas's reassuring presence.

They were silent for a few moments, allowing the aura of the crisp autumn night to soothe their tiredness.

"Thomas?"

"Yes, darlin'?"

Bree was silent for a moment, her pending question hanging in the air. She paused for so long that Thomas propped himself up on his elbow and peered at her through the darkness.

Before he could speak, however, Bree's voice broke the stillness. "This is so great!"

Thomas was taken aback for a moment, then he began to chuckle. "Yep. It's pretty great all right."

Bree giggled. "I'm so glad we're here. The kids love it."

Thomas smiled in the darkness, but Bree heard the emotion in his voice when he softly said, "And we love having them—having all of you—with us."

A few moments of silence passed between them, then Thomas began to speak. "You know, sis, I don't think you and them younguns can ever imagine how much you've blessed this old man's life." He paused before continuing. "I mean, my life is good. I love my son. It's just nice to have something young and fresh around. It makes some of the pain from the past seem not so burdensome."

Bree stifled a yawn, and Thomas spoke quickly. "I'm sorry, honey. I'm probably keeping you awake."

"Oh, no! I'm fine, Thomas. I'm just relaxing. Please . . . continue."

Thomas began to speak, completing the history he had begun telling Bree a few weeks earlier.

"My poor, sweet Linda. She was never the same after we lost Tom."

The rest of Thomas's story revealed how he had felt himself wither and die inside as he watched the closed coffin containing his eldest son being lowered into the dark, unforgiving earth. He was inconsolable. He turned inward, blind to the needs of his wife and younger sons. They were a family split apart by the hands of a distant war, and they were unable to bridge the chasm that was threatening to rend their lives.

Thomas had turned from his family and found solace in the amber depths of a liquor bottle. Somehow, though, he was able to maintain a semblance of sobriety during working hours, and years passed before anyone realized, or admitted to, the depth of his drinking problem.

Carl stayed on the ranch after his return from Vietnam, drifting through the days and finally coming to terms with the changes that his brother's death had wrought. He moved into the bunkhouse with the other single ranch hands, distancing himself from the pain of his parents' distress. Linda continued to provide for the physical needs of her family, hiding behind the wall of her silence. "Michael was so little. Somehow, she took care of him, but it wasn't the same. She was grieving so hard for Tom that she forgot Michael needed her.

"I also forgot that Michael needed me. And Linda and Carl. They needed me too. But I forgot about them. I forgot about them all."

"How old was Michael?"

"He was still a baby when Tom was killed. He was born that year, a few months before Tom was drafted. The aimlessness of our lives came to an abrupt end, literally for Carl and Linda, seven years after Tom's death." Thomas explained how the ranch had been shaken by the sudden loss of Richard Sheridan, Steve's grandfather. His life had been claimed by a sudden, massive heart attack. The Sunday following his funeral, Linda succeeded in getting Thomas, Carl, and Michael to accompany her into town to attend church. She tearfully pled with them, insisting that they all needed to do this as a family.

Carl and Michael weren't hard to convince, and Thomas went along only because it was easier than resisting. He knew that he wouldn't sit through the service anyway, and he didn't. As soon as Linda and the boys were settled in a back pew of the small Methodist church, Thomas excused himself and disappeared through the back door.

By the time he drained the large bottle of cheap whiskey, Linda and Carl were waiting for him in their old, battered pickup. Linda told him that Michael was staying in town, having been invited to have dinner with a friend. Staggering only slightly, Thomas climbed behind the wheel, silent and morose as he peeled out of the parking lot of the small church.

The first leg of the trip home took place without incident, and it wasn't until Thomas crested the mountain summit and headed down the curving road into the high valley that the accident occurred. The strong alcohol finally kicked in, and Thomas felt himself floating, free from the pain of his sorrow. The truck picked up speed as it careened down the winding mountain road. Linda and Carl begged Thomas to slow down, but in his drunken stupor, he lost control of the vehicle. As it flew over a small precipice and wrapped around a giant tamarack, Thomas was thrown free.

Carl and Linda died instantly.

Thomas awakened three days later, sober and devastated with the knowledge that he had caused the death of his wife and son. He felt the hopelessness and despair of his guilt even as he continued to crave the stupefying effects of his whiskey bottle. Deep inside, however, he found a reservoir of determination. He still had Michael. Michael gave purpose to his life.

Instead of turning to the bottle as he had in the past, Thomas turned to Lucas Sheridan, Steve's father and the new owner and boss of the ranch. Lucas was dealing with his own feelings of loss as he attempted to take his father's place in running the ranch. Together, Thomas and Lucas found the strength to continue on, and they forged a bond of mutual strength and support.

Two weeks after leaving the hospital, barely on his feet after the devastating automobile accident that had claimed the lives of his beloved wife and son, Thomas was introduced to the Mormon missionaries. A friend from Alcoholics Anonymous told him about the Latter-day Saint Church, sharing their belief in eternal life and eternal families. Thomas was so intrigued by the idea that he agreed to meet with the young representatives of the Church.

He still kept in touch with the two young men who had taught him the gospel. The comfort and the peace he felt after hearing their message convinced him that he wanted what they offered. Their message of hope, salvation, and eternal love struck a chord in his aching heart. He had grasped the gospel's promise of eternity and never looked back.

He quietly went about his business, living his life patterned after the truths he had found, finding peace and reassurance in the knowledge that Linda, Tom, and Carl were together, and that one day he and Michael could be reunited with them.

His heart ached painfully with the understanding that he had caused the deaths of his wife and son, yet he had found a joy stemming from his newly found faith in God and the wondrous plan designed to reunite families in His kingdom.

"I've been sober ever since, Bree."

Bree smiled. "I'm so glad you found something to help you heal. Michael needed you back then. He still does."

"I know, sweetheart. I need him too. He's done real good. He used to have a problem with his temper. Everything he went through as a kid—my drinking, losing his mom and brothers. He had some problems. But as he's grown up, he's changed. That tempestuous, angry kid has grown into a well-balanced, even-tempered man. The Church has helped there.

"During the time right after I was baptized, I was still struggling. I'm afraid I wasn't there for Michael, not like I needed to be." Thomas's sadness seemed to overcome him for a moment, but then he straightened his shoulders and his voice became firm again. "The bishop and Michael's teachers really took him under their wings. He changed. He's grown into a great man."

Bree spoke cautiously. "Someone mentioned that he used to have problems. I found it hard to believe, though. He's always so gentle with the animals, with the kids," Bree paused, "with me."

"That's the real Michael, not the angry kid he used to be."

"I'm glad he has you for a father. You've done a good job."

"It's not because of me, Bree. Michael needed a lot more than what I could give him. It was God and the people at church who really changed him. You know, you really should come to church with me one of these days."

"I know. One of these days, Thomas. Just not yet." Bree couldn't explain her hesitancy in going with him. "I hope it doesn't hurt your feelings when I turn down your invitation."

Thomas smiled gently at Bree, "Oh, no. It doesn't hurt my feelings. I just miss you on Sundays. I think Michael does too."

Bree allowed a gentle smile to grace her lips, a faint tinge of pink staining her cheeks. "I know. He's asked me to go to church too. So have Brock and Shari. I told them the same thing I told you. Maybe one of these days. Just not yet."

Bree settled back into her sleeping bag, drawing the edges close under her chin. The peaceful night lulled her into a drowsy state of half-sleep. She yawned deeply and laughed when she heard an answering yawn from the old man resting in his bedroll next to her.

"Good night, Thomas."

"Good night, darlin'. Sweet dreams."

Bree closed her eyes and turned toward the children. She fell asleep, her lips curved with a smile of contentment and gratitude in her heart for the sweet man who had adopted the Nelson siblings as his surrogate grandchildren.

Chapter 19

As the night passed, the darkness broken only by the distant stars, Bree slept next to Thomas, comfortably safe in his company. While she slumbered, she was unaware of the phantomlike figure wandering silently through camp, his mind in turmoil and his hands hanging by his side. His fingers flexed and released in clutching movements as he rounded the corner of the chuckwagon. He stood and watched the sleeping woman and gasped at the intensity of the fury he felt when he realized that the old man had become his adversary.

The nearness of the sleeping children also fueled his unreasonable rage. It had been years since he had felt such anger, but this summer he had found himself fighting it constantly. He felt lost and confused as a result of the tempestuous emotions boiling in his heart. He loved Bree so much. He loved everything about her, including her devotion to Brock and Shari. Where did this intense resentment come from?

And Thomas! How could he be so searingly jealous of an old man?

Questions about the old man and the children flew in his head, causing a frenzy of confusion. Were they going to be a problem? Did they pose a threat to his plans for Bree?

The man shivered at the unbidden and unwelcome thought that entered his head. *If so, they will have to go.*

Chapter 20

The eastern ridges of the mountain valley came alive with the glow of day as the diamond-bright stars faded in the approaching dawn. Bree pulled her heavy denim jacket closer around her shoulders while she finished the morning preparations for breakfast. Camp had begun stirring an hour ago when the first glint of morning was only a faint line on the horizon. She had climbed out of the warm nest of her sleeping bag, softly calling to Brock and Shari until they turned with a groan and followed her out into the cold, morning air.

She gave them both a short list of chores to do, and Bree smiled when they eagerly accepted her mandates with no arguments or whining, too excited to waste time fussing about a few chores. They washed up and dressed in clean clothes, not wanting to waste a moment of that day's adventures.

The rest of the ranch hands were quick in rising, and the day soon got underway. The sounds of bellowing cattle and whinnying horses accompanied the symphony of nature, greeting the awakening world.

Bree was kept busy cooking breakfast, and the warming ovens kept the stacks of hotcakes and piles of bacon and eggs warm. When she was finally able to take a moment and catch her breath, she leaned her back against the side of the chuckwagon, her eyes taking on a faraway look as she studied the emerging vista of the high mountain pastures and the far-reaching mountain range. Bree felt a quiet reverence encompass her, and she realized how beautiful the world was. She felt an overwhelming sense of gratitude for the chance she had to live in such a lovely part of the country.

"Stop daydreaming and get those victuals served, woman."

Bree jumped and then turned to smile at Ben as he came up behind her, bringing her out of her reverie. "Patience, cowboy. Haven't you learned that you have to wait for all good things?" Bree's voice was teasing.

Just then, Steve Sheridan walked over to join them and asked, "How soon till breakfast is ready, Bree?"

"It's ready now, Steve. I was just getting ready to call everyone."

As she finished ringing the bell, Bree turned to greet Sarah, who had joined them, a wide-brimmed hat perched jauntily on her head. Her brown eyes were soft and loving as she put her hand through the crook of Steve's arm and stood close to him. "Something smells wonderful, Bree. I'm starving. It always surprises me how hungry I get when I sleep out in the open."

"Everything is ready, so help yourself."

Sarah took a plate from Bree, and soon a line of hungry men joined her, filling their plates high with food. Bree grinned when she noticed Michael helping Brock and Shari, his face aglow as he helped the two youngsters through the breakfast line. Brock and Shari smiled at her when they filed past. She returned their grins and then transferred her gaze to Michael.

She felt her heart flutter from the intensity of Michael's look. The emotion in his expression was serious, and Bree felt drawn to him in a way that she had never before experienced. Finally, someone called his name, and Michael broke his gaze away from Bree, his face softening and his smile teasing. He left her with a flirtatious wink.

Bree felt her breath catch in her lungs. She seemed unable to take her eyes off the retreating figure of the young cowboy. She pursed her lips and finally expelled the air she had been holding in her lungs. She felt flushed and flustered by her emotions, confused by the brief and wordless encounter. But she was excited too. With a determined set to her jaw, Bree turned back to the tasks at hand.

Later, after Sarah helped Bree put the last of the dishes away, the older woman said, "I can't wait until tonight. I talked Steve into joining me at the hot springs later this evening. After a day in the saddle, a nice, long soak in that hot mineral water will be so relaxing and therapeutic."

"That does sound nice. Are the hot springs close?"

"Not too far away, maybe three or four miles along the slope of the western ridge over there." Bree followed Sarah's pointing finger to the distant horizon, where the grasses of the valley rose to meet the base of the mountain.

"What are your plans for the rest of today, Sarah?"

"I'm not sure," Sarah answered. "I think I'll ride with the men. They can always use an extra hand to search the foothills for the livestock. It's amazing how many hiding places the cattle can find. And heaven forbid they should wander into the woods."

Bree grimaced, grateful that she had her responsibilities to keep her busy in camp. Even though she loved her mount, a lovely bay mare Steve had given her, she was still a little nervous on horseback, and she wouldn't want to ride all day long. She would probably take Sunflower out for a ride in the afternoon. She was getting more comfortable riding, but she still preferred to keep her two feet on the ground.

Sarah smiled when Bree voiced her preference. "I understand. I grew up with horses and riding with the cattle. It can be pretty daunting if you're not used to it."

As the morning sun rose higher in the sky, the mists and dew of the new dawn melted away, but the air maintained its crisp coolness, and Bree knew that winter was just around the corner. She thought enviously about Sarah's planned tryst with Steve at the hot springs that evening. The hot water would feel wonderful, and Bree thought about how lovely it would be to relax in the warm, therapeutic spring.

With a gleam in her eye, she had a sudden thought. *Why not!* Smiling at the daring plan formulating in her mind, Bree set about scrubbing and peeling potatoes and carrots for the beef stew she was making for lunch. *If I plan this right, I can save myself a few hours labor later on this afternoon!* Her face was bright with anticipation, and her thoughts resounded with silent encouragement. This whole roundup was an adventure, and why should she limit herself?

With a soft sigh, Bree realized that there was another reason she longed for some time on her own. Her life since coming to the ranch had been filled with busy, hectic days. There were times she longed for solitude, and suddenly Bree became aware of a hunger gnawing at her spirit. It was a yearning to be by herself, to be unencumbered by responsibility. She loved Brock and Shari, and she would never do anything to separate herself from them, but like most adults with children entrusted to their care, she seldom had time for herself. She merely wished for a couple of hours to be on her own in a peaceful setting to contemplate the events that were taking place in her life.

She had so many things to ponder. Her heart was being drawn inexorably toward a blue-eyed cowboy, and she wondered if this was what it felt like to be falling in love. She didn't know. But she hoped so. Thoughts of Michael also included his father, Thomas, and the gentle influence he was having on her family. She had been touched by the story of his struggles and his losses, but she had also been impressed by his faith. She sensed there was something in that faith that could bring her solace, especially when the grief and sorrow she felt for her parents swelled to the surface.

Looking around the deserted campground, Bree realized that she didn't need to leave in order to find solitude. Yet she knew that if she stayed in camp, she would inevitably fill her time with chores. She felt something compelling and urgent pulling her to ride away, even if for just a couple of hours.

The children were enjoying themselves, riding with the cowboys under the careful and watchful eye of Thomas and Michael. Bree knew she didn't have to worry about them, so why not have an adventure of her own? She would take Sunflower and go exploring this afternoon. With any kind of luck, she would find the hot springs. If not, that would be okay too.

Eagerly she refocused her attention on the tasks at hand. An hour later, Bree stepped away from the chuckwagon, a large pot of aromatic stew bubbling away on the burner and a pan of sourdough biscuits baking in the oven. Lunch would be ready on time. She had tossed extra potatoes and vegetables into the pot so there would be enough of the stew left over to serve as a side dish with tonight's dinner of pan-fried steak.

Later, after the bustle and noise of the lunchtime routine had faded and the cowboys, accompanied by Bree's excited siblings, had returned to their afternoon work, Bree made sure the chuckwagon was clean and tidy. She safely stored the leftover stew, wrapped the leftover biscuits in plastic wrap to keep them fresh, and shook the sealed container of marinating beefsteak. Everything was set for dinner. When she returned from her excursion, it would take but a few minutes to grill the steaks and warm up the stew. Bree pinned a hastily scribbled note on the corkboard at the back of the chuckwagon, knowing that either Ben Laird or Steve Sheridan would automatically check the message board upon arriving back at camp.

Bree smiled to herself, confident that should anyone arrive back at camp and wonder about her absence, they would find her note and realize she was safe. Her note stated that she would be back by five o'clock just on the cusp of sundown, and an hour before supper was to be served.

It took Bree several minutes to saddle Sunflower, but she was soon on her way, walking the gentle mare toward the western ridge, mentally following the direction pointed out that morning by Sarah. The late afternoon sun felt warm on her shoulders while the chill of an autumn breeze made her feel grateful for the warmth of her padded jacket and the comfort of the softly knitted scarf draped around her neck. It was a soft shade of periwinkle blue, reflecting the color of her eyes, and Bree treasured the scarf because it was the last gift she had received from her parents.

Bree felt tears well in her eyes, the thought of her missing parents more poignant in the face of the happiness she and her siblings had found on the Sheridans ranch. She knew that her parents would want her to be happy, and she gratefully acknowledged the blessings that had come into her life. She loved her job, and she loved Steve and Sarah Sheridan. They had drawn Bree, Brock, and Shari into the lives of the ranching family with loving warmth and acceptance that left Bree breathless. In addition, there were the friendships of so many others: Thomas, the Larsens, Ben Laird and his nephew Chuck. And Michael.

Especially Michael. He was fast becoming the best friend Bree had ever known. They spent as much time together as they could. Even when they were separated, Bree felt his presence. The memory of his searching eyes, the warmth of his smile, the sound of his voice, and the touch of his hands all combined to send shivers of delight coursing over her skin.

Bree's eyes were dreamy, her mind faraway, when all of a sudden Sunflower stumbled. Bree automatically clutched the reins tighter and strengthened the grip of her knees on the side of the saddle.

Righting herself as Sunflower regained her footing, Bree clicked to the horse and said, "Whoa, girl." She took a few minutes to look around, realizing that she had traveled farther than she had intended. She had left behind the grassy mountain meadow and was surrounded by the heavy shrubbery and underbrush that covered the mountainside. Towering trees shaded the earth, and Bree wondered how Sunflower could have found the winding path that they were following.

"I guess I overshot the hot springs," Bree said aloud to herself. Patting the mare on the neck, she continued, "We better turn around, girl. If this path led us here, it can lead us back out."

Gathering up the reins, Bree pulled to her right, trying to get Sunflower turned. The mare became jumpy and unexpectedly stubborn. She shied from Bree's command, and, unsure of how to handle the suddenly uncooperative horse, Bree tightened her hold. The mare responded to Bree's nervousness with an increase in her flightiness, and a sudden loud snapping in the nearby underbrush caused the horse to rear back on her hind legs.

Bree lost her grip and found herself flying through the air. She landed on her back, and lay there, winded. With a gasp of dismay, she watched as Sunflower turned and bolted back down the mountainside. Bree sat up and brushed at the leaves and dust covering her jacket and clinging to the back of her hair.

Standing up and grimacing at the twinge of discomfort from her hard landing, she looked around. She was standing on a rugged but clearly marked path. Stones and broken branches littered the path, and she could only assume they had been the cause of Sunflower's earlier stumble. The heavy foliage shrouded the forest in gloom, and Bree suddenly became worried. It seemed darker than she expected it to be for the time of day. She looked at her wristwatch and realized that it was later than she had thought. "I must have really been daydreaming," Bree muttered to herself. With a resigned sigh, she turned and started to follow her runaway mount. "I better get started back. I have a long walk ahead of me."

Bree immediately thought about the children, as well as Steve and Sarah, Thomas, and Michael. They would all worry about her when she didn't appear back at camp by five o'clock, and it was already past four-thirty. She knew that she must have ridden for over two hours. And it would take her much longer than that to walk the distance back to camp. Her thoughts brightened when she realized that they would likely send out a search party for her.

That thought brought her some relief, but she also felt guilty knowing that she was causing them worry and extra work. Determinedly, Bree tugged on the tail of her jacket and loosened the knot of her scarf. She had just started to walk when the sound of breaking twigs sounded in the twilight gloominess of the forest. Bree jumped, startled at the sudden sound. Her heart rate increased and she paused, unexpectedly wary. It was the same kind of sound that had spooked Sunflower. Bree swallowed the lump of fear in her throat, and glancing over her shoulder, she began to walk, quickening her pace as she kept looking around. Her eyes darted from shadow to shadow, and she gulped when she realized how quickly the evening's obscurity was descending on the mountainside.

Chapter 21

The man was hidden by the dense underbrush, concealed even further by the dusky shadows that were cloaking the winding mountain trail. He had been following Bree for over an hour, having caught sight of her riding toward the western ridge. He had been curious when her mount entered the forested mountainside and had cantered his mount to catch up with her.

His first thought had been to join her, to take advantage of the opportunity to spend some time alone with her. But once he drew close enough to see her face, he could see that she was lost in thought. *Maybe she's thinking about me!*

Excitement and desire had swept over him, and he decided to follow her at a distance. He had ridden the ranch more than Bree, including exploring the mountain trails, and he knew that there was a parallel path a few feet away. He had turned his horse in that direction, staying with her but never close enough to give away his presence.

He had taken pleasure in her nearness while becoming more and more disinclined to reveal his presence. He wondered about her purpose in riding and soon realized that she had no idea she had wandered so far away from camp. His realization was confirmed when he saw the sudden stiffening of her shoulders and how she halted her mount. He sensed her confused uncertainty when she turned her head back and forth, studying the dappled grayness of the forested surroundings.

His horse had suddenly stepped back, becoming antsy at the stillness caused by his staying hand on the reins. The loud snapping of a branch under the horse's hoof caused Bree's mount to startle and rear, and the man watched as Bree landed hard. His first instinct had been to run to her, to make sure she was unhurt.

When her horse bolted and she sat up, gazing after it with a dumbfounded look on her face, the idea of revealing his presence repulsed him. He grinned, a wicked light of anticipation shining from his eyes. He would continue to follow her, to see what she would do, how she would react.

I'll follow her, then when I can, I'll get in front of her. Maybe if I frighten her enough, when she sees me, she'll run right into my arms.

The cruelty of his plan failed to impact his conscience. Dismounting, he tugged lightly on the horse's reins, causing it to follow him as he walked slowly down the parallel trail. It was getting darker and more difficult to maintain sight of Bree through the ground cover. He sped up, determined not to lose contact with her. Even though he could no longer clearly see her, he sensed her anxiety. He anticipated with selfish satisfaction the moment she would rush into his arms, seeking safety from the danger stalking her through the night.

Chapter 22

Trudging through the inky canopy of the forest, Bree found herself shedding the uneasiness that had befallen her immediately following her fall from Sunflower. She felt oddly safe wrapped in the cocoon of darkness and isolation. The nocturnal sounds of the woodland had ceased to frighten her, and Bree found herself enjoying the hike along the mountain trail. The chill of the autumn night spurred a brisk pace, and she felt invigorated.

The moon had appeared, full and shimmering in the night sky, giving depth to the wooded land, when a sharp noise to her left chased away the enjoyable sensations of her solitary traipse. Suddenly, Bree felt the imminence of danger, and she froze, aware of the foolishness of her situation. As she realized her folly, a specter moved and separated from the darkness.

* * *

The man, still and watchful, felt his pulse quicken. He continued to follow her as the woods thinned and she approached the valley floor. The thick ground cover, however, provided him coverage, and he took a step toward her. The leaves, dry and brittle, crackled loudly in the hush of the night.

Bree, standing motionless, stirred when the crackling leaves penetrated the quiet. When the man took another step, the rustle and snap of breaking twigs sounded loudly in the darkness. She turned her head, and only the curtain of night kept her from seeing him.

Hidden by the safety of the nighttime shadows, the man smiled, taking another step forward. Bree stood poised for flight. Licking his hard lips, the excitement of his game coursing through him like fire, the man whispered softly in the night, the sound carrying eerily through the dark on waves of terror, "I'm coming for you soon. Are you afraid, my darling?"

* * *

When the quietly spoken words reached Bree, she felt her heart turn to ice, and she cursed her own stupidity for being caught alone in the middle of the woods. She had felt so safe since coming to the Sheridans' ranch and had never imagined herself being in danger. Not here. Not now. But there was menace lurking in the shadows, and Bree was terrified. Turning, she began running as if all the demons of purgatory were pursuing her. She knew that her first line of defense was to get away, to run from the peril stalking her in the dark.

All of a sudden, the cold penetrated the layers of her clothing, and she realized that she was chilled to the bone. She felt like she was moving in slow motion as she clumsily fled through the forest. Whiplike fingers of tangled underbrush tore at Bree's clothing and cut the unprotected softness of her bare hands and face. Heedless to the pain, she stumbled along, breathless and exhausted, but every twist in the trail seemed masked with danger, and she didn't dare stop. The threat behind her was too close, too real.

Suddenly, Bree screamed as she was grabbed from the side of the trail. Fighting in a frenzy of terror, she lashed out at her captor. The stinging pain of flesh being ripped and torn brought realization to her fevered mind. She was caught in the brambles of a wild rosebush, its sharp thorns tangled in the soft yarn of her scarf. With a sob, Bree fought the offending rose branch, the sweet scent of dried blooms mocking her efforts to free herself. Disregarding the pain caused by the sharp thorns tearing the tender flesh of her hands, Bree looked over her shoulder in desperation.

The sound of slow, deliberate footsteps following her down the rock-strewn path reached her ears, and Bree gave a small cry of vexation. As the footsteps drew nearer, she tore the tangled scarf from around her neck. Dropping it, she quickly turned and stumbled over a protruding root. Bleeding hands quickly reached out to break her fall, and she hastened to her feet and continued her stumbling race down the winding trail.

* * *

When the man rounded a bend in the path, he stared at the frightened figure racing ahead of him in the dark. He gasped, watching her retreating figure being consumed by the folds of blackness.

Having lost sight of her, he turned his gaze to the tangled scarf hanging lifelessly on the wild rosebush. Reaching out, he grasped the fabric, clenching its soft folds in his tight grip. Slowly, he raised his hand and buried his face in the softness of the knitted material. Closing his eyes, he breathed in Bree's sweet scent.

With slow deliberation, the man reached into his pocket and brought out a small, gleaming object. With the flick of his finger, a blade, sharp and deadly, appeared. His jaw tensed as he stretched the scarf toward him. In a cold, calculating move, he struck quickly. The knife's blinding edge sliced through the tangled threads of yarn, freeing the garment to fall into his cruel grasp. Raising the perfumed folds to his face once more, he inhaled deeply before he whispered, "Don't be afraid, my darling."

With sudden speed, he pocketed the wicked knife and stuffed Bree's scarf down the front of his zippered jacket. If he was going to reach Bree first when she stumbled into camp, he had to get moving. With quick purpose, he mounted his horse and spurred it to a gallop, crashing through the underbrush, no longer worried about keeping his presence hidden from Bree. She knew he was there. If the loud noise of his retreat added to her fear, all the better.

Chapter 23

With a gasp of relief, Bree broke through the dense cover of thorny underbrush and sprinted out into the moonlit clearing. With a gasp of relief, she saw Sunflower standing with her head down, grazing on the meadow grass. With a silent prayer of gratitude that the gentle mare hadn't bolted all the way back to camp, Bree approached her and leaned against the mare's sturdy side. As the cold night air brushed over her sweat-drenched body, Bree shivered violently. Hastily, she mounted Sunflower and turned her toward camp.

Cold and frightened, Bree rode hard, fighting down the waves of terror washing over her. She had to get control. Soon, her choking, air-starved lungs relaxed their labored efforts and her pulse slowed, the adrenaline fading from her veins. She brushed a quivering hand across her face. Her cheeks felt stiff and unnatural, a mixture of dried tears and cold.

It wasn't long before she caught sight of a distant, glowing fire. Bree raced toward it, keeping her eyes fixed on the blazing light that welcomed her with its proffered protection. Trotting into the campground, Sunflower came to a stop, and Bree slowly dismounted. Her hair was a tangled mess hanging wildly down her back, and her eyes were large in her pale face. Her lips were dry and cracked, and angry red welts crossed her face and the backs of her hands. Wincing as she dropped the reins, Bree looked down at her hands. Angry, jagged lacerations that were weeping blood marred the softness of her palms.

The sound of her approach alerted the small group of people surrounding the fire. Two small shadows separated themselves from the crowd and came hurtling through the darkness. Bree found herself engulfed by her brother and sister. She dropped to her knees and returned their embrace, swallowing a silent sob.

"What happened to you, sissy?" "Where were you, Bree?" Brock and Shari asked their questions simultaneously.

Bree drew back and smiled at them. "I got lost in the woods for a little while, but I'm okay now."

Shari lifted a finger and pointed at Bree's face. "You're bleeding!" The little girl's chin quivered at the sight of Bree's injuries.

Brock stared at Bree, his mouth open and his eyes wide with worry. Seeing their concern, Bree tried to downplay her pain. "I'm okay, really. I just had a run-in with some bushes."

"Hey, Bree!"

Bree glanced up at Chuck Laird, who was hovering behind the children, the flickering light from the fire circle casting him in an eerie silhouette. Behind him was another figure, but Bree was focused on Chuck, and she overlooked the other man's presence.

Standing up, Bree took Brock and Shari by the hand and walked closer to the light of the fire. Chuck stared at her face. With growing concern, he shouted, "What in tarnation happened to you, Bree?"

A loud exclamation drew Bree's attention to the other man, standing behind Chuck.

Ben Laird stepped up to her and tilted her chin so that he could get a better look at the angry red welts covering her face. "Gracious, girl. Looks like the bush won this battle!"

Bree tried to smile, but fatigue and shock were setting in, and all she could do was nod. She suddenly found herself blinking back tears, impatient at her lack of control as the events of the last few hours caught up with her. Ben groaned, "Oh, Bree." Ignoring the irritation that flashed across his nephew's expressive face, Ben drew Bree into his arms, offering her the comfort of a hug.

Bree relaxed against him, but Ben exclaimed loudly when her knees buckled. Thanks to quick reflexes, he caught her just before she fell, then lifted her into his arms and carried her over to the fire. He set her down on the softness of his sleeping bag that was stretched out on the ground in front of the fire. "Hey, Chuck, get me the first-aid kit, would you please?"

Brock and Shari, concerned for their sister, followed Ben into the fire's glow. Chuck, who was standing behind Brock and Shari, stared at Bree.

"C'mon, Chuck, I need that first aid kit," Ben repeated.

At his uncle's impatient request, Chuck turned and said, "Sure. Hang in there, Bree. We'll get you fixed up."

Several minutes later, Brock and Shari settled down next to Bree, who sat wrapped in a blanket, her face cleaned and her scratches anointed with a soothing salve. Ben had muttered words of dismay when he saw her torn and bleeding hands. He had gently cleaned and bound them in soft, sterile gauze.

Just as they finished, the sound of pounding hooves sounded in the distance, and additional riders joined the small group surrounding the fire. Michael Reilly and Steve Sheridan dismounted and turned their horses loose to graze, with Sarah and Thomas right behind them. Soon Bree was surrounded by a group of her concerned friends.

Looking stern, his eyes fastened on Bree's pale and tired face, Steve demanded, "What's going on here?"

Ben looked up at his boss, his voice quiet. "Bree had a little accident. We just got her cleaned up, and she was going to tell us what happened."

Michael shouldered past Steve and knelt beside Ben, his hands reaching out to Bree as he gently stroked her cheek, his eyes resting on the angry-looking scratches marring the perfection of her skin. "Back off, Steve. She's in shock," Michael responded to Steve's curt inquiry.

Steve's lips pursed, and he glared at Michael's back for a few seconds. Taking a deep breath, he lifted his chin and gazed at the sparkling stars overhead, gathering his patience until he could say in a quieter voice, "I'm sorry, Bree." Sarah stepped up next to her husband and laid a gentle hand on his forearm, knowing that he often spoke brusquely when he was concerned.

Looking down at Bree, Steve joined the other men squatting next to the girl. "It's been a long night." Taking off his Stetson and running a hand through his matted hair, he looked down. "We were really worried about you when you didn't come back. We've been out looking."

Sarah dropped down beside Bree and said, "It's late. Let's eat, and then I think the kids should get ready and go to bed. Bree can fill us in on her little adventure after that."

Bree shifted on the ground and made an attempt to rise. Sarah put a restraining hand on her shoulder, "Oh, no you don't. I didn't mean for you to get the food on. I'll take care of that. From what I can see, you have everything almost ready." Sarah stood up and said, "Chuck, why don't you come help me?"

The young man arose, his eyes never leaving Bree's face. He stood for a moment, staring at her before he turned to follow Sarah to the chuckwagon.

Ben watched his nephew watching Bree, his gaze narrowing and a strange flicker of emotion on his face. "Thomas, why don't you come help me get the horses taken care of?" Before turning away, Ben let his gaze linger on Bree's face also. "I'm glad you made it back safely, Bree."

Bree smiled wanly. "Thank you, Ben, for taking such good care of me. I appreciate you."

Ben nodded and quietly responded, "You're welcome, honey."

Bree watched the tall foreman walk away, then turned when Thomas leaned down and kissed her gently on the cheek. He straightened slowly as if his joints were aching and turned toward Brock and Shari. "Why don't you younguns come and help an old man with his chores?"

Bree gave the children a quick squeeze before urging them to go with their old friend. Thomas, Brock, and Shari followed Ben's retreating figure, leaving Michael and Bree alone by the fire. Michael scooted over, sitting where Ben had squatted next to Bree.

Bree sighed and turned to face Michael. She found his gaze fastened on her, his eyes concerned as they studied the bruises and scratches marring the flawlessness of her skin. She returned his stare for several moments, suddenly feeling infused with glowing warmth that had nothing to do with the fiery embers crackling nearby.

A shimmer of moisture seemed to glisten in Michael's eyes as he whispered her name. "Bree!"

Bree's lips curved sweetly, no words needed to express the emotions in her. She found herself in Michael's arms, the muted sounds of activity in the camp fading as she felt herself relax into his embrace. His arms were strong and safe as he held her to his chest. With extreme care, Michael tilted her chin so that her lips were poised to greet his kiss.

Several minutes later, Bree stirred when Sarah approached with two plates loaded with food. Bree accepted Sarah's offering, though it was awkward handling the plate and fork with her bandaged hands. Somehow, she managed to begin eating. With a knowing smile and a twinkle in her eyes, Sarah quickly left the two to eat their meal alone.

Bree and Michael shared a few additional minutes of privacy while they ate, but their time alone was cut short when Brock and Shari scurried over to Bree.

Bree reached out and rumpled Brock's hair when he dropped down onto the ground next to her. "What've you been up to, buddy?"

"We helped do the dishes."

"You did!"

"Uh-huh! Us and Thomas did the dishes."

"I'm going to have to remember that when we get back home. I could sure use a couple of good helpers in the kitchen. Do you want to come do my dishes for me every day?"

Michael and Bree burst out laughing at the look of consternation that settled on the boy's face. Bree could tell that he wanted to shout a definite "No!" But she also knew he was afraid of hurting her feelings. Taking pity on Brock, she reached for him and gave him a quick hug, "That's okay, squirt. Doing the dishes is my job. You just do your own chores, and I'll be happy."

Just then, Thomas came for the children. "C'mon kids, me and Sarah are gonna help you get ready for bed. Sis," he looked at Bree, "we'll be back in a jiffy?"

Stretching, feeling sore and battered, Bree nodded. "Thanks, Thomas."

Just then, Steve and Ben joined them. Steve tilted his hat to the back of his head and said, "Kids, are you heading for bed? I need my two newest cowhands rested and ready to ride in the morning."

Brock and Shari grinned at Steve before wrapping their arms around Bree, hugging her intensely but being mindful of her scratched face. "I love you, sissy," Shari whispered into Bree's ear.

"I love you, too, punkin." Bree tugged one of Shari's pigtails.

"You, too, spud!" She slapped Brock's backside as he jumped up and grinned at her before trotting after Thomas.

"They're sure good kids."

Bree glanced up at Ben, momentarily startled at his height as she craned her neck backward. "Thank you, Ben. They are good kids."

Ben and Steve settled themselves on the ground next to Bree and Michael. They chatted quietly until Thomas and Sarah, who reported that Brock and Shari were already asleep, joined them.

"Okay, Bree. Why don't you tell us about your adventure tonight?" Steve's voice was grim.

Bree began describing her adventure in the forest. "I was so envious of your plan to go swimming at the hot springs. It sounded so wonderful, and I guess I thought I could find it on my own." Understanding seemed to soften the eyes of all the men but one.

* * *

He sat on the hard ground, his eyes glowing with a maelstrom of emotions as he listened to the musical cadence of Bree's voice describe her encounter with him as he stalked her through the night.

She left out some of the details and minimized the frenzy of her escape from him, but his heart beat faster as he remembered the excitement that had driven him to pursue her through the darkness of the night. And as she wound up her story, he joined the others in murmuring words of dismay and concern.

* * *

Sarah reached for Bree's hands. "Oh, honey. I can't imagine how frightened you must have been." With a stern look, she turned toward her husband. "Steve, what are we going to do about this?"

Steve removed his hat from his head and sat twirling it in his large, rough-workened hands. "We definitely need to notify the sheriff. He'll want to talk to you, Bree."

Bree nodded before answering, "But how will he find out who it was? I couldn't see him in the dark." She shivered. "And I didn't recognize his voice." Her words trailed off before she continued softly,

"He only spoke the one time."

The group sitting around the fire fell silent, each lost in their own thoughts.

Chapter 24

The October sky was filled with high clouds, casting the mountain valley with the soft, gray light of an early winter. Bree wiped down the kitchen counters, her eyes on the windowpane, her thoughts far away. The condensation running down the cold glass seemed to hypnotize her as her mind wandered over the past three weeks.

Steve had insisted that she and the children leave the roundup a day early, assuring her that Sarah and Thomas could cover her cooking duties. He had wanted her to talk to the sheriff as soon as possible. Sheriff Hambly had been kind and understanding, but beyond interviewing Bree and then returning with Steve to camp to interrogate the cowhands, there had been little he could do.

Steve, Thomas, and Michael had made sure one of them stayed close to Bree at all times. Sarah had hovered like a mother hen, making Bree nervous and jittery. She had finally talked to Sarah, reassuring her that there was nothing to worry about. Bree told her that with Steve, Thomas, and Michael looking out for her, she felt safe. Bree had laughingly told Sarah how Ben and Chuck Laird both argued with Steve that they should be allowed to share the duties of protecting Bree, and in exasperation, Steve had finally relented.

"I have five knights standing ready to protect me, Sarah. How can I worry with all that gallantry surrounding me?" Sarah had laughed with her and had left, her concerns appeased.

After a week, things had settled down again, with no further threats against Bree, and eventually the men had eased up their vigilance. She was grateful for their concern but even more grateful for the return to normalcy. She had hated the constant reminder of that night on the mountainside, and with her friends hovering around her, she had been unable to forget the fear of that night.

Realizing that winter was coming and yet feeling secure and safe in the confines of the warm kitchen, Bree smiled and brought her thoughts back to the present. She had a free afternoon ahead of her. Lunch was over, and a casserole for dinner was in the oven set to time bake. Fresh, homemade dinner rolls were cooling on the counter, filling the kitchen with mouthwatering aromas. The vegetables were peeled and ready to be steamed, and chocolate pudding was chilling in the fridge.

Looking at her watch, Bree murmured, "Five hours. I have five hours until dinner needs to be served." Stretching her shoulders tiredly, she realized how badly she needed a break. A smile teased the corners of her lips as she thought about the hours ahead. *Too bad Michael is out of town. I'd love to spend the afternoon with him.*

Bree's eyes sparkled with remembered pleasure. She and Michael were definitely moving forward in their relationship. It was a known fact that they were seeing each other, and Bree blushed remembering the teasing remarks that had been thrown at her the night before. Lex Larsen had walked in on her and Michael, and they had sprung apart, Bree's lips tingling from Michael's kisses. She smiled, recalling Michael's bashful response to Lex's teasing. Bree really hadn't minded; she liked having people know that she and Michael were a couple.

Bree frowned as she recalled another incident from the night before. Chuck had come into the kitchen after dinner. Bree was alone, finishing up the dishes, and Chuck had stolen up behind her, wrapping his arms around her waist. He had nuzzled her neck, ignoring Bree's efforts to free herself.

He had once again become persistent in his pursuit of Bree, and his intentions were clear. For a while after his fight with Michael, Chuck had backed off, seeming to accept the course of friendship dictated by Bree. But lately he had begun anew his campaign to come between her and Michael, convinced that Bree was making a mistake. He had told Bree that he loved her and that one day she would see that he was the man for her, not Michael. He refused to listen to her denials, and she was becoming angry with him.

Her anger had given her the strength to break away from his embrace the night before. She had spun away from him, slapping him across the cheek. He had stared at her in shocked surprise, and Bree had felt terrible. She tried to tell him she still wanted to be his friend, but she hated his uninvited advances.

He wouldn't listen, and instead he had stared at her, the shock on his face turning to hurt and finally to anger. He then stalked from the room, his shoulders stiff and his hands hanging at his side, his fingers clenched. The memory of his departure and the cloud of his rage caused Bree to frown.

"No! I won't let him ruin my afternoon!" Bree's voice sounded oddly detached as she berated herself in the silence of the kitchen. Pushing away the disturbing thoughts, Bree reached for her denim jacket and left the room.

She breathed deeply, relishing the refreshing chill of the autumn day. It was so beautiful on the Sheridans' ranch. Even with the difficulties caused by Chuck's unrequited crush, Bree was almost overwhelmed by the feelings of gratitude and happiness she felt. With a sudden shift in thought, she felt the unbidden idea to join Thomas, Michael, and the children for church the next Sunday.

They continued to urge her to attend with them, and with a smile of anticipation, she imagined their delight when she finally agreed to accompany them. With lightness in her heart and a skip in her walk, Bree hurried across the ranch compound. Before she had traversed half the distance to her house, a voice called to her.

"You off on a break?"

Turning to smile at Ben Laird, Bree answered, "Yep, dinner's in the oven and the dishes are all done, so I'm heading home for a little quiet time."

"How 'bout saddling up a horse and going for a little ride with me? It's a great day."

Bree was tempted to accept his offer, but lately she had started noticing a look in his eyes that bespoke of a deeper intent behind his invitation. Ben was a nice man, but she was afraid that he would see her acceptance as a sign that she was open to further pursuit.

I don't know what it is with these Laird men! Weeks ago, Bree had recognized Ben's interest in her. He had been so protective and solicitous after her terrifying experience on the roundup, and while she appreciated his friendship, she certainly wasn't romantically interested in him. *At least he's not being pushy about it! He seems to accept the fact that I'm interested in Michael. I hope so.* Bree realized that she valued the ranch foreman's friendship, and she was grateful that he seemed to understand.

She still found herself reluctant to accept his invitation, however. With regret, she turned him down. It was a gorgeous October afternoon, and a ride across the open acres of mountain meadow would have been delightful—but it wasn't worth the possible outcome if Ben was encouraged to pursue her.

With a smile to soften her rejection, Bree replied, "No thanks, Ben. The kids won't be home from school yet, and I really would like to take advantage of the quiet at home and get a few things done."

Ben's answering smile appeared to be understanding. "Maybe another time then." He paused as he reflected, "I really shouldn't go for a ride either. There's a bunch of chores waiting to be done. I better get back to work." Tilting his hat in farewell, he said, "Enjoy your afternoon, Bree."

Ben straightened his hat as he turned and left her with a smile that didn't quite reach his eyes. Bree turned from him, immediately forgetting his invitation. She walked across the ranch yard and had a sudden idea. She had some errands to run in town, and if she left now, she was sure she would have time to complete them and be back in time to serve supper. She would have to hurry, but after glancing at her watch, she made up her mind.

As soon as she got home, she made a quick phone call. "Sarah? Hi, it's Bree. I'm fine, thanks. I have a favor to ask, though. I have a little spare time, and I need to run to Sun Valley and run a few errands. I should have plenty of time to make it back before supper, but . . . you will? Thank you so much, Sarah. You're the best."

Bree hung up the phone, grateful for Sarah's willing assistance. Bree hadn't even had to voice her request before Sarah had broken in and said that she would oversee the completion of dinner for Bree. Now all she had to do was stop in at the school and speak to Brock and Shari to let them know where she was going. Grabbing a lightweight jacket, her purse, and the truck keys, Bree ran from the house and hurried to the small building that housed the schoolroom.

Entering the doorway, Bree smiled as she heard the music of children's laughter and young voices eagerly participating in their lessons. Shyly, she knocked on the door and got the attention of Mary Smith, the teacher. "May I speak to Brock and Shari for just a moment, please?"

Nodding her head and smiling her consent, Mary encouraged the two youngsters to join Bree at the back of the room.

"Hi, Bree!" Brock enthusiastically greeted his oldest sister and threw his arms around her waist in an impulsive hug.

"Hey, buddy. How's it going?"

"Good! I learned three new words today!" Brock was learning to read, and he was excited about his blossoming skills. He loved the books available at school and was showing the signs of becoming an avid reader.

"Good for you! I am so proud of you!" Rumpling his hair, Bree turned to Shari. "How 'bout you, sis?"

"It's good."

Bree smiled at her sister, knowing that Shari's two-word answer was on the mark. It was good. School. Her job. Their family. All of it was good. Smiling, Bree informed the kids that she was heading into town.

"I shouldn't be late, but in case I get held up, I want you two to stay at the dining hall. You can get your homework done and visit with the guys."

"Can't we go back home after dinner, Bree? Please!"

"Yeah! There's a good show on TV tonight that we really want to see." Shari supported Brock's plea.

"I don't know. If I'm out after dark, I don't know if I want the two of you staying alone."

"We won't be alone, Bree. There's lots of people on the ranch."

Bree looked at the pleading faces of her young siblings. They both looked so little, and she was torn. Her instincts told her to ignore their pleas, but a part of her agreed with them. Loving and supportive people surrounded them. Their friends, the Larsens, lived in the house next door, and there were plenty of other people around to watch over them and to be there if the need arose.

Feeling a tug at her conscience, Bree gave in and said, "Okay. If I get held up and I'm not back by the time dinner's over, you can go back to the house. Make sure you close the curtains and lock the doors."

Brock and Shari jumped up and down in eagerness to reassure their concerned sister. "We'll be good! And we won't fight!"

Bree smiled, knowing that they were telling the truth. They were both good kids, and they rarely fought. Bending down, she kissed them both on the cheek and shooed them back to their desks.

With a final wave, Bree turned and left the happy schoolroom. As she hurried to the small truck she had purchased from her former employer, Mel, she glanced at the sky and frowned at the sight of dark clouds lowering in the sky. She pushed aside a niggling twinge of doubt, frowned at the rolling, black thunderhead building in the distance, and pushed on the accelerator, spurred by a sudden twinge of anxiety.

Chapter 25

The man watched the cloud of dust dissipate in the air. He had watched Bree as she hurried away from the schoolhouse, frustration tightening his gut. There were too many people in his way—namely her brother and sister. Her love for the kids was admirable. In fact, her devotion to them was one of the things he had first loved about Bree. But the fires of jealousy were starting to burn in his gut, driving out reason.

And her friendship with Thomas ate at him. How could she spend so much time with the old man? If she knew his history, how he had destroyed—killed—his own family, she would abhor him, just as he himself despised the old man.

He felt impotent in his efforts to manipulate Bree's emotions. She offered him friendship, and she seemed to care for him, but it wasn't enough. He had tried to bury the frustration and anger, but he still felt it welling in his heart, eating at him and driving him to the brink of doing something mad. Something dangerous.

If that's what it takes, though, I'll do it! Shifting his hat back onto his head, the man stared into the distance, his eyes tracing the path Bree's truck had taken.

When you come home, I'll be waiting for you, my darling.

Chapter 26

Hours later, frustrated and dismayed at the length of time she had been away from the ranch, Bree muttered a silent curse at the unfortunate luck that had kept her out so late. During her absence, the dark clouds had continued to build, bringing the scent of rain to the mountains. She still had to stop in at the grocery store, but the rising storm overshadowed the pleasure she had experienced so far from her afternoon outing.

She had reached Sun Valley in good time and had visited the bank to cash her latest paycheck. She took the time to speak to the bank manager, a kind, middle-aged man, and asked him about setting up a trust for Brock and Shari. He had recommended establishing savings accounts for the two youngsters, instead of a trust, so Bree had decided to start out small, investing $25 from her paychecks for each child.

She then visited the hardware store. She had some minor home repairs to make, and rather than depend on Steve or Michael to do the work for her, Bree wanted to do it herself. During the months since her parents' accident, she had developed a fierce sense of independence. She realized that she couldn't do everything on her own, but she was determined to do what she could.

Taking one last look at the darkening skies, she hurried in to the small grocery store. She needed to pick up a few items for the ranch, things that she had forgotten to add to her monthly order. Steve usually had Ben order all of the supplies for the ranch, and Bree would turn in her shopping list to him. She was getting better at placing her monthly orders, but it seemed as if there was always some extra little item that she forgot.

She also wanted to pick up some munchies for the kids to have at home. Brock and Shari were typical kids and loved having between-meal snacks. Bree felt a surge of pleasure at the knowledge that she could now indulge their cravings, if only a little. Smiling to herself, she added a bag of miniature candy bars, a box of snack cakes, and a large box of microwave popcorn to her shopping cart. It was fun being able to buy the kids extra treats.

After completing her shopping, Bree hurried to her truck, realizing she was going to miss supper. With a grimace, she glanced at the sky. Dusk was descending quickly, and with it the wind was starting to pick up and blow. Flashes of lightning split the gloomy skies, followed by crashes of thunder that seemed to shake the ground. The scent of rain was strong, and Bree quickened her pace, reaching her truck just as the first heavy drops began to fall. Quickly unloading the shopping cart and transferring her groceries into the passenger side of the cab, she pushed the cart aside and hopped into the truck.

Inserting the key into the ignition and turning it, Bree's attempt to start the old truck failed. Pumping the gas pedal and turning the key again, the engine still refused to turn over.

"Oh, brother. This is all I need," she muttered under her breath.

Bree sat in silence, the rain splattering the dusty windshield as she contemplated her options. There was a garage a couple blocks down the road, and if she hurried she might be able to reach them before they closed. It just meant walking there in the rain. Shrugging into her jacket, Bree was grateful for its meager protection. She climbed from the stalled vehicle and began running down the street.

Two minutes later she arrived, panting and soaking wet, at the service station, grateful to see the "Open" sign hanging in the window. The mechanic on duty was kind and helpful and accompanied her back to her car with his tools. It took awhile for him to find out what was wrong, but he eventually was able to get the truck started. He recommended a good tune-up and reassured Bree that he would follow her out of town for a couple of miles to ensure her vehicle kept running.

As she drove higher into the mountains, the storm's intensity increased and Bree silently cursed the fates that had kept her away from home for so long. Her underlying sense of worry had not decreased even though the mechanic had lent her his cell phone to call both Brock and Shari. She told them that they should go next door to the Larsens until she arrived. She didn't want them home alone during the storm. Bree knew how terrifyingly hostile lightning storms could be in the mountains.

She crested the mountain and began the final descent into the valley below, the wet, gleaming surface of the unpaved road stretching before her like the writhing back of a snake. She shivered uncontrollably as the wickedness of the storm heightened.

Several minutes later, the towering outline of a giant cottonwood tree broke through the darkness of the night, and Bree sighed in relief at the sight of the massive sentinel marking the turn into her driveway. As she brought the truck to a stop and turned off the ignition, she became aware of the unnatural silence surrounding her in the cocoonlike stillness of the cab.

The havoc of the raging storm seemed remote and faraway, but Bree knew that her secure isolation was only an illusion. With a grimace she slowly opened the door and stepped out into the torrent of bone-chilling rain. The wind caught at her hair, tangling its long tresses, and she shivered as Medusa-like strands stung her sensitive cheeks.

She frowned, glancing at the unlit windows of her home, and as she approached the front door of the darkened house, a jagged flash of lightning ripped through the skies, followed quickly by a deafening clap of thunder. The ground literally shook beneath her feet, and Bree jumped, her throat suddenly knotted by a lump of fear. The yawning blackness of the unshuttered windows loomed before her, empty and unfriendly. *Brock and Shari must be next door.* Her warm and inviting home suddenly seemed remote and lonely. Trying to shake away the disturbing premonitions, Bree moved toward the front door. *I'll just go in and see if the lights are working before I go get the kids.* Her feet carried her up the three shallow steps of the landing. She stopped, and her outstretched hand became still as the small ring of keys fell from her fingers.

The howling of the wind and the clatter of the storm receded, making her own labored breathing the only sound of which she was conscious. The door was ajar, a thin line of deeper blackness delineating the opening. *How many times have I reminded Brock to make sure the door is latched behind him when he closes the door!* Bree's mental wanderings did nothing to soothe the nervousness that was causing her legs to tremble. The steady beat of her racing heart reverberated and echoed in her ears as, with an unsteady hand, Bree reached for the door and gently pushed.

Quietly, the door swung inward. She swallowed once, breaking the statuelike stillness that had claimed her from the moment she had first noticed the door standing slightly ajar. Gulping again and feeling as if the house were consuming her with its intimidating blackness, she stepped across the threshold, automatically pulling the door closed behind her, her fingers finding and twisting the lock out of habit. With groping hands, she searched for and found the light switch.

Clicking it once, twice, three times, the darkness remained. Bree assumed the storm must have caused a power failure. *I have some candles in the bathroom closet. I'll get them lit, and then I can go bring the kids home.* With faltering steps, she made her way deeper into the bowels of the house. The quiet shuffle of her feet was accompanied by the choking, rasping sound of her breath. Pausing in the doorway leading into the living room, her vision adjusted to the dim, muted light coming through the lace-curtained window. Bree berated herself for feeling so scared. This was her home, her refuge. There should be nothing here to alarm her.

But she was inexplicably frightened. The shadows from the thrashing branches of nearby trees seemed to leap and dance about the room, excited by the frenzied onslaught of the continuing storm. Their shadows, snaking and writhing across the walls, beckoned her forward.

Even as her mind shouted *"No!"* her feet moved, taking her to the opposite side of the room. Suddenly, her senses came alive, and the fear that had gripped her only moments before as she entered the quiet, empty house increased. As she stood listening for some sign of life in the darkened, tomblike house, a blinding flash of lightning suddenly illuminated the room. Thunder crashed and rumbled overhead, drowning out her tortured cry. "The children!" Bree knew something was terribly wrong. She should be surrounded by the light and laughter of a home brightened with the welcoming laughter of her younger brother and sister, not the fearful darkness and eerie quiet that surrounded her.

The floor behind her creaked, and she spun around, turning her back on the silence. Her mouth fell open in a silent scream as a giant shadow bore down on her, its threatening, upraised arm moving too quickly for her to evade its danger.

Chapter 27

Booming thunder resonated throughout the darkness of the house. Darkness was interrupted by flashes of light, and snakelike fingers of shadow flickered across the crumpled figure lying in the middle of the floor.

Interspersed with the crashing clamor of the storm was the sound of someone frantically beating on the front door. The man jumped away from Bree, his chest heaving from the exertion and the emotion of fighting with her. An expression of profound fear crossed his features, and he backed away from her lifeless form. *Had he killed her?*

Tears sprang to his eyes. He hadn't meant to kill her. He hadn't meant to hurt her. But when she started to fight him, and when her fingernails scraped down his cheek, he had lost his temper.

Frustrated rage welled in his heart, driving away the fear and the grief. *It's your fault, Bree! You shouldn't have fought me!*

* * *

A momentary lull in the storm caused Thomas Reilly to pause in the middle of his conversation with Lex Larsen. He had been visiting the Larsens, just as he had visited the other families on the ranch that night, reassuring himself that they were safe from the onslaught of the storm. His aged bones creaked with cold discomfort, but he had felt a compulsion to leave the security of his own home, to fight his way through the storm, in order to check on his friends and their families.

The Nelson home was his final destination, but during the momentary lapse of noise from the storm, another sound intruded on the night. Thomas felt the hair on the back of his neck stand on end, and his eyes widened with alarm when he recognized Bree's voice raised in frenzied screams of terror. He raced across the yard separating the Larsens' home from that of the Nelsons'. He was unaware of Lex following closely behind him, his only focus the young woman whose cries were suddenly silenced.

* * *

With a desperate lunge, the man spun and ran from the room. He had to get out. He couldn't be caught. And he still had the kids to think of. The din of splintering wood and the cry of frantic voices coming from the front of the house propelled the man out of the house. He dove through the back window, kicking the fallen screen aside. He ran through the storm and climbed into the cab of his truck.

It was a good thing he had hidden the truck at the back of the house. He had the kids tied up in the back, covered with a rainproof tarp. He would proceed with his original plans and take the kids to the cabin, keeping them there until he decided what to do with them. He drove away, the storm masking the sounds of his escape, his gloved hands gripping the steering wheel, tears rolling down his cheeks.

Meanwhile, Thomas knelt over Bree's inert form, Lex squatting beside him. Thomas's aged hands trembled as he felt for a pulse at the base of her throat. She was so still and so pale. But she was alive.

Chapter 28

The quiet of the night pulsed with underlying danger. Its blackness, total and enveloping, was like a weight crushing her soul. Struggling to breathe, Bree fought the waves of terror emanating from the dark. Only the unknown menace lurking in its shadows broke the silence of the night. And as the fear escalated, threatening to consume her, Bree began to cry.

The salty tears coursing down her cheeks and washing over the surface of her face soaked into the hollow of her pillow. The dampness and convulsive shudders brought consciousness, and Bree awoke. Suddenly, the unknown menace was gone. In its place was nothing. A void, more terrifying in its reality, replaced the fearful imaginings of a sleeping mind.

The muted light coming through the slatted blinds of the hospital window became a focal point for Bree's trancelike gaze. As the actuality of the room, sterile and safe, penetrated the terror surrounding her, Bree slowly began to loosen her deathlike grip on the blankets. Her shaking sobs turned into small, hiccuping gulps as she blinked her eyes, trying to dispel the last lingering traces of moisture. Lying back against the stiff, white pillow, Bree allowed her mind to wander to the events of the last two days.

There was little that she could remember about the dream that had awakened her, much less about the night that had spawned the seed of her horrifying nightmares. She remembered the storm and the shadows and the quiet, the quiet that had been so unnatural.

Bree shook her head to clear it of the confusion and fear clouding her thoughts, and she felt her heart constrict with sorrow as she thought of Brock and Shari. Where were they? Who had taken them from the safety of their home? Were they frightened? Hurt? Were they still alive? Why had this happened?

The question that hammered in Bree's mind more loudly than the others, however, was the question of her own culpability. The loneliness and the grief were almost too much to bear, and worst of all was the overwhelming guilt. If only she hadn't left the children alone that night. She mentally berated herself for not listening to those first stirrings of unease.

If she had been home, she might have been able to protect Brock and Shari, and now they wouldn't be missing.

Or she might be dead.

The police and the doctors told her that she had been lucky to survive the vicious attack. But she didn't feel lucky. How could she feel lucky when her whole life had been destroyed?

She felt so alone and so frightened. Clutching the white cotton blanket to her chest, Bree closed her eyes and willed the heartache away. She shivered from the fear creeping along her spine, bringing back the haunting pain of the nightmares that had plagued her all night.

She had awakened, screaming and hysterical at one point, drenched with perspiration. She had lain in bed, shivering and trembling, wishing that a nurse would come and offer her the relief of a painkiller. But no one had come, and she had been too paralyzed with fear to move and find the call button that would have summoned help. She had looked around, hoping to find someone sitting in the bedside chair. Thomas, Sarah, and Steve had all been to visit her. But they had all gone home the night before to get some rest.

She was alone. And she was frightened.

Bree wearily wiped a shaking hand across her face. Tired and weak from the restless night, she knew that her struggles had just begun. She knew that she would have to resolve the questions and the guilt. She had no other choice. With a grim determination born of desperation, Bree threw back the covers and climbed out of bed. Her bare feet made a soft padding sound as she crossed the floor to the bathroom. She thought she might be going home later that day, and she was ready.

Despite the fear and the grief swamping her, Bree was driven by her determination to find the children. She knew that Sheriff Hambly had launched a full, all-out search for Brock and Shari. He had interviewed her for hours, the nurses hovering anxiously as he had questioned her.

Bree had cried with frustration because she was unable to answer his questions. No, she hadn't seen her attacker. No, he hadn't spoken to her. And, no, there had been nothing to identify him. Nothing. The sheriff had taken scrapings from under her fingernails. Her defensive action of scratching the man might provide some proof after a DNA test was run, but it would take several days, maybe even a week, before the results came back. For now, Bree felt helpless and impotent. There were no other clues.

The storm had washed away any footprints or tire tracks, and there had been no fingerprints found at the house other than Bree's and the children's.

Bending over the white, porcelain sink, Bree splashed her face with cool water. The shock of the cold water against her flushed skin made her shiver, and she hurriedly grabbed for a fluffy, white towel. After drying her face, Bree studied her reflection in the mirror. She grimaced at the masklike face staring back at her.

Her finely etched features looked drawn and fragile. Her eyes were rimmed with shadows and looked large and bruised in the paleness of her face. Bree lowered her lashes, allowing the thick fringe to cover the blank, empty gaze staring back at her from the mirror. She didn't want to see the questions and the doubts and the fears lurking behind the facade of her wide, blue eyes. Turning toward the shower cubicle, Bree reached in and turned on the faucet. The forceful spray enticed her to hurry, and she stripped off the limp, colorless hospital gown before stepping under the steaming cascade of hot, soothing water.

As she shampooed her mass of auburn curls, Bree felt a sense of release from some of the stress. The act of showering and washing her hair was so normal that she allowed herself the luxury of believing that nothing had changed. But when she stepped from the warmth of the steamy cubicle, she knew that everything had changed and that her momentary sense of normalcy had been nothing more than an illusion, washed away with the soap and lather of her morning shower.

After drying and dressing, Bree crossed back to her bed, where she hastily straightened the bedclothes. Wearily, she climbed back under the covers. It was time to begin making some adjustments, but as she laid her head back against the pillow, she didn't know if she was up to the challenge.

Knowing that she would be released later that day, however, gave Bree the impetus to start trying to make some decisions. She closed her eyes and tried to concentrate on those choices that would impact her immediate future. But it proved too difficult at that moment, and she sighed, giving in to the weariness.

Just then, the muffled clanking sounds coming from the hospital corridor heralded the commencement of the day's activities. Breakfast carts, pushed by harried aides and orderlies, rattled along the hall, and it wasn't long before the door leading into Bree's room swung inward. A handsome young orderly, his muscled arms bulging with strength, approached Bree with a covered tray.

"Good morning, Miss Nelson. My name is Rob Carlton, and I'll be working the day shift today. If there's anything I can do for you, please let me know."

His cheerful greeting went unanswered as Bree averted her gaze, unwilling to meet his open, friendly stare. With a curious glance at her drawn, expressionless face, Rob smiled as he placed Bree's breakfast tray before her. Removing the insulated cover from a steaming bowl of oatmeal, he began to list the items on the tray, pointing to each one with a well-manicured finger. Bree looked down as he pointed to each dish and became mesmerized by his hands.

The background lighting of the room receded into blackness. The husky voice of the orderly faded into nothingness, and Bree's heart began to race. A roaring filled her ears, and fine beads of sweat lined her brow. The threat was very real, and a scream began to build deep in her throat.

She closed her eyes and was once again surrounded by a darkness that was broken only by intermittent flashes of lightning. The leering, evil face loomed over her, his visage filling her with the horror of remembered pain. The shadow's mouth hung open, and his maniacal laughter filled the emptiness of Bree's consciousness. His hands, large and bruising, were around her neck, choking out the very essence of her life. With a wild cry, Bree reached up with her hand, her fingers curled into sharp, nailed claws.

Suddenly, Bree heard another voice. "Miss Nelson. It's okay. You're safe."

Safe? Was she safe? Would she ever be safe again? Opening her eyes, Bree blinked, clearing her mind of the fearful images, and found herself staring into the kind, brown eyes of the concerned orderly.

"Can I have the nurse bring you something?"

Bree tightened her jaw, aching for the comforting, mindless relief of the pain medication she had been receiving. Clenching her hands under the blanket she murmured, "No. Nothing. Thank you."

"Are you sure?" At Bree's silent nod, Rob turned to leave, giving her one last sympathetic look. Bree was unaware of his compassion as she sat clutching the hospital blanket to her breast. Drawing in a shaky breath, she released the folds of fabric and reached for a spoon. Determined to conquer her fears and embarrassed by her hysterical reaction to the orderly's hands, she quickly began to eat and was only minimally comforted by the mundane routine.

The thick, tasteless cereal soon lost its appeal, and Bree dropped her spoon. Reaching for the cup of lukewarm orange juice, she quickly swallowed the liquid. With a grimace, she pushed the remainder of the breakfast tray away, its contents immediately forgotten.

With a shuddering sigh, Bree leaned back against the soft support of the pillow. Pulling the covers up to her chin, she let her gaze wander slowly about the room. Its impersonal decor was a surprising balm to her troubled spirits, and she dreaded the moment when she would have to leave its safety. This room had been her haven for the past two days, and she shuddered when she thought about having to face the outside world.

That time was coming soon. Her doctors had told her that she was ready to leave, and she wanted to leave. She hated the enforced inactivity that kept her from participating in the search for Brock and Shari. She had been promised that her physical injuries were healing, and she had also been assured her that once she was away from the hospital and had to face up to her fears, her emotional scars would also begin to heal.

Why, then, did she feel so unprepared to face the future? Bree knew the answer. She was afraid.

The police had no leads on the identity of the man who had wreaked such havoc on her life. There were no clues as to what had happened to Brock and Shari. Even though a massive search was underway, Bree knew that until she could remember more about that night, the police would be hindered in their ability to help her. They needed facts, and Bree had none to give.

The only fact that mattered to Bree was that the children were missing and that the man who had taken her family—and who had threatened her life—was still at large. Bree knew that he would be coming back. She was afraid and alone, and all she could do was wait for his return.

Chapter 29

The man jumped off the cot, cursing at the grimy feeling of his soiled clothes and the rumpled sheet covering the thin mattress. He needed to go check on the kids. He had them in the root cellar beneath the cabin, its door hidden by the surrounding foliage at the back of the house. He had kept them bound and gagged most of the time, only releasing them a couple of times a day so that they could eat and move around a bit. They were filthy and frightened, and he meant to keep them that way.

He would have to untie them, though. It was time for him to return to the ranch, and he didn't know how long it would be before he could make it back up to the cabin. They would have to be able to access the meager store of food and water that he would leave them, things he had pilfered from the dining hall. He quickly snatched up two plastic jugs of water and a burlap bag containing the food.

Stalking across the creaky wood floor, he threw the door of the cabin open and made his way outside. The freshness and beauty of the day was a cruel contradiction to the ugliness filling his heart. Pulling on the rusted handle of the root cellar door, the man made his way down the dank, narrow stairs. The interior of the cellar was dim and smelly, and he could barely make out the recumbent forms lying on the floor.

He stood over the two children, their frightened eyes adjusting to the intrusion of light. Shari whimpered in the back of her throat, the dirty rag stuffed in her mouth absorbing the sound. She flinched and stared as the man reached down and untied her wrists. She didn't trust him and she was frightened, so she lay still as he untied her ankles, then watched as he reached over and untied Brock, who was lying quietly, also watching.

The man stood over the children, his hardened heart untouched by their grimy, dirt-smeared faces. Streaks traced the paths of fallen tears, and two sets of eyes pled for mercy. Reaching down, he pulled the filthy rags out of their mouths. Shari and Brock worked their jaws, which had grown stiff and sore. Dry tongues flicked over cracked lips.

When the man turned to leave, Brock managed to croak, "Don't leave us."

The man turned and sneered, "You're not afraid of being alone, are you?"

"Please. It's so dark in here." Shari's words were raspy, and she flinched as the man laughed out loud.

"Don't want to be alone. Don't want to be in the dark. Babies," he snarled. "Okay. Here." He reached behind him and pulled a flashlight out of his pocket, then tossed it on the ground at Shari's feet. "Maybe that'll help."

Without another word, he left, and as the cellar door slammed shut, Brock crawled over to Shari. For the first time in two days, he felt loving arms around him. As the darkness engulfed them once again, Shari and Brock cried, frightened and desperate.

The man slid the hasp of the rusted lock into place and securely clamped the padlock. The old, wooden door, though gray and weathered with age, was thick and strong. There was no way the two children could break through its barrier. With a smile of satisfaction, he strode to the front of the cabin and reentered the dim, shabby interior.

Walking across the room, he came to a stop in front of the cloudy, broken mirror hanging near the black, potbellied stove. Examining his face, he noted that the scratches were almost healed and barely noticeable. He fingered the three-day growth of beard that covered his dirty, unwashed face and grimaced in distaste as he ran his hands through the thick, greasy strands of his hair. He hated filth and disorder, and this dingy, dirty room had been his prison for the past two days, but the dilapidated cabin was remote and had been the perfect place to bring the kids.

He'd had to make some quick alterations to his original plans. Bree was supposed to be with them, and he had intended to take her far away. But when he had been interrupted that night and had to leave Bree behind, he had driven crazily along the narrow, winding roads. Eventually his mind had finally cleared, and he had turned toward the cabin. It was high in the mountains, remote and forgotten. He knew that a search for the brats would be initiated, and he had actually returned to the ranch later that night, volunteering to "search" the section of mountain nearest the cabin. He hadn't worried about returning to the ranch over the past two days, knowing that his absence would be attributed to his "dedication" to helping find the missing children.

He'd had one moment of doubt when he remembered that Jonathan Smith had been with him when he'd discovered the cabin. He realized that it was time for him to return, to keep his ears open. If Jonathan showed any sign of remembering, he'd have a problem on his hands to take care of.

With pleasure! While hiding for the two days, he'd had too much time to think. Gone was any tenderness for Bree or the children. He no longer dreamed of spending his life with Bree. She had caused him too much grief and heartache. In his convoluted mind, she became the root of the evil looming in his heart. And she was going to have to pay.

He thought about the children. If Bree still lived, she would be overcome with worry and grief. Maybe he would have to arrange a little family reunion. Or, not. With a grim smile, he made his preparations. He was going home. And if Bree were alive, she'd soon find out how dangerous it had been to fight him.

Chapter 30

Steve Sheridan left the huge barn, closing the large, cedar door firmly, frustrated by the ongoing demands of his job, tasks that couldn't be delayed even in the face of the traumatic events that were taking place on the ranch. Thomas was inside, hastily completing the necessary tasks of preparing for the delivery of the bull the ranch had recently purchased, anxious to return to the search for his young friends.

The bull being delivered was from choice stock with a great pedigree. The fact that the bull had been up for sale had drawn ranchers from four surrounding states to the auction house located in Butte, Montana. Steve's pleasure at successfully outbidding the competing ranchers vying for the bull was totally erased by the devastating events that had taken place on his ranch. The sale had been a week ago, and he had returned jubilant. He had made arrangements for the bull to be shipped to Idaho. He had sent Michael to Idaho Falls to meet the train, and Michael had returned just that morning, towing the stock trailer and glad to be home.

Michael's first thought had been to see Bree, and his face had gone ghostly pale when his father broke the news to him about the children's disappearance and the attack on Bree. He had hammered the sheriff with question after question, demanding that he do everything possible to find the two children. Sheriff Hambly had assured him that everything was being done that could be. Tangible clues were nonexistent. Whoever had perpetrated the horrendous deed had been clever. It was like an invisible force had entered and destroyed the sanctity of the Nelsons' home. Everyone living on the ranch had been questioned, but there wasn't one solid lead.

Fear seemed to permeate the ranch. Steve felt it, and he knew that Sarah did too. He couldn't imagine how devastating this must be for Bree. Anger boiled in Steve's heart, and he vowed that he would do anything within his power to protect her and to find the children.

Just then, the phone hanging on the wall above the foreman's desk rang. Steve picked it up on the first ring.

"Mr. Sheridan?"

"Speaking."

"This is Dr. Wilson from Sun Valley Memorial Hospital."

Steve felt his gut tighten with apprehension, "Yes, Dr. Wilson. Is everything okay?"

"Yes, I was just calling to let you know that we're going to release Miss Nelson this afternoon."

Steve felt the tension in his shoulders lessen as he questioned the doctor. After receiving the information he sought, Steve quickly bid the doctor good-bye. He held onto the receiver of the phone as he pressed the intercom button connecting him to the cookhouse. He knew Sarah had been planning to help the other wives and volunteers prepare food for the searchers. A woman's voice answered after the third ring.

"Oh, hi, Steve, this is Tina." Tina Larsen was Lex's wife, a cheery, attractive brunette who had become good friends with Bree.

"I'm trying to find Sarah, Tina."

"She went back to your house this morning. When she found out we had so much help here, she said that she had a lot to do at home."

"Thanks, Tina." Steve looked puzzled as he buzzed the intercom to the house.

Sarah answered immediately.

"Hi, honey. I just got off the phone with Bree's doctor. He's sending her home this afternoon."

Steve heard the emotion in Sarah's voice when she said, "I want to go pick her up, Steve."

Steve sighed, sharing his wife's desire. "I know, babe. But I can't go with you. I have to get that new bull settled before I can do much of anything."

"You don't have to go with me."

"I don't want you going alone."

"But Steve . . ."

"No! Sarah, listen to me. Until this maniac, whoever he is, is found, you're not going anywhere by yourself."

Sarah sighed, acknowledging the wisdom of her husband's edict. "But who . . ."

Steve quickly reviewed in his mind the activities of all his ranch hands. "I'll send Ben. I saw him just a few minutes ago. He just got back from town. I'll grab him before he gets involved in another project."

"Okay. I love you, Steve."

"I love you, too, Sarah. Talk to you later."

After setting the phone back on its cradle, Steve fought down the surge of frustration that welled up as he reviewed everything that had to be done that afternoon. He couldn't possibly leave the ranch to drive in to Sun Valley and pick Bree up. And Michael and Thomas weren't available. They had joined the sheriff and his men, along with the rest of the ranch hands, in the organized search for the children. Chuck was absent too. In fact, Steve realized that he hadn't seen several of his ranch hands for days. *I guess they're so involved with the search that they're not taking the time to come in to rest.* Steve could understand the mania driving his men and the sheriff's deputies. They all had one focus: to find the children and to apprehend the person who had caused such havoc in their lives.

Heading for the foreman's quarters located behind the barn, Steve called out for Ben Laird. If he couldn't go for Bree himself, then he would send the next best man.

Ben had come to the ranch six years ago and had proven himself to be a valuable asset to the management of the ranch. No task was too menial or too difficult for him to accomplish. Steve had known right from the start that he and Ben would make a productive partnership because of their similarities. They were both focused on success.

Ben had succeeded. He had stepped in when Sarah's father had retired and moved with his wife to southern Idaho. Ben had also proven himself to be a top-notch foreman, earning the respect of his employer and the ranch hands.

"You called, boss?" Ben answered, his voice low, a slight drawl emphasizing the charm of his soft voice.

Glancing at the man, Steve was startled by the intensity of Ben's gaze. Steve was a tall man, and it was disconcerting for him to face another man at eye level. He mocked himself, realizing that after six years he should be used to the feeling by now.

Steve said, "Yeah, Ben. I'm glad you're back from town. Things went okay, I take it?"

Ben nodded and murmured that he had managed to wrap up the tasks that had kept him busy that morning—ordering supplies and making preparations to keep the men searching for the children fed and equipped with whatever they might need.

"I need you to do me a favor, Ben. Bree's being discharged from the hospital this afternoon, and I'd like you to go pick her up. I wish I'd known earlier, so you could have just stayed in town instead of having to make a second trip. I'd go myself, but I can't leave."

Appearing surprised at Steve's request, Ben nodded and said, "Sure, boss. I'd be happy to do that. It's gonna be hard for that little lady to come back to an empty house."

Steve felt a shiver go up his back at the thought of Bree having to return to the place where she had faced so much horror. Making a snap decision, he said, "I don't want her going back to her house just yet. Bring her on up to the homestead. I'll fix things with Sarah, and we'll let Bree stay with us for a while."

Cracking a crooked grin, Ben looked relieved. "Sounds like a good idea. What time do I need to go get her?"

"Not until later this afternoon."

"What's later this afternoon?"

The voice from behind them startled Steve and Ben. They turned and saw Chuck Laird standing there, his tall, gangly form leaning against the wall. A strange light shone in his eyes, and his posture appeared rigid. He looked tired and grungy, and Steve realized he had been right in his earlier assumption. Chuck obviously had been hard at work scouring the mountainside for the missing children.

Ben stared at his nephew for a few seconds before answering, "Steve asked me to run in to Sun Valley and pick Bree up. She's coming home this afternoon."

Chuck crossed his arms over his chest. "I could go get her if you want."

Steve responded before Ben could speak, "No, that's okay, Chuck. Thanks for the offer, though. Ben will go get her."

"But . . ."

Steve's jaw worked with tension, fighting to dampen down the surge of irritation at Chuck. "No arguments, Chuck. You look exhausted, and I don't want to risk you having an accident, either on your way there or on the way back."

Chuck stared at his boss and then transferred his gaze to his uncle. Breathing deeply, he nodded his head once. Pulling his hat low over his forehead, Chuck said, "Fine. Just thought I'd offer. I better go and rejoin the search. I just came back to get something to eat."

Chuck turned to leave, but before he could take a step, his uncle placed a firm hand on his shoulder. "Stay focused on the search, boy. That's the most important thing right now."

"Right. Thanks, Uncle Ben."

Steve and Ben watched the boy leave before turning back to the matters at hand. After filling Ben in on the details of Bree's release, Steve left the barn and headed for the house. He needed to talk to Sarah about Bree's impending visit. He was sure there would be no problem, but he quickly rehearsed in his mind just how he would approach Sarah with his request.

Mounting the wide, wooden steps leading to the front verandah, Steve called out, "Sarah! Honey, I need to talk to you."

The screen door slammed behind him, and Steve heard his wife answer him from a room at the back of the house. Heading toward her voice, he found her in the sunroom off the large, spacious kitchen. Looking around, Steve's face registered surprise at the changes to the room.

The furniture was clustered at one end of the long, narrow room, the brightly colored cushions offering an appealing contrast to the white wicker. Abundant green plants flourished in the light streaming through the large, open windows and gave the room a feeling of light and beauty. Sarah was standing over a narrow daybed, smoothing out a white eyelet quilt. Bright cushions of pink, blue, yellow, and green were scattered across the bed, picking up the colors in the floral pattern of the thick cushions padding the wicker furniture. The cozy breakfast nook had been changed into a lovely, welcoming bedroom, and Sarah turned to Steve, a self-conscious look on her face.

"Hi, honey. I'm sorry I didn't have a chance to ask you first."

Sarah paused, and Steve began to smile. Teasing, he approached Sarah and placed his hands on her shoulders. Looking down into her upturned face, he asked sternly, "Ask me what?"

Seeing the glint of humor in his bright blue eyes, Sarah slipped her arms around his waist and rested her head against his shoulder. "I knew you wouldn't mind if we had Bree come stay with us for a few days. I don't want her being by herself just yet. Before he left to join the search, I had Thomas help me move the bed down here. I didn't want Bree to have to climb up and down the stairs. She needs to focus all of her energy on getting better, not climbing stairs," Sarah paused before continuing, "and not worrying and being afraid in that house all by herself."

Tenderness washed over Steve. His wife's compassion overwhelmed him, and he kissed the top of her smooth, blond head. "You must be a mind reader. I was just coming to ask you if you would mind having her stay with us. The room looks great, honey."

Pleased with Steve's approval, Sarah stepped back and looked up into her husband's face, her deep brown eyes warm and glowing.

Encouraged by her response, Steve reached out and tugged a lock of her shining hair. With a quick movement, he grabbed her and pressed a quick, intense kiss to her smiling mouth. "Gotta go, honey. Ben will be bringing Bree back from the hospital soon. I want to be done with my chores so I can be here. And I need to call the sheriff and make sure he's going to follow through with assigning someone to stay close to Bree. I don't want her—or you—to be left unguarded, even for a moment!" With that, Steve put his Stetson on his head and strode purposefully out the door.

* * *

Later that afternoon, after having prepared a large pot of home-made chicken and noodles, a batch of freshly baked rolls, and a rich, chocolate layer cake, Sarah felt ready to welcome their guest. The sunroom looked cozy and inviting, the house was sparkling and clean, and the air was filled with the aroma of the freshly baked bread.

Just then, the front door swung open, and Sarah hurried into the front hall. Steve stood in the entryway, studying the handful of mail that he had just brought in. "Any sign of them yet?" Sarah asked.

Shaking his head no, Steve walked toward her. Silently he took her in his arms and held her close, sharing the support and strength of their love. Sarah felt her lips begin to tremble. Her heart was full to the point of overflowing with the depth of emotion she felt for this giant of a man. She loved him so passionately, and as Sarah nestled in Steve's arms, she was grateful for his strength and for his presence. If anyone could keep her safe, it was her husband.

Chapter 31

The elevator doors slid open, and Bree's heart thumped loudly in her ears. She clasped her hands tightly together while the softly perfumed volunteer pushed her wheelchair toward the front entrance of the hospital. The light chattering of the kind, elderly woman made no impression on Bree. She strained to concentrate on what the woman was saying, but all she could think about was the seemingly impossible task facing her. She dreaded going back home. Home, as she had known it, no longer existed. All that was left was the shell of a home, a house filled only with furniture, memories, and unanswered questions.

The radiant afternoon sunshine blinded Bree, and she blinked rapidly, trying to adjust to the glaring light. The warmth and the brightness of the autumn sky seemed to mock the winter chill in her heart, and she closed her eyes against its intrusion. A quiet voice, friendly and familiar, greeted her, and Bree wearily opened her eyes.

A large shadow suddenly blocked the blinding rays of the sun. The silhouette gave her a start, and she had to fight down the rising surge of fear. Breathing in deeply, Bree glanced up and found herself looking into the rugged, familiar face of Ben Laird. She tried to force a smile in response to his greeting.

Bree rose from the wheelchair, and when her elderly companion turned to leave, she grabbed the woman's soft, wrinkled hand and whispered, "Thank you," her blue eyes large and imploring in a silent, unspoken plea.

"You're very welcome, honey. God bless you." The volunteer, her eyes misty with understanding and compassion, leaned in and impulsively brushed Bree's cheek with a quick, feather-soft kiss.

Bree watched the retreating woman until the yellow-smocked figure had vanished. With a trembling hand held to her mouth, Bree turned toward the waiting man and, with a muffled sob, silently shook her head at his inquiry, "Are you okay, Bree?"

Seeing his concerned, puzzled expression, Bree closed her eyes momentarily, took another deep breath, and resolutely straightened her shoulders. Lowering her hands, she gave him an apologetic smile and said, "Yes, Ben, I'm fine. Thank you."

After closing the passenger door, Ben walked quickly around the front of the cab of his large, red pickup and climbed into the driver's seat. Bree felt her lips curve with a hint of genuine amusement as she watched Ben fold his long, lanky form into the confined space behind the steering wheel.

Catching her glimmer of a smile, Ben cracked a disarming grin and said, "These long legs of mine can be a bit of a problem at times."

Settling herself for the long drive to the ranch, Bree listened to Ben's friendly chatter, grateful for the distraction of his ramblings. He didn't seem to mind that it was a one-sided conversation and began telling her about his mother and siblings, who lived in eastern Oregon. He chuckled, remembering how grateful he always felt when it was time to return to the ranch after visiting them. "I usually go visit sometime in the fall after the roundup is finished. I'm glad I didn't go this year, though. This is where I need to be, where I'm needed. We're gonna find those sweet kids, Bree. We won't give up until we do."

"Thank you, Ben." Bree's eyes filled with tears, and she blinked impatiently, not wanting to give into her emotions again.

"Michael was sure upset when he got back this morning and found out about everything."

"Michael's been gone?" Bree asked.

"Yep. He went to Idaho Falls to pick up that bull Steve bought. He's out with the sheriff's men right now, or I'm sure he'd be here."

Bree nodded her understanding. She had been surprised and hurt when Michael hadn't come to visit her. She knew he had been out of town, but she hadn't realized he was going to be gone so long. Sarah and Steve had been to visit, sitting with her while she slept, clasping her hand while the sheriff grilled her, holding her when she cried.

Thomas had stopped by, but he hadn't stayed long. He had become emotional during the visit, and Bree had been glad when he had left. He had reassured her that he was praying for her, and while she appreciated the sentiment, Bree wasn't sure she had the faith to believe it would help. Her faith had been badly bruised during the past few days, and she ached with barren hopelessness.

Bree again blinked back the quick tears that threatened to spill from her haunted, bruised eyes. Thoughts of Thomas automatically led her thoughts to Brock and Shari. She was so worried about them. They were so young, and she knew they had to be terrified—if they were still alive.

The thought that they might be dead was enough to break her heart, but not knowing for sure was devastating. If she only knew one way or the other, she might be able to find some resolution. If they were dead, she could grieve and hopefully find some closure, maybe eventually move on with her life.

Until she knew for sure, though, she would move heaven and earth to find them. Even if she had to get out and scour the countryside herself, Bree realized that she couldn't give up hope that they were still alive. She would find the strength to keep the search going, to do whatever she had to do to find them. She was determined to know one way or the other.

Bree's silence became heavy in the quiet of the cab, and Ben looked over at her. She was turned toward the side window, lost deep in thought. He studied her delicate profile. Her skin, though marred by purple bruises, appeared pale and translucent in the glow of the afternoon sun. Her eyes were downcast, and the thick fringe of long eyelashes cast sweeping shadows across the contours of her wan cheeks.

Bree was unaware of Ben's silent study. She was staring out the window at the passing scenery. They had long since left behind the golden meadows of the Wood River Valley and were now ascending high into the rugged beauty of the central Sawtooth Mountains. Bree appreciated the grandeur of the towering trees and the massive outcroppings of granite that lined the mountain road. When the truck crested the summit, she drew in her breath at the majesty of the panorama spread before them. There was restorative magic in the spirit of the mountains.

Ben slowed down, noticing the direction of her gaze. When the truck rolled to a stop, Bree opened her door and slowly clambered out into the pine-scented air. Her limbs ached with stiffness, and her head throbbed from the movement. She walked over to the stone wall that served as a buffer between the road and the sharp drop-off and stood there silently, drinking in the splendor. Her broken spirit and frightened soul were slightly soothed by the healing of nature's balm.

Mountains and valleys stretched on, seemingly forever. The deep green of the pine-covered ridges faded into the distance, blurring into shades of mauve and blue. The azure sky was deep and far-reaching with puffs of drifting, white clouds dotting its limitless expanse. Closing her eyes, Bree drew in a deep breath of the marvelously clean, crisp air. Slowly, she exhaled and opened her eyes, turning to glance at the man standing by her side. "Thank you for stopping here, Ben. I needed this."

Ben smiled down at her, his dark eyes riveted on her upraised face. He reached out, placing a large hand on the fragile point of her shoulder, and squeezed gently.

The magic of the moment dissipated when Ben touched Bree. She cast a brief look up at him, startled and uncomfortable by his unexpected touch. The strength of his hand frightened her, and she realized that his appearance was deceptive. He appeared long and lanky, but his touch made her realize that he was all muscle and sinew. Turning toward the truck, she said over her shoulder, "I suppose we had better be on our way."

Ben's hand dropped to his side as Bree stepped away from him. His eyes narrowed as he followed her and climbed behind the wheel of the truck.

The remainder of the drive was done in silence, with both Bree and Ben lost in their thoughts. Bree felt uncomfortable. She had sensed Ben's anger over her rebuff, but she felt too apathetic to care and breathed a silent sigh of relief when they drove through the main gates leading to the ranch.

Bree looked over her shoulder with a puzzled expression when Ben passed by the graveled entrance leading to her small house. Seeing her confusion, Ben quickly explained, "The boss said that I should bring you to the homestead when we got back."

Bree felt a wave of relief. She silently looked back at the house, wondering how a building that looked so peaceful and inviting could fill her with such dread. The large cottonwood tree stood like a sentry guarding the entrance of the driveway, and she noted that its leaves had turned the bright, golden yellow of autumn. Soon those leaves would start to fall, and the tree's twisted branches would be as empty and as bare as her heart.

After Ben pulled the truck to a stop in front of the wide verandah of the homestead, the front door of the large, impressive log structure swung open. Steve hurried down the steps followed closely by Sarah. Bree could see the piercing blue of Steve's eyes glowing in his dark, tanned face, and his square jaw was firm as he broke into a warm smile. His features were softened by the fleeting appearance of grooved dimples.

Bree sat waiting, her bruised eyes brightening slightly while she watched Steve and Sarah approach the side of the truck. Steve reached for the door and pulled it open. He assisted Bree to step out of the cab and put an arm around her shoulders, hugging her briefly. Sarah was beside him, offering Bree her hand. Bree smiled at her, suddenly uncomfortable from Steve's embrace. It seemed as though every man who touched her was now suspect and caused her to fear. First it had been the hospital orderly, then Ben. And now, Steve.

Stepping away from him, Bree turned to Sarah.

"Bree, welcome home." Sarah took Bree into her arms, holding her close. Bree closed her eyes, relishing the warmth and safety of Sarah's welcome.

Sarah, keeping an arm wrapped supportively around Bree, led the way into the house. They entered the front foyer and continued on to the back of the house. Bree, though weary and heartsore, glanced appreciatively around the cheerful, attractive room and realized how much work had gone into making her feel welcome. She sat down on the edge of the daybed.

Sarah sat down beside her and gathered Bree into her arms, her voice soft and warm against Bree's cheek as she whispered, "We want you to spend as much time as you need with us, Bree. We know how difficult this homecoming must be for you." Sarah felt Bree begin to tremble. She drew her closer into her embrace and continued, "I know, honey. It's an awful burden you have to bear, but we're here for you."

Steve watched his wife comforting the lonely, frightened girl. Leaning down, he placed a warm hand on Sarah's shoulder, caressing her with a loving touch as he reached for Bree's hand. Smiling, he echoed his wife's words, "We'll always be here for you, Bree. Whatever you need, just let us know."

Withdrawing his hand from Bree's soft grasp, Steve turned to Sarah and said, "I have to get to work now. I'll be back later this evening." He leaned down and placed a tender, lingering kiss against her slightly parted lips.

Steve turned away and heard Sarah ask Bree, "How would a nice cup of herbal tea taste? I have either chamomile or spiced apple."

"The spiced apple would be nice, thank you." Bree wanly smiled her gratitude as Sarah entered the nearby kitchen. With a sigh, Bree kicked her shoes off and swung her feet off the floor. Leaning back against the soft pile of brightly colored cushions, she allowed the quiet solitude of the room to wash over her troubled spirits.

She felt comforted and warmed by the knowledge that Steve and Sarah both cared about her. Here in their home, Bree felt that she might be able to begin the healing process. She knew that they could offer her strength and resolution until she could find it on her own. She needed their courage, especially as the days ahead loomed empty and uncertain. She felt her eyelids droop and allowed herself to rest knowing that Sarah and Steve were close by, watching over her, protecting her.

An hour later, the touch of a soft hand against her cheek woke Bree up from her nap. The kitchen was filled with the aroma of chicken soup and freshly baked bread. Warm sunlight shone across the foot of Bree's bed, warming her feet. She lay in a daze for a moment, trying to focus on the figure sitting on the bed beside her. Sudden recognition lit her eyes and tears welled up as she was gathered into Michael's strong embrace.

He held her for what seemed an eternity, his chin resting on top of her head while she sobbed against his chest. His hands caressed her back, his quiet, whispered words consoling her spirit.

Finally, Bree pushed away from his hold and wiped her eyes with a shaky hand. Michael shifted his hands and lifted her onto his lap. He held her as if she were a child.

"I'm so sorry this has happened to you, Bree." Michael's voice was hoarse with suppressed emotion. "And I'm so sorry I wasn't here for you."

Bree tightened her hold on his neck, clinging to him, unable to say a word.

They were unaware of the young man watching them from the French doors leading out into the backyard.

* * *

Chuck Laird felt his heart twist with envy. He didn't stand a chance with Bree. Sure, she seemed to like him, but watching her with Michael, he saw the love in her eyes and the tenderness in her touch. He turned and ran, grief mingling with the jealousy. *I won't give up! One day she'll see. She'll see him for what he is . . . and she'll turn to me!*

* * *

Several minutes later, Michael rose and said, "I'm sorry, Bree, but I have to go. I only had a few minutes. Sheriff Hambly has us all on a pretty rigid schedule, and my break is about over. I need to get back out there."

Bree smiled through her tears. She didn't want him to leave, and yet she did. She knew that she could trust Michael to do his best searching for the children. He seemed to love them almost as much as she did. "You go, Michael. Go find Brock and Shari for me!"

Their kiss only lasted a few seconds, but Bree felt the promises of a lifetime in the motion. Michael then lifted his head and stared into her blue eyes. "Thank you, Michael. I know if anyone can find them, you can!"

Michael stood upright, his eyes sad. "I won't be back until we do find them. I promise you that!" he pledged. He turned to leave, his voice raised as he called, "Sarah! I'm leaving."

Sarah Sheridan entered the kitchen. "I'm here, Michael. You go ahead." Sarah waved Michael off, then turned toward Bree. "Now, what can I get you? I have a pot of yummy chicken and noodles. Would you like some?"

Bree nodded her head absentmindedly. "I suppose I should eat a little something."

"Maybe I should offer Deputy Odham a bowl of soup too." Sarah left for a moment to check with the young man who had been assigned to stay close to the homestead. Jeff Odham came into the kitchen with Sarah, grateful for her thoughtfulness. After introducing himself to Bree, he sat across the table from her and explained how he would be pulling the twelve-hour shift from 8:00 A.M. to 8:00 P.M. "Don Haynes will cover the night shift. You'll like him. He can seem like a grouchy old codger, but he has a heart of gold."

Bree smiled at the deputy and thanked him for his attentiveness. She looked up at Sarah, who was holding out two bowls brimming with savory soup. Deputy Odham quickly finished his, then donned his hat, tipping it to the two women in farewell. "I better get back out there and patrol the grounds some more. I'll check in with you every hour or so."

"Thank you, Deputy. We appreciate you." Sarah walked the young man to the back door, then went back to the table and sat down next to Bree. She reached for Bree's hand, and the two women settled down to visit and console each other, aware of the late after-noon sun settling in the cradle of the western mountain ridge, heralding dusk, which was a mere hour away. The inevitability of nightfall would complicate the ongoing search, but Bree found comfort in the knowledge that the search would continue, regardless of the time of day.

Later that evening Bree lay on the firm mattress of the daybed, covered with the softness of Sarah's homemade quilt. Her eyes were droopy with weariness, but her heart was heavy with sorrow. Silent tears leaked from under her closed lids as she willed herself to go to sleep. She was so very tired. Her exhausted body craved sleep, but her weary mind betrayed her with thoughts of her missing brother and sister, whirling with memories of her parents. She missed them all so much. She didn't want to feel so alone. Or so frightened.

Finally, with a huff of irritation, Bree flung the covers back and swung her legs over the edge of the bed. She sat for a moment holding her head with both hands until a surge of dizziness passed. She stood and walked into the kitchen, flicking on the soft overhead light. Her trembling fingers reached for the small amber bottle sitting next to the sink. The doctor had sent her home with a prescription for a sleep aid, and although she had initially been determined not to take it, she was desperate for sleep. If she didn't get a decent night's sleep, she would be worthless when the sun rose the next morning. And more than anything, she wanted to be alert and ready for action when word came that the children had been found. Quickly swallowing two of the powerful tablets, Bree closed her eyes and rested against the sink, a deep sigh calming her nerves.

Slowly she opened her eyes, reached for the light switch, and then padded back across the darkened room to her bed. She crawled under the covers and turned on her side, determined to stop thinking, if even for just a few hours, about the possibility that Brock and Shari might never be found. Twenty minutes later her deep, even breathing indicated the granting of her wish as she fell into the forgetfulness of sedative-induced slumber.

Chapter 32

Ebony skies canopied the high mountain valley. Stars glittered like ice chips floating in a pool of black water. The ranch buildings were quiet, the women and children cloistered within the fragile safety of their homes. The men, weary and determined, were still searching for Brock and Shari. One man spurred his horse, the sharp metal points digging cruelly into the sides of his mount. He pulled his broad-brimmed hat low over eyes that had become hard and cold.

He was riding toward the ranch, having been ordered by the sheriff to take a break. His diligence in searching the mountainside had been duly noted and appreciated. The sheriff and his deputies were now making sure the searchers were taking care of themselves, eating and resting when needed.

He didn't mind returning to the ranch. He had plans. He felt Bree's spirit calling to him, and he found himself responding with an eagerness that made him breathless. Part of him responded to Bree with the boyish giddiness of a first crush, while the harsh reality of his obsession drove him to unspeakable lengths.

Galloping into the ranch yard, he pulled hard on his horse's reins, dust and debris flying as the strong legs and hoofs responded to the command. Quickly dismounting, he led the stallion into the barn. He accomplished the unsaddling and bedding down of his horse in record time.

After leaving the barn, he stood in the moonlight and checked his watch. 2:00 A.M. It had been a long day and a long night. Soon he'd be able to crash and get some much-needed sleep, but not yet. He had something more pressing to do.

Stealthily glancing over his shoulder to make sure he wasn't being observed and keeping his eye out for the deputy patrolling the grounds, he made his way to the homestead. He circled the large structure, entering the backyard. He knew that the doors were never locked, and he also knew that there was a minimal chance of being overheard by the sleeping inhabitants if he entered through the back door. Steve was still on the mountainside searching, and he was sure Sarah and Bree would both be asleep.

The backyard was filled with shadows and ghostly shapes from the abundant foliage decorating the garden. The trees waving in the gentle breeze cast sheltering shadows around the man who paused outside the French doors. He watched, hidden in the night, listening for a few seconds. Finally determining he was safe, he carefully turned the doorknob and slowly opened the door. He stepped inside.

He squinted as his eyes adjusted to the darkness of the unlit room. *Something's different. There's more furniture here.* Suddenly he realized what he was staring at. It was a bed, and in that bed was a slight figure. *Bree!* He felt his heart race with excitement. This was so easy! She was right here, right in front of him.

He stood in the dim glow of moonlight filtering through the window, transfixed by the sight before him. Knowing that the ranch was basically deserted and that he was safe from prying eyes, the man crossed the sun room floor, confidence and bravado evident in his swaggering gait. His feet carried him over to the bed, where he stood watching Bree, listening to the sound of her deep, even breathing. The filtered moonlight coming through the window threw his silhouette into relief against the paleness of the walls, and his giant, distorted shape loomed threateningly over the girl who slept, unaware of the man's presence.

His breathing quickened, and he fingered the sheath of the deadly knife enfolded in the pocket of his coat. His face was cold and impassive, with only his eyes showing any anger and obsession. His fingers twitched as he listened to her soft breathing.

Leaning down, he brushed her face in a cold caress as he whispered, "Tomorrow, Bree. Sleep tonight, my darling. I'll be back for you tomorrow."

His diabolical promise lingered in the air as he turned and silently left the slumbering girl, her dreams disturbed only by the hazy image of the danger waiting for her to awake.

Chapter 33

The dim interior of the musty cellar reeked. Shari and Brock had cried the first few days when their bodily functions had demanded relief. Now, the fact that they had to live in their own waste mattered very little.

They huddled together under a pile of old, dirty quilts. At least he had brought them blankets and heavy clothing. It had turned so cold, and they had shivered together for several hours before he returned. Their food and water supply was meager but adequate. They had learned quickly that in order to survive, they would need to ration it. Once he brought them the clothes and the blankets, the cold was no longer such a deadly opponent.

They rarely spoke. It was too cold, and they were too hungry. The food and blankets were enough to keep them alive, but not enough to bring any measurable comfort. The first few hours after their shackles had been removed, they had used the flashlight to explore the small cell. Shari had clawed at the dirt walls but found them to be as dense as granite. The door, though old and gray, was solid and strong. There was no hope for escape.

They had tried to keep track of the days and nights, but with no light from outside, it had been impossible. The long, frightening days and nights had turned into one continuous nightmare. Though the darkness and the cold and the hunger threatened to consume them, Brock and Shari found a way to survive.

Thomas had taken them to church, and they had found that they loved the classes for children, the stories of Jesus, and especially singing time. So every time they ate a meager meal, they would sing one of the songs they had learned at Primary and say a simple prayer.

Their faith carried tremendous strength. Though they were hungry and cold, Shari and Brock were able to keep their spirits centered on the knowledge that they would be rescued. Their situation seemed hopeless, but they did not doubt that somehow they would survive.

At the same moment that their sister was sleeping, trying to evade her ever-present nightmares, Brock and Shari were softly singing words of comfort and hope. Thomas had told them about Jesus Christ and had shown them how to walk in the light of His love. He had taught them how to pray to their Father, and they had no doubt that the light of their loving Savior would lead them home.

Chapter 34

"Bree, are you sure you're ready for this?"

Bree looked up at the woman standing beside her and smiled, her eyes reflecting her determination. "Yes, I'm sure. I just need to go to the house . . . to be there for a few minutes. I won't stay very long, I promise. I have to prepare myself for when the kids get back, they'll expect me to be there, and even if I'm still staying here, I need to be able to pick up and go home when they need me to. I've got to confront my fears." Bree shuddered. The day had passed slowly for her, filled with long hours of pacing, worrying, and fearful musings. Her determination to visit her home, to begin preparing herself emotionally for the children's homecoming, gave her a sense of purpose.

Following Bree down the hall, Sarah ran a hand through her hair, mussing its tidy look. "Bree, wait. I just don't feel good about this, honey. You just came home yesterday. At least let me go with you!"

Bree stopped in front of the door and turned to face her friend. She reached for Sarah's hands. "It's going to be okay. Yesterday I didn't think I could ever face going back to my own house, but I think that's where I need to be. For Brock and for Shari. But in order to be there, I have to start now, preparing myself to go back. I need to do this for myself. And I need to do it *by* myself. Please understand!"

A trace of her deeper emotions momentarily darkened Bree's eyes. "I know it doesn't look good, Sarah. Sheriff Hambly told me that with each passing day, the chance that Brock and Shari will be found grows slimmer. But I can't give up hope. I have to believe that they'll be found." Giving Sarah's hands one final squeeze, Bree loosened her hold and said, "They won't let me take part in the search, so all I can do is wait and prepare myself so that I'll be ready for them. Just in case. I promise I won't stay long. It's already three o'clock, and it's going to get dark soon." Bree gulped. "I know I'm not ready to be there by myself after dark. I promise, I won't be more than a half hour. Besides," Bree smiled grimly, "Deputy Odham is never very far away."

Sarah smiled her understanding. She looked like she was going to say something more, but just then, the phone rang and Sarah turned to answer it, waving at Bree over her shoulder.

Bree heard Sarah say, "Hi, darling. What is it? Oh! My goodness! Yes, I'll be ready in a few minutes."

Bree walked away from the homestead, missing Sarah's immediate companionship. She looked around, squinting in the gathering gloom, trying to locate Deputy Odham. *He must be doing his rounds of the outbuildings.* Bree thought about searching for him to tell him where she was going, but it was cold and the afternoon skies were already darkening. *No, I'll just run ahead. I won't be there very long. and I want to get back before it gets any darker.*

The sky was heavy with gray, snow-filled clouds. Bree took a deep breath of the cold, crisp air and shivered when a strong gust of wind cut through her clothing. The golden-brown carpet of leaves crackled underfoot as the wind sent them dancing across the yard. She pulled her denim jacket closer around her shoulders in an effort to ward off the chill of the unexpectedly cold, autumn night air.

Bree shivered again, quickening her pace, intent on reaching the sheltering warmth of her house. Since the night of the attack, Lex Larsen had been going over daily to make sure the house was secure. Bree knew that it would be clean and warm, if not exactly welcoming. Secretly, her heart hurt at the thought of going into the quiet, lonely house, but she knew it was the right thing to do.

She knew she couldn't stay with the Sheridans forever, and today's visit was the first step toward returning to her own home. Steve and Sarah had been so loving and supportive, and while she genuinely appreciated their hospitality, there had been a sense of unease disturbing the surface tranquility.

Bree knew that the uncomfortable feelings stemmed from the fear that she kept hidden. She tried so hard to put on a brave front, but she lived in terror each day. Extending her stay with the Sheridans wasn't the answer. She felt that she had to face her fear head on.

The lonely, black hours of night were the worst. Bree dreaded the onset of evening, and she shivered as she walked through the gathering gloom of dusk, contemplating her self-appointed task. Shrugging her shoulders in an attempt to physically gird herself up, Bree reprimanded herself. She had to move on. She had to be strong for herself and for the children.

Looking up into the gray, dismal sky, Bree noted the small flakes of snow beginning to fall, filling the air with a flurry of white. She shivered again as tiny fingers of ice touched her chilled skin.

Weary and weighted down by the fear, Bree reached her house. As she mounted the shallow steps of the landing, she looked into the mailbox. She gave a small exclamation of surprise when she saw that there was actually something there. Reaching in, she pulled out the small, white envelope. Her name was written across the front in bold, dark pencil strokes. The letter had obviously been hand delivered, as there was no return address and no postmark. With shaking fingers, she pulled out the single folded page of notebook paper, her face blanching to the color of parchment as she read the words.

I haven't forgotten you, Bree. Be afraid, my darling.

Bree closed her eyes, her chest heaving with the effort of controlling the terror raging in her head. "No, no, no. It's not real. It's not real."

When she opened her eyes and stared down at the black letters, terrifying in their total anonymity, she cried out, knowing that she would be a fool to deny the reality of the threat. And she had been a fool to come to the house by herself.

Turning quickly, the vile letter clamped in her frozen hands, Bree stumbled down the icy steps of her house. With a scream, she fell short as hands reached out to grab her upper arms. Bree began to struggle.

"Bree, what's wrong? Why are you out here all alone?"

Bree's haze of terror began to fade. She recognized Ben's voice and sank against him. Taking a moment to gather her wits, Bree pushed away from the ranch foreman's safe embrace. She quickly explained her purpose for being at the house, then shook her head. "But I was a fool. It's too early and too dangerous. Look!"

Bree thrust the letter into Ben's hands. He quickly scanned the penciled lines, his face pale and his expression grim. "C'mon, Bree. Let's get you back to the ranch house."

Bree accepted Ben's support, and they quickly made their way across the compound. Ben knocked once on the front door but didn't wait for an answer. He pushed it open, ushering Bree in ahead of him. "Steve! Sarah!"

His shouted greeting was met with silence. With a frown, Ben urged Bree into the sitting room. The remnants of a fire continued to warm the room. Striding back through the door, he called over his shoulder, "I'll be right back, Bree."

Bree silently acknowledged his words. She stood quietly in the middle of the room, then stepped toward the fireplace and knelt down in front of it, holding her chilled hands to its warmth.

"Bree?"

"I'm over here, Ben. By the fireplace."

Ben joined Bree by the hearth and looked down on her bent head. "It looks like Steve and Sarah have gone out."

Bree remembered the phone ringing earlier, just as she left the homestead that afternoon. She recollected Sarah's voice saying, *Hi, darling. What is it? Oh! My goodness! Yes, I'll be ready in a few minutes.*

She looked up at Ben. "Sarah got a phone call earlier. I think it was from Steve. It sounded like he was asking her to go somewhere with him."

Ben scratched his head, confusion and uncertainty etched on his handsome face. "Look, Bree, I need to go find the deputy. I want him to see that letter as soon as possible. But I don't want to leave you here alone."

Bree pushed herself off the floor. "I'll be fine. I'm sure Sarah and Steve will be home any minute." Bree pushed a weary hand through her hair, tucking it behind her ears. "I'll make sure the doors are all locked. And I'll keep all the lights on!"

Ben smiled gently at Bree's remarks. "Keeping the lights all on is going to keep you safe?"

"It'll make me feel safer!"

"Okay. Listen, sweetheart, walk me to the door. I want to hear that dead bolt latching before I leave you."

Bree followed Ben out of the den. She stood in the hallway while he quickly went through the house checking to make sure the windows were securely latched and the back doors were tightly locked. "Okay, everything's secure." Coming up behind her, Ben touched her shoulder. "You sure you're going to be okay?

"Yes! I'll be fine." Bree paused a moment as a shiver of apprehension crawled down her spine. "You won't be long, will you? You will come back?"

"Of course I'll come back. As soon as I find Deputy Odham I'll come back and keep you company until Steve and Sarah come home."

"I'd appreciate that, Ben. Thank you."

Ben opened the door, and Bree looked around him, gasping at the intensity of the darkening sky. Nightfall had descended quickly, and with it had come a heavy curtain of drifting snow.

"What a night! I hope Steve and Sarah get home soon!"

Bree echoed Ben's sentiments, closing the door and twisting the bolt. She heard Ben's muffled footfall on the snow-encrusted steps and turned away, missing his reassuring presence. She retraced her steps back into the den, and before settling down on the comfortable couch, she threw two heavy logs onto the dying embers of the fire. She sat on the sofa, warmed by the flames and lulled into a stupor of thought. Bree was unaware of the passage of time until the ringing of the phone summoned her across the room. She lifted the receiver and held her breath until she heard the voice on the other end.

"Bree? It's me, Ben."

"Did you find the deputy?"

"No, I didn't. Lex said he thought he saw Deputy Odham driving away with Sarah and Steve an hour or so ago. Listen, Lex is going to organize a few men to patrol the ranch buildings. There aren't too many men available; they're all still out searching. This snow has everyone worried, but I think I need to get this letter to the sheriff as quickly as possible, so I'm going to see if I can go track him down."

"That's a good idea. Is he still up on the mountain at the command station?"

"I think so. He's working like a madman. That's the first place I'm going to look anyway."

"Please be careful."

"I'll be fine. The command station is only a few miles out. They've set up some tents as the central point for the search. They've got portable propane heaters and camp stoves set up so I'll be able to warm up once I get there. And they have a makeshift lean-to for the horses."

"Are you going to ride your horse?" Bree asked in surprise.

"Yeah, it'll be quicker to ride. I won't have to worry about following the established roads."

"Okay, but please . . . be careful."

Bree replaced the receiver, grateful for Ben's concern. With a sigh she sank onto the sofa cushions and leaned back, closing her eyes. She lay there thinking about that day's events, reliving the determination she had felt at the idea of going home for a while, of exerting her independence. Then she relived the moments spent on the front step of her house, the heinous note clasped in her trembling fingers. Images of Ben, his comforting voice, mixed with Sarah's voiced concerns for Bree's planned visit home. Bree felt overwhelmed by it all. Tears threatened to choke her when the faces of her little brother and sister rose before her, an insubstantial and fleeting specter.

Suddenly, the loving features of her parents replaced Brock's and Shari's images and Bree began to sob. The emotions of the past few days descended on her, crushing her will and breaking her spirit. "Oh, Mommy and Daddy!" Bree's cries were those of a little girl. She yearned to feel the comfort of her parents' arms encircling her, ensuring her that she and the children were safe. "I miss you so much."

Bree cried until exhaustion overtook her and she fell into a troubled sleep. An hour later, she was awakened by the shrill ringing of the telephone. She sat up, disoriented by the quiet, empty house. She jumped when the phone rang again, and she leaped to her feet. She was across the room in a second, her hands flying to the receiver sitting on Steve's desk. *Maybe it's Ben with some news. Or it could be Steve and Sarah!* Without hesitation, she brought the phone to her ear and said, "Hello."

Bree's features froze, and in a fearful trance she slowly sank onto the wooden chair next to the desk. The cool plastic resting against her cheek seemed to spark with evil as she listened to the silence.

Seconds seemed to stretch into minutes, and then, as she had known he would, he spoke. "Be afraid, my darling."

Chapter 35

The piercing echo of Bree's scream reached through the phone lines, bringing a malicious smile to the lips of the steely eyed man on the other end. The hair on the back of his neck was raised, and he felt his skin prickle. The excitement was almost too much for him, and his maniacal laughter blended with the tortured strains of her voice. The phone line suddenly went silent, and the man's laughter died as he threw down the receiver.

He began to pace back and forth across the carpeted floor of the office, his muscles tense and tight. He fought to keep himself under control. The fires of obsession and rage burning in his gut urged him to go to her now. He had, in fact, planned on ending it all tonight. He had promised her that he would come for her today, but he found that he didn't want to end the game just yet.

She was suffering, and he wanted it to continue. If asked, he wouldn't have been able to point to any one incident that had turned him from loving Bree to hating her. But he felt that she deserved to suffer, and he was going to make sure her life turned into a living nightmare. He hated her for looking so lovely and so calm. He knew that the calm was just a mask. She was slowly dying on the inside, and he relished the agony she was suffering.

With a grim smile of fiendish pleasure, he walked over to the large, oak desk and sat down. Pulling out a blank sheet of paper, he grabbed a heavy-leaded pencil and began to write.

Chapter 36

The loud laughter mocked her terror, and Bree slammed the phone down. She stood tense and terrified. Her screams died in the silence of the snowy night, and a sudden sob broke her stillness. She had to leave. She couldn't stay in this house, knowing that he was near, watching and waiting for her. She had been a fool to stay alone, to make herself more vulnerable to his mania.

Bree's hands flew up, covering her face. After a few seconds of deep breathing, her fingers slid into her hair, grasping and pulling at her own locks. She felt like she was going crazy. She squeezed her eyes tightly closed and willed herself to find a sense of calm.

That will fled, however, when she opened her eyes and found herself staring at the top of Steve's desk. A cry of sheer terror tore from her throat, and she ran to the front door. With stiff, clumsy hands, she fought with the locks. She couldn't make her fingers work and cried out in frustration as she pulled and tugged on the stubborn dead bolt. Finally, with a gasp of relief, the knob turned in her hands, and Bree wrenched the door open. Stumbling down the slick, icy steps, she ran.

Nightfall had come quickly, cloaking the ranch in a veil of snow. The cold mocked the flames of fear driving Bree through the darkness. The blackness was not only that of the nighttime; it was a void so deeply embedded in her heart that she knew she would never again find the light. The horridness of the phone call, combined with the hideous truth of what she had seen on Steve's desk, rose in her throat like bile. She suddenly stopped and turned her face upwards, the falling snow caressing her fevered skin with taunting gentleness.

The coldness of the night found an answering echo in the frozen depths of her soul, and she opened her lips, a silent cry of anguish rising to the heavens. Steve's desktop had been littered with papers, pens, and pencils.

And on one sheet of paper had been scribbles, unintelligible words and figures that made no sense to Bree. The only fact that had registered had been the boldness and the strength of the heavy pencil strokes.

Her mind reeled at the idea that the same hand responsible for those meaningless scribbles had also been responsible for the ugly, horrifying words that had called her *darling* and had warned her to be afraid. He couldn't have made the terrifying phone call. He wasn't home. He and Sarah were together. But were they?

All at once, Bree realized that there was no one she could trust. She didn't even trust the sheriff. His apparent efforts to solve the crime seemed so ineffectual and so inadequate. She cried from the very depths of her being for someone to trust. Frantically, she looked around. Where were the deputies who were supposed to be patrolling the ranch, assigned to keep her safe?

She felt so alone and frightened, and as the snow continued to cascade over her, its caress feather soft, Bree sank to her knees and allowed the overwhelming feelings to flow over her. She rocked back and forth, her mind numb with the ache of needing someone to trust. Minutes passed as the cold night wrapped her in its icy embrace, and suddenly her movements stilled and she again raised her face to the sky. A name came to her, and as it whispered itself to her heart, a fleeting glimmer of hope crossed her pale countenance.

Thomas.

She needed Thomas. His name became a mantra as she rose from her knees and slowly began the short trek across the deserted ranch compound.

She reached the door of his small cabin and hesitated. She had no idea how late it was or even if he would be home. The windows of his cabin were darkened, peaceful silence reflected in the ebony glass. He was probably asleep. Or maybe he was out searching. Was Michael home? *Why didn't his name come to me first? Why Thomas and not Michael?*

She thought she might be falling in love with Michael, but did she trust him? Uncertainty warred with her craving need for someone to talk to. She stood in indecision on the stoop, her hand poised to knock but something holding her back from doing so.

And while she stood there, shivering from the cold and the fear, a phantomlike figure lurked nearby, watching and waiting in menacing silence.

Chapter 37

Bree wasn't the only person whose emotions were in turmoil that night. The ominous figure standing so tall and silent in the cold darkness felt his anger burn. His confusion clouded the determination of his demented plan. He hated her with every breath he took.

But every time he looked into her lovely face or heard the musical sound of her laughter, obsession churned and mixed with the fledgling hatred embedded in his gut. Desire for her would sweep over him with bittersweet longing. How could he love her but hate her at the same time? There were times he questioned his plans for her.

Yet even after the softer feelings emerged, bringing a hint of humane enlightenment, the insidious veil of his hatred fell once more, conquering the softness. He watched her poised on the front step of the old man's house, and he clenched his hands and gritted his teeth. There were too many other people pulling at her, trying to take her away from him. He knew with a certainty that there was only one way that he could completely own her.

He had to kill her.

Chapter 38

"Shari?"

"Huh?"

"Would you tell me a story?"

Six-year-old Brock's voice was weak, barely a whisper in the cavernous gloom of their earthen prison cell. Both children were slipping into the grasp of despair. Shari tried to remember Bree's face. She was so pretty, and her face had always carried such a countenance of love that her eyes seemed to glow. But that glow was dimming with each passing day. Shari found herself fighting back tears as she struggled to remember the warmth and the light of Bree's love.

She was only seven years old. By most standards she was barely older than a baby, and listening to Brock's plea, she felt like a baby. She didn't want to tell him a story. All she wanted to do was curl up on the floor, suck her thumb, and cry.

"Please!"

Shari felt the touch of her brother's small, cold fingers when he slipped his hand into hers, somehow finding her despite the thick darkness that had become their world. Her heart melted as she felt him curl up beside her. She put her arms around him and drew him close. "What kind of story?"

After a few seconds of contemplative silence, Brock whispered softly, "Tell me a Jesus story."

His request touched her heart, and Shari felt warmth in her entire body. It not only covered and soothed and warmed her skin, she felt it bring comfort to her very soul. Snuggling closer to Brock, her grimy, dirty cheek resting atop the soft shock of red curls outgrowing his former buzz cut, Shari felt a smile spread across her face.

While the night deepened outside and as the early snowfall shrouded the cellar door beneath which they were trapped, a golden aura seemed to surround the two lost children. As Shari's quiet voice repeated the stories of Jesus that Brock yearned to hear, it was as if the Savior Himself knelt beside the two small bodies huddled together in the dark.

Chapter 39

"Mercy sakes, Bree! What are you doing out on a night like this?" Thomas wiped the sleep from his eyes, staring in shock at the shivering girl standing on his porch. "Never mind that. Come in, child." With a gentle hand, Thomas pulled Bree into his house and the safety of his presence.

"Oh, Thomas," Bree cried, crumpling against him.

"Hush, child, you hush now." Holding her, Thomas felt her trembling and realized that she was on the verge of collapse. With tenderness, he guided her into the small front room. He snatched a soft, knitted afghan from off the back of the couch and wrapped Bree in its comforting warmth.

"Where's Michael?" Bree asked.

"He's out with the sheriff's men. He came in for a quick bite to eat, but he couldn't stand the thought of the kids being out there in the snow." Thomas paused, working through the lump in his throat. "I wanted to be out there too. But he wouldn't let me. He was probably right. These old bones wouldn't have been much use out in that cold. But that's okay. I'm here, and obviously this is where I need to be."

Thomas got up from the couch and soon had a fire crackling in the fireplace. After making sure that Bree was comfortably settled, he hurried into the kitchen. She could hear him banging pans and rifling through the cupboards. Soon he returned and pressed a cup of steaming hot chocolate into her hands.

He waited in silence until she drained the cup. Sitting beside Bree, Thomas took her hands in his and looked deep into her eyes. Since she had returned to the ranch, he had tried to talk to her, to get her to share the deep pain. But she always downplayed her fear, and it broke his heart.

All he could offer was his love and his faith. She accepted his love, but her dread prevented her from sharing his faith. He could hold her close in a warm, grandfatherly embrace, but he knew her fear remained undimmed.

Something told him that tonight would be different. As the fire crackled and the snow continued to fall outside, gently frosting the world in a layer of glistening white, Bree turned to Thomas and poured out her heart to him. She told him about going back to her house that afternoon.

"I need to prepare myself to move back home. But I don't want to be alone."

Thomas felt his heart squeeze with sorrow at the words stated so quietly yet with such a depth of feeling.

"I know, child. None of us wants to be alone."

Rising from the couch, Bree walked over to the front room window and stood watching the drifting snow. She felt as though the pristine beauty was a mockery of the cold and ugly horror that filled her life. Closing her eyes, she forced herself to forget the repugnant image of violence that crowded her mind. Instead, she concentrated on the picture-perfect beauty of the world cloaked in a mantel of white.

By morning, the trees would be frosted with layers of sparkling snow, their thick green needles peeking out from beneath a heavy cap of glistening white. The ground would be covered with a crystalline and pure carpet, unmarred by the trampling of human feet. The mountains would tower above the unspoiled landscape, their crags and peaks reflecting the wintry splendor of the valley below.

As Bree's mental imagery began to work its magic, she felt her tense muscles relax. She opened her eyes to gaze out upon the softly falling snow and allowed the peace of the moment to wash over her. Turning from the loveliness of the wintry night, Bree returned to Thomas's side. She began telling him about finding the note in her mailbox, what it said, and how it made her feel.

Thomas's face turned as gray as the smoke rising from the burning logs. He closed his eyes and whispered, "Oh, child, you've got to call the sheriff."

"I know. Ben Laird found me. I don't know what I would have done if he hadn't shown up. He took me back to the ranch house. But Steve and Sarah weren't home. I don't know where they were. The house was so empty, but Ben reassured me and helped me feel safe. But then he left to go find the sheriff. And then . . ." Bree's voice trailed off as she remembered the horror of the menacing voice reaching her through the phone line.

Thomas watched Bree's face blanch. "There's more?"

Bree then told him the rest. She told him about the phone call, the hideous threat and the maniacal laughter. "And then," Bree paused as she relived what had followed. As briefly as possible, she told Thomas about finding the papers covered in bold, black-penciled letters. What confused and frightened Bree the most, however, was the fact that she had seen those papers on Steve's desk.

Thomas stared at her in disbelief. "You must be wrong, Bree. There's no way."

Bree's eyes filled with tears. "I know. I can't believe it either. But I can't deny what I saw."

Thomas wiped a hand across his aged face and groaned. Bree cried, "I don't know what to do." Her words echoed the depth of her despair. "If there's even a chance that . . ."

"Please, don't say it, Bree. I can't believe it."

"But Thomas, what if . . ."

"No, it's not possible."

Thomas and Bree sat together, the gravity of her unspoken accusation making them both numb with horrific denial.

Finally Thomas spoke, "Bree, honey, I'm sorry if I sound like I don't believe you. But those pencil marks—is that all you're basing your suspicions on?"

"Yes."

Thomas fell silent as he contemplated what Bree had told him. Taking a deep breath, he looked at her and said, "I think we should talk to him."

For a moment Bree looked terrified. But then she calmed herself and agreed, "Yes, we owe him that, don't we?"

"I think so. Honey, I honestly can't believe he's involved. I'd trust Steve . . . with my life."

"I trusted him, too, Thomas. Now, I just don't know. I'd think I could believe it of anyone else. But not Steve. And not you."

Thomas frowned. "What about Michael?"

Bree caught her breath, her face freezing with doubt. Finally she choked out, her voice barely discernible over the crackle and hiss of the burning logs in the fireplace, "I don't know." Flashing through her mind were the faces of the men she knew—Michael, Steve, Ben, Chuck, Lex Larsen, Jonathan Smith, Thomas. Did she really know any of them? Did she trust them?

Thomas felt the pain behind Bree's words as he reached for her. "Honey, I know you don't completely believe me when I tell you how important prayer is, but I think that's what we need to do."

Bree felt her face settle into gentle repose as she said, "I don't *not* believe you, Thomas."

"Will you pray with me about this, Bree?"

Bree silently nodded. Thomas smiled gently, urging her, "Kneel with me."

Bree followed Thomas as he slipped off the couch and knelt in front of the fire. The heat from the flames warmed their skin, and Thomas began to pray, his words simple but heartfelt. Bree felt a tingling glow as she listened carefully to his words.

She was amazed at how naturally he prayed, as though he were speaking to someone in the room with them. She felt tempted to peek but quelled the childlike urge and refocused her attention on what he was saying. He closed his prayer with a soft, "Amen." Bree blinked her eyes rapidly against the unexpected tears.

Thomas slowly rose to his feet and reached a hand down to assist Bree. She stood beside him and put her arm around his waist. Leaning her head on his shoulder, she said, "Thank you. I think that helped."

"I'm glad, child. I think we should try and get some sleep. I think I know what I need to do, but there's no sense in waking everyone up tonight."

"What are you going to do, Thomas?"

"I'm going to talk to Steve. And Michael."

"Do you want me to be there?"

"No, that's okay. I'll do it. When I see them tomorrow, I'll find some time to pull them aside. I'm not sure yet exactly what I'll say, but I know the Lord will help me."

"Thomas, where does your faith come from?"

Bree's question took him by surprise. He thought for a moment before answering, "Why, I think it comes from in here." He tapped himself on the chest. "It's in here, and it's just a matter of finding it and then helping it grow."

"How do you do that? Help it grow?"

Scratching his head, Thomas realized that Bree was on the threshold of taking a very important step. He remembered back to the days when he was first learning about the gospel, and he decided to share with her something that the missionaries had told him. "Our faith is like our bodies. In order for us to be strong and healthy, we need to exercise. Exercise strengthens our muscles and helps our bodies function the way Heavenly Father meant them to function." Thomas looked at her out of the corner of his eye, and he saw her listening carefully, "Our faith is just like that. It's there, but sometimes it's just buried a little deeper and can be weak from not being used. You have to exercise it to help it grow."

"Okay?"

Thomas smiled when he heard the unspoken question and continued, "All you have to do to exercise your faith is to believe. Let God know that you trust Him and that you'll try to follow Him. Soon, you'll find it easier to believe and easier to follow. It just goes from there."

Bree nodded gently, knowing that she would have to think about what Thomas had told her. She wanted to find her faith. She recognized what it meant to Thomas, and she saw how much comfort it gave him. She wanted that for herself.

Suddenly, she remembered the hope she had expressed to Sarah that the kids would be found. And she started to smile, realizing that she had already found her faith. It was just a matter of doing what Thomas said and putting her trust in God so that it could be exercised and strengthened.

"Thank you, Thomas. I feel much better."

Thomas could see in her eyes that something had changed. There was a glimmer of light that shone in the wide, blue gaze, and he smiled down at her. "I'm glad, child. Here, let's get you some blankets and a pillow, and you can sleep here tonight. I'll stoke the fire up so it can keep you company while you sleep."

Soon, the little house was quiet and still. Once Thomas was sure Bree had fallen asleep, he made a quick phone call, letting the sheriff's office know of the latest incident. He was informed that the deputy on duty would be by shortly to take their statements. He asked if Bree could give her statement in the morning, but assured the dispatcher that he would wait up to talk to Deputy Hayes.

The deputy arrived within minutes, disturbed that something had happened on his watch. Thomas shared with him as many details as he could remember. Deputy Hayes took down the report and promised to be back at 7:00 the next morning to talk to Bree.

It was 1:00 A.M. before Thomas went to bed, his heart hurting for his young friend but grateful for the chance he'd had to pray with her. Thomas and Bree both slept a little easier, their earlier fear and dismay soothed by the balm of their shared faith. Thomas's faith was anchored deeply in his past, and Bree's was like a newborn, tender and dependent, but filled with eternal potential.

Chapter 40

"Here, Brock, have a drink."

Shari handed her little brother the water bottle and listened while he drank thirstily. The slurping sounds he made seemed loud in the darkness, and she felt concern for his seemingly unquenchable thirst. She reached for the bottle, her fingers clumsy as they searched blindly.

"Let me have it back, Brock. We can't drink it all right now."

"But I'm still thirsty."

Shari heard the pleading in his voice and knew it wasn't just the water he was longing for. She licked her own dry, cracked lips. "I know. Me too. But we have to save some for later."

"Do you think he'll be back?"

"I dunno."

"I hope so." Brock's voice was tiny and filled with yearning. Even though the man's actions were mean, he was an adult, and in Brock's mind that made him want to trust the man. Shari cringed at the thought of the man's return. He scared her. It wasn't just that he had taken them from their home, and it wasn't only because he kept them locked in the cellar. There was something different about him that she found frightening. She couldn't have explained what it was; she didn't know the words to describe the pure evil she saw in his eyes. The purity of her spirit, however, recoiled from the sinister aura that permeated the room when he entered.

Shari blanched and shut her eyes tightly, her lips moving in silent prayer, pleading for comfort for herself and Brock. Seconds later, she opened her eyes and reached for Brock's hand. She squeezed his fingers and smiled, resting her head on the cold, damp wall behind her.

"Remember the picnics we had with Bree? And the one when we had a water fight?"

Brock started to giggle. He slid down onto his side, his head lying in Shari's lap. He closed his eyes, feeling surprisingly warm and happy while he listened to Shari's voice. He fell asleep with happy memories of Bree dancing in his dreams.

Shari's voice soon faded, and she felt her head nod forward. Her chin rested on her chest, and as the two children slept, a spirit of peace wrapped them protectively against the cold and dismal reality of their imprisonment.

Chapter 41

Bree arose early the following morning, feeling unexpectedly refreshed and bearing the spark of renewed hope in her heart. She spoke with Deputy Hayes and Deputy Odham, giving them a complete account of her experiences the night before. They promised that they would fill the sheriff in on the events. Before leaving, Deputy Odham took Bree's hand and said, "We'll make sure we stay extra close to you, young lady. But please, no more going off by yourself like you did last night!"

Bree promised, and then she insisted to Thomas that she felt well enough to go to the cookhouse and work. "I can't just lie around today. I'll go crazy if I can't help in some way." Thomas nodded his understanding when she continued, "They're my baby sister and brother. The sheriff won't let me help search for them, but I have to do something."

Later that day, Bree was finishing the dishes from lunch and found herself unexpectedly tired. Sarah had helped her with the preparations for breakfast. She had told Bree about Steve's phone call the evening before and how the sheriff had supposedly asked them to meet him at the command center. "But when we got there, the sheriff wasn't around. He'd gone back to Sun Valley for the night." Sarah then told Bree how Steve had felt compelled to join the search since they were already out. "The storm was increasing, and he was so worried about the children. But he wouldn't let me drive home alone. I stayed at the command center all night." Sarah had answered Bree's concerned inquiry about sleep with a tired laugh. "Oh, I managed to get a couple of catnaps in. The propane heaters are keeping the tents warm, and there were blankets to snuggle up with. But I am tired."

After breakfast had been served, Sarah returned to her home for a few hours of much-deserved sleep. Mary Smith and Tina Larsen had stayed with Bree to help with the cleanup, but the ladies had left before lunch, trusting Bree's reassurance that she was up to the task of taking care of the meal on her own.

The clamor of loud voices coming from the dining hall was a sharp contrast to the silence of the empty kitchen. Bree stood hunched over the sink full of soapy water, staring out at the brown countryside. The previous night's unexpected snowfall had melted quickly with the rising of the morning's sun. The trees and the grass were shedding their summer coat of green, and the world was a mixture of brown and gold and rust. The towering pine trees high on the mountain ridges in the distance offered a muted contrast of dark green to the amber of the ranch's fields and pastures.

The entire ranch was caught in a whirlwind of activity as the search for the missing children escalated. Thomas's prayer from the night before had given Bree a foundation of faith and hope, and she knew that somehow, everything was going to be okay. Yet she was realistic enough to know that she still had a huge burden to deal with, and she was still afraid.

But Thomas had shown her that she didn't need to let the fear destroy her.

Bree gazed out of the frosted windowpane. The rising sun filled the bowl of the valley with golden light, and the glory of the autumn scenery beckoned her forward into a day that seemed brighter, offering a beacon of hope.

The condensation running down the frosted pane of the kitchen window streaked its misty surface with rivers of tearlike droplets, and Bree found herself crying. It seemed like she had cried the tears of a lifetime over the past week, but this time, she felt cleansed from the weight of all that had been threatening her.

Lost deep in thought, Bree was startled when the kitchen door swung inward. Surprised by the unexpected intrusion, she sniffled and wiped at her moist eyes. She quelled an exclamation of surprise, staring at the man coming toward her.

"Hello, Bree. I haven't seen you for a while."

Bree's face was ghostly white and absent of any expression as Chuck approached her. He brought with him an unexpected aura of menace. Whether the threat was real or not, to Bree he seemed to epitomize every haunting moment from the last week. She shuddered from the memory of their last encounter when he had tried to force himself on her a second time.

Maybe I should tell the sheriff how weird Chuck has been acting—how he's changed since we worked together in Boise. Her eyes darted to the phone hanging on the wall across the room.

Chuck's advance toward her, however, drew Bree's attention, and she realized the futility of trying to reach the phone. Chuck's face was drawn and gray, as if he had been up all night. What frightened Bree was the coldness that emanated from his eyes.

He stepped in front of her, staring her in the face, but not touching her. "I never meant for any of this to happen."

"Any of what, Chuck? I don't understand." Bree's words didn't reflect the horrified thoughts screaming through her mind. *Chuck! It couldn't be! What was he trying to say?*

"I never meant to fall in love with you." His quietly spoken words died in the silence of the kitchen. Chuck turned abruptly and left Bree without a backward glance.

Chapter 42

"Turn on the flashlight, Brock. Please. I want to see how much food is left."

"I can't, Shari. The batteries are almost dead." Brock's young voice was faint in the heavy darkness.

They hadn't had a visit from their prison guard for a long time. Shari knew that they didn't have much food left, and they were almost out of water. She couldn't help but wonder if he had forgotten them.

"I don't like the dark, Shari." Brock's voice broke as he began to cry. He had been such a brave boy for so long. He still wanted to be brave, but sometimes it was too hard. He was so tired and hungry—and so scared.

Shari crawled back toward him. She found him in the dark, and they wrapped their arms around each other.

"What're we gonna do, Shari?" Brock's voice was a whisper that stirred the lank strands of his sister's hair.

"I don't know." She knew they should pray. That's what Thomas would tell them to do. But for the moment, she was too tired and too weak.

"I'm tired."

Shari felt the weight of responsibility as six-year-old Brock nestled his head on her shoulder. "Go to sleep. Maybe when we wake up we'll feel better."

"Shari?"

"Huh?"

"Why do you think it's taking so long for Heavenly Father to answer our prayers?"

Shari thought for a moment, and then her answer came simply. "Maybe whoever He's trying to tell to help us isn't listening."

"Thomas would be listening."

"I know. Maybe Thomas isn't s'posed to find us."

"You think Bree is listening?" Brock's simple query gave Shari an idea.

"I don't know." Suddenly Shari felt her spirit revive as she knew what they needed to do. "Let's ask Him to help her listen."

Chapter 43

Thomas stretched, his back aching from the long hours spent in the saddle. He refused to give in to the weakness of his aging body. High in the forested depths of the mountain, he felt an odd sensation of nearness. To the children? To God? He couldn't identify it, but it kept him in the saddle. He had been thinking about his promise to Bree about talking to Steve and Michael. He hadn't had the chance to talk to either man yet, but he would at the first opportunity.

Suddenly, Thomas's eyes caught a movement further along the trail he was following. Then a flash of color appeared. His mouth fell open in surprise. *Wonder what he's doing here?*

Thomas reflected on the assignments handed out that morning and knew that the other man had been given an area to search miles away from his own assigned post. Spurring his horse, Thomas had just decided to hail the other man when he unexpectedly disappeared from view.

"Now where in tarnation does he think he's going?" Thomas muttered the words out loud, turning his gray mare, Clementine. She was prancing impatiently, and he had to forcibly hold her back from following the other horse. He quickly scanned the surrounding terrain and recognized a long-forgotten logging road on the far side of the mountains that rimmed the southwestern edge of the ranch.

"He's not supposed to be this far south," Thomas muttered to himself, still confused at seeing the familiar rider.

Before he could think about what he was doing, Thomas conceded to his mare's instincts and turned her southwest. High overhead, an eagle soared and circled the old man as he followed the disappearing figure along the heavily wooded western ridge.

Chapter 44

With one quick glance over his shoulder, the man guided his horse through the brush and found the trail he knew was there. He felt compelled to check on the children and had purposely ignored the directives that he had been given that morning. He was cautious, though, in order to avoid the other searchers. He didn't want anyone to see him or question him about his presence in the southwestern sector of the search grid. Should he encounter any of them, however, he did have a story outlined in his head. But he was confident in his efforts to remain unseen.

He patted his bulging saddlebags, knowing that the supplies he had pilfered the night before wouldn't be missed with all the hoopla going on. He knew that the kids were probably getting low on food, and he didn't want anything to happen to them. At least not yet. Besides, if things went as planned, this would be the last time he would have to bring food to the brats.

His gut still burned with gall when he remembered the night on the roundup when Bree had spent the night sleeping next to Thomas. He didn't know why that memory was so raw. He also didn't know what he was going to do about the old man. "I'll figure somethin' out, though." Muttering to himself, he issued a warning, "Be careful, Thomas. You don't want to get in my way."

Chapter 45

Thomas almost missed the trail leading upward into the densely wooded mountainside. He sat for a moment scratching his head, wondering where the man could have disappeared. Just as he was ready to retrace his steps, he saw the trail.

It was narrow and overgrown, but Thomas saw the broken branches that indicated someone had recently passed by. Urging Clementine forward, he wound his way up the mountainside.

After riding for ten minutes, he broke out of the woods and found himself on a rutted logging road. He was dumbfounded. "Now which way?" Rubbing his stubbled chin, he listened to Clementine whinny as she tossed her head to the right.

"That way, girl?" Thomas asked his mount. "Okay, I'll trust your instincts."

Muttering under his breath, his curiosity building, Thomas rode on. "Yep, they've been this way. Looky there." Thomas squinted his eyes and wrinkled his nose at the pungent scent of horse manure that assailed his nostrils.

After riding another ten minutes, Thomas started to wonder if he was on a wild goose chase when the narrow road ended in a clearing. He stared at the small, weathered cabin nestled in the bosom of the trees fifty feet across the clearing.

"Wonder what he's doin' here." Thomas dismounted and dropped the reins as Clementine lowered her head and began to graze on the wilting grass poking through a thin layer of fallen leaves.

Hesitantly, Thomas looked around before striding toward the front stoop of the cabin. He knocked on the door, and when there was no answer, he tried the handle. Looking down, he saw the hasp and closed padlock that kept the door securely shut. Stepping to the left of the door, he sidled up to the grimy window set high in the wall of the cabin. Using his shirtsleeve, he wiped at the dirt covering the pane. When he had cleared a small spot, he used his hands to frame the hole as he put his face close to the window. Peering into the murky depths of the cabin's interior, he was unable to see much of anything.

Just then, he heard a rustle from behind and he turned, his smile of greeting fading when he saw the upraised hand bearing down on him. "Hey! What the . . ."

Thomas's words died unspoken as the hand wielded its weapon, and he crumpled to the ground, the bleeding wound on his forehead covering his face in crimson.

Chapter 46

"Stupid old man. I knew you were going to be a problem."

Minutes earlier, he had been alerted to Thomas's presence by the knocking on the door. He had been in the process of unlocking the door to the cellar, his food-laden saddlebags slung over his shoulder, and at the sound of the banging on the door, he had dropped the bags and quickly refastened the padlock.

Silently creeping around the side of the cabin, he had seen Thomas stepping up to the window. Cursing under his breath, he quickly looked around for a weapon. His gaze landed on the rusty head of an old hammer lying half-hidden in the snow. He'd quickly picked it up, and, grasping it securely, he'd snuck up behind the old man.

As Thomas turned, he saw the old man's expression change from recognition and greeting to comprehension and fear. The hammer had descended too quickly for Thomas to do more than cry out once.

Standing over Thomas's inert form, the man rubbed his face in agitation. "I knew you were going to be a problem," he repeated.

Pacing in a circle, his thoughts racing, he frantically tried to decide what to do next. Stopping midstride, he looked at his watch and cursed at the lateness of the hour. He glanced at the sky and noticed the gossamer haze of evening descending. It was time to go. He'd have to deal with Thomas later.

"For now, old man, I guess you get to be reunited with the brats." Bending over, he grabbed Thomas by the upper arms and started to drag him around the back of the house. He only took a moment to unlock the door and toss the saddlebags of food down the gaping hole before he kicked Thomas's unresponsive body forward. As the old man's body disappeared into the blackness, he slammed the door shut and slapped the padlock.

Cursing, he rounded the cabin and ran toward his horse. After he mounted, he heard the whinny of a second horse and watched in disbelief as Thomas's mare reared and spun. The old Appaloosa disappeared down the road, its reins flying behind and the empty stirrups slapping its haunches, matching the sound of its beating hooves.

Chapter 47

The dusky lavender skies softened the air with gentle color, and Sarah rode her mount along the logging road, wondering if she had ridden too far south. She was searching the sector next to Thomas, but she had lost her bearings and had become separated from her partner. Relaxing back in the saddle and pushing her hat to the back of her head, Sarah glanced around. It was such a beautiful setting. The spirit of the land alone was enough to help her relax and clear her mind. She closed her eyes and breathed deeply of the perfumed air. It was a relief, even if just temporarily, from the terrible stress and fear that had permeated the entire community.

Without warning, the crashing and snorting of a horse breaking through the nearby brush startled Sarah. "What in the world?" She stared at the familiar Appaloosa as it came rearing through the clearing, riderless. She watched it disappear down the road, an expression of deep concern turning her countenance gray.

Before she could utter another word, a second horse came crashing through the brush. Startled, she screamed as its rider shouted in surprise, his curse renting the air.

With a hand held to her breast, her breath coming in gasps, Sarah stared at the familiar figure astride the powerful stallion.

"Sarah, thank goodness you're here."

"That was Thomas's horse!"

"I know. There's been an accident. I was just riding for help."

"Thomas! Is he hurt?"

"I don't know. I think so."

"Take me to him, now!"

* *

Sarah's unexpected demand caused the man to breathe a frustrated sigh. Everything was falling apart. His cool demeanor hid a raging tumult of emotions.

Seeing Sarah sitting astride her horse in the middle of the old logging road had taken him by surprise. He hadn't expected anyone else to be so close. But when Sarah issued her command, his quick-thinking mind was released from the strangling vine of frustration that had choked his thoughts.

He had to get control of the situation—and fast! Taking Sarah to Thomas might be just the answer. He'd have time to think it through while he led her back to the cabin. Wheeling his horse, he re-entered the forest, Sarah close behind.

* * *

Sarah's mind was in a whirl. Questions stormed in her subconscious, but she was unable to catch hold of any particular one. Her heart was heavy with the thought that Thomas was injured, and her concern crowded the questions aside.

Soon, the two riders cantered into the clearing, and Sarah followed her escort's example by quickly dismounting.

"Follow me. He's around here."

Puzzled, Sarah ran around the side of the cabin. As she came to a stop beside him, she looked around. "Where is he?"

"He's in the cellar."

"What's he doing down there? And why is it padlocked?"

The man straightened from his hunched posture as he finished unlocking the padlock. He then turned and looked at Sarah, his face cold and unfriendly.

Sarah gasped, the blood draining from her face as she felt the anger and the hate emanating from his burning eyes. Sensing imminent danger, she turned on her heels and started to dart away.

With a cry of terror, she was thrown down the stairs, the door slamming shut, encasing her in cavernous blackness.

Chapter 48

Shari and Brock cried out in fear when the light from above slashed through the coal-black interior of the cellar. The light was accompanied by ear-shattering screams. Suddenly, the screams ended and were replaced by the sound of someone crashing down the stairs. After the sounds died, the dank room seemed silently spooky.

"Shari, where's the flashlight?" Brock's voice trembled as he cried out to his sister.

"It's right here, but the batteries are almost gone." Shari was sitting cross-legged, Thomas's head resting in her lap. He was still unconscious, but he moaned when Shari shifted to hand the flashlight to Brock. She gently stroked the old man's cheek, trying again to brush away some of the congealing blood that was pooling in the crevices of his aged face.

"Quick! Turn it on."

"Shari?" Sarah's voice was hesitant in the darkness. She could barely believe the reality of the familiar voices. When Brock had first spoken, Sarah had lain on the floor, dazed and in pain, certain she was dreaming. But when Shari answered Brock, Sarah's heart had leapt at the realization that she was awake and lucid and that the voices truly belonged to her young friends.

Brock turned on the flashlight, its feeble light flickering through the darkness. "Sarah!" he exclaimed.

Sarah sat up, shaking her head and rubbing her bruised limbs. Brock threw himself across the narrow space and wrapped his skinny arms around her neck.

"Brock?" Sarah's voice was tremulous, and she still couldn't seem to quite take in the fact that she had found the children. Her arms closed around the young boy, and she held him tightly, feeling the trembling of his body. She became aware of how bony and cold he felt, and when the sour scent of his unwashed body assaulted her nostrils, she realized that the two children had been in this cold, dank prison for days.

"Shari?"

"I'm here, Sarah." Shari was crying too. For so long, she and Brock had been alone. They had been afraid. But now, all of a sudden, they had not one but two adults with them.

Stuttering, Shari sobbed, "T-T-Thomas is here, too. A-a-a-and he's hurt real bad."

Setting Brock aside, Sarah grabbed for the flashlight that had fallen to the floor unheeded and waved its dim beam around the small enclosure. She rested the light on the huddled figures of Shari and Thomas.

For a second, she stared into Shari's face. She saw the tangled mass of auburn curls, the dirt-streaked face, and the thinness of the girl's frame. Sarah felt tears roll down her own cheeks as she reached out with a gentle hand and stroked the little girl's face.

"Oh, honey." She was unable to say anything more, but Shari's deep blue eyes shone back at her.

With a gasp, she transferred her gaze to Thomas's silent features. She saw the gaping wound on his forehead, the surrounding skin purple and swollen. She felt for his pulse and sighed with relief when she felt it under her fingertips.

Sarah closed her eyes and couldn't help the little cry of despair that escaped her lips. The hideous truth hit her. She knew who was behind all this evil. The children had been his prisoners, and now she and Thomas had joined them.

With a cry, she thought of Bree and knew that there was nothing she could do to save the young woman who had become like her adoptive daughter. Sarah felt her heart shatter as she asked, "Why?"

The face of their captor rose before her, and Sarah began to sob. "It couldn't be." The reality of his identity was too dreadful, and Sarah clenched her eyes tightly closed while she prayed.

Chapter 49

Dinner was long past; the majority of the men had rejoined the sheriff's deputies as they continued scouring the hills for the children. There were several women from the ranch and from town who had volunteered to help in the kitchen, and Bree had been enormously grateful for their assistance. But they had left to return to their own homes. The cookhouse was eerily quiet, and Bree shivered, the hair on the back of her neck rising. It was like a hidden draft of cold air was passing over her shoulders. She drew on her heavy jacket, wrapping herself in its cozy warmth.

Bree dimmed the lights and wandered to the kitchen door, hesitant to leave the safe confines of the cookhouse. She hadn't seen Sarah or Thomas that evening. She assumed they were still searching, and she was grateful for their commitment to finding Brock and Shari.

Bree stepped outside and shivered in the cold night air. The ranch was still and quiet, with only the occasional bawling cow or neighing horse to break the silence. Bree noticed that most of the houses were dark. It was late. She had delayed leaving the kitchen, wary of returning to an empty house. *Maybe Sarah is already home!*

During the weeks following the roundup, Bree had balked at the cloistering protection offered by her friends. But she had welcomed their presence and diligence over the last few days since her return from the hospital. She knew that everyone was busy searching for the children, and she was glad they were. But she missed the solace that another person's presence provided. *I shouldn't be afraid here. This is my home!* Bree felt the darkness of the night crowding in on her thoughts, slowing her steps as she walked toward the homestead, wondering if Deputy Hayes was close. Maybe he would come into the house with her and stay to keep her company.

She glanced down the road toward her own little home. It broke her heart to think about the once-cheerful abode. Where it had once been filled with children's laughter and hours of happy togetherness, it was now void and empty. Bree almost cried from the grief, loneliness, and fear.

Get a grip, for heaven's sake! she silently berated herself as she walked across the dark compound toward the homestead. The stars shining overhead did little to penetrate the blackness encasing her heart. She struggled to remember Thomas's teachings on faith and hope. If she could find strength in those precepts, she might make it through the night on her own.

Approaching the front door, Bree slowed and finally came to a stop, wondering why she was so hesitant to go inside. She had only known security and safety in Steve and Sarah's home. *Why am I so afraid?* She waited at the bottom of the front steps, her hand gripping the railing. Bowing her head, Bree listened inwardly and heard Thomas's voice coaching her, telling her how to pray.

A minute later she lifted her head and, with a determined gleam in her eye, mounted the steps, unlocked the door, and entered the empty house. She closed and latched the door behind her, locking out the fear that had accompanied her on her walk through the night and placing a barrier between herself and the man skulking in the shadows.

Chapter 50

The following morning, the last of the men were filing their way past Bree so she could dish up their breakfast. She was tired from not having slept much the night before but bolstered with courage from the prayers that had soothed her fears.

Steve was the last in line, his rugged clothes dust covered and his face drawn and tired. He had been up all night, like most of the men participating in the search. He knew that Sarah wouldn't worry about him. She would know where he was. He stopped in front of Bree, holding out a plate.

Bree stared into his weary face. His skin looked pasty, while the stubble covering his chin had a definite hint of gray. "Are you okay, Steve? You look like you're about ready to collapse." Bree stared into Steve's eyes and knew with a surety that her doubts regarding his trustworthiness had been faulty. She didn't know if Thomas had spoken to Steve, but she now knew that it was unnecessary. She found herself hoping to find Thomas first, to tell him that her fears had been unfounded. She could only envision the hurt that would darken Steve's eyes if he were to hear of her former suspicions.

Steve, unaware of Bree's thoughts, returned her look, his eyes missing their usual sparkle. His mouth was grim and unsmiling. His countenance softened, however, in the face of Bree's concern. "I'm fine, sweetie. Just tired. It's been a long night."

"Have any clues been found?"

Steve dropped his gaze from Bree's face. "I'm sorry, but no. There's been no sign."

Tears filled Bree's eyes, and she fought to maintain her composure. Steve looked at her again before setting his plate on the serving bar. He reached for her hands and squeezed them. "We're not giving up, though. You can't give up your hope, Bree. Do you understand?"

Bree nodded wordlessly, blinking rapidly. She overcame the urge to cry and pulled her hands out of Steve's grasp. "I want to help. I want to go riding with you today."

Steve shook his head vehemently. "No, it's not safe for you out there."

"But Steve, I feel like I'm going crazy . . . I can't stand it."

Steve was just about to relent but was interrupted by Mary Smith's approach. "Steve, I was looking for Sarah. I wanted to talk to her about her idea of having a counselor come in and talk to all of the children." Mary paused and appeared to have a difficult time finding the words to complete her thoughts. "You know—about everything that has been happening lately. They're all pretty scared. Have you seen her this morning?"

"No, I just rode in a few minutes ago. I haven't been home all night. She's probably still at the homestead."

Mary was shaking her head. "I don't think so. I was just there."

Puzzled, Steve looked at Bree. "Have you seen Sarah this morning, Bree?"

Bree answered, "No. I was kind of wondering where she was too. She's been here every morning to help with breakfast. I got up early this morning and didn't see her before I left the house. I wonder if she's still asleep."

Mary was moving her head back and forth vigorously. "Nope, that house is empty."

"Did you check the barn, Mary? Is her horse there?"

"I don't know. I can go check."

"No, that's okay, Mary. I'll go. If I find her, I'll let her know you were looking for her."

Mary turned and left the room, hurrying to finish her preparations for that morning's school lessons. Just after she left, Michael came running in, his face pale and creased with worry. "Steve!" Chuck Laird, who was breathing heavily, followed him closely.

"Michael, what's wrong?"

Michael was gasping as if he had been running. He struggled to catch his breath before he could answer. His nervous energy spread to the group, and Bree felt her stomach tighten with anxiety. Steve's eyes were squinted, and he was staring at Michael with a frightening intensity.

Finally, Michael gasped, "Sarah! My dad! I think something's happened to them. Chuck and I were searching the eastern ridges together before coming in for breakfast, and when we came out of the woods, we found their horses. Both of them. But there was no sign of Sarah or my dad."

Bree whimpered, her hands flying to her face. She felt tears gather in her eyes as Steve spun on his heel and raced for the wall phone. He was shouting into the receiver and the dining room seemed to erupt in mass confusion as the cowboys and deputies who had been break-fasting heard the news of the missing man and woman.

Steve hung up the phone and shouted out above the din filling the room, "Has anyone seen Thomas or Sarah?"

His question was met with silence. "Come on, guys, speak up. I need to know if anyone has seen them."

Jon Smith, his usually cheerful face drawn with worry, spoke up, "Steve, we were just sitting here jawin' 'bout the search and discussin' how things have been goin'. We was sharin' stories 'bout last night's ride and someone . . ." Jon scratched his head as he tried to remember. Giving up, he continued, "I don't rightly recall who 'xactly, but they said they saw Thomas and Sarah ridin' off together."

"Together?"

"That's what it sounds like."

"Thanks, Jon. Does anyone remember anything else?"

Lex Larsen spoke up next, his quiet, surprisingly cultured voice a sharp contrast to Jonathan's western drawl. "They were seen heading toward the northeast slopes of the valley, Steve." Looking around at the other men for confirmation, he continued, "That was last night. Right before dusk."

The other men in the group nodded their heads in agreement. Steve stood with his hands on his hips, his head bowed in thought. Finally, he looked up and pushed his Stetson to the back of his head.

"We need to get back out there. I know you're all tired, but this is serious. I just talked to the sheriff. He's rounding up some more men and will be here soon. He told me to go ahead and organize today's search."

Steve's authoritative voice hid the turmoil raging inside his head. Sarah was missing. Quickly, he gave the men assignments, using a map of the ranch hanging on the wall to point out the sectors each man was to ride.

Bree stood watching all of the activity, disconcerted and frightened. She listened as Steve gave orders for the men to check in every few hours for updates and new information.

"Do you all have firearms?"

As each man in the group patted their side holsters or held up a rifle scabbard, Steve said, "If you find anything, fire off three shots as a signal and keep in touch with your radios."

Steve quickly gave the men specific instructions. "We'll ride in pairs, but then split up once we get to the base of the mountains. We'll be able to cover more ground that way. We'll concentrate on the north, northeast, and eastern slopes, since that's where they were last seen."

Scratching his head, Steve thought a moment before continuing, "We'll send someone out to the opposite areas, too." Looking around he said, "Where's Ben?"

"I'm right here, boss."

"You still riding that fast stallion?"

Ben grinned fleetingly at Steve's reference to the fact that his black stallion, Mustang, was known for his speed. "You betcha."

"Good. I want you to take the south side of the valley. That horse of yours should cover a lot of ground. Cover the perimeter starting from where the rest of us will be searching from the north to the east. Chuck, you take the southwest. You'll be the only two not paired up, so I want you to keep an especially careful eye open."

Looking at the men grouped around him, Steve said, "Everyone clear? Good. Let's ride. Oh . . ." Pausing a moment, Steve turned back to Bree. His heart nearly broke when he saw her standing behind the serving table. She looked so young and frightened. "Bree…"

She stared back at him, and before she could stop herself, she flew around the table and threw herself into his arms. He held her as she sobbed, tears in his own eyes. It was only with intense will that he was able to hold them back. He stroked her hair for a moment before setting her away from him. "Listen, Bree, honey, you've got to stay strong. Stay here. Cook. Keep busy. We're going to need lots of food for the men searching. Do whatever you can to stay busy. And stay safe." Steve's words didn't come close to expressing the depth of his fear.

Taking a deep breath, Steve handed Bree his handkerchief. "Here, wipe your eyes. Then go call Tina Larsen or Mary Smith. Have one of them come over here. I don't want you alone. Make sure Deputy Odham is close."

Bree nodded as she handed his handkerchief back to him, damp with her tears. "I will, Steve." She bit her lip in an effort to control the trembling making it difficult for her to speak. "Go find them. You have to find them!"

"I know, baby. I will."

Bree glanced away from his stern face, and her eyes fastened on Michael. He was standing a few feet away, the expression on his face inscrutable. She saw his eyes soften as he met her gaze. Her heart began thudding in her ears when he stepped toward her.

He came up to her and took her hand. He then squeezed her fingers and bent down to place a light kiss on her cheek. "Stay safe, Bree. Stay here, and stay safe." Michael's voice cracked. "I don't think I could bear it if anything happened to you."

"I'll be okay, Michael. It's Brock and Shari, and Thomas and Sarah you need to be thinking about."

Before Michael could answer, Chuck Laird approached Bree. His eyes were shielded by sunglasses, but his mouth was unsmiling. He shouldered past Michael and put a hand on Bree's shoulder. She was surprised at the strength in his hand and involuntarily took a step backward.

An involuntary twitch curved the corner of Chuck's lips downward. He let his hand fall to his side. "Don't worry about anything, Bree. Everything will be okay soon. I know it."

She stared at Chuck as he turned and strode across the floor, following the other men who were leaving.

"Don't mind him, Bree."

Bree transferred her surprised gaze to the figure of Ben Laird. She hadn't heard him approach. She tried to smile at him, but her roiling emotions made it impossible. He reached out and stroked her cheek with his forefinger. "It's okay. I know how hard this is for you. We won't give up until this is over and we find the kids." Ben cast a quick look at Michael, who was still holding Bree's hand. "Thomas and Sarah, too."

"Thank you, Ben. I appreciate you."

Ben smiled grimly at Bree's sincere words. Tipping his hat with the same finger that had caressed her cheek, the tall foreman turned and left.

Michael looked down at Bree. He dropped her hand and put his arms around her, holding her close for several minutes before he, too, left. Bree wiped away the tears trickling down her cheeks, Michael's softly spoken words of tender support lingering in her ear.

Bree walked to the door and watched the men mount their saddled horses and ride away. The sun was barely cresting the eastern sky, but already the day felt endless. Bree watched until they were out of sight before she turned to go back inside to call Tina. She knew that Mary Smith would be busy teaching school. The parents of the children had all agreed that their activities should remain uninterrupted. Closing the door and latching it securely, Bree turned her back on the ranch yard unaware of the lone rider who had lingered, hiding in the shadows of the barn's immense and gloomy interior.

Chapter 51

That was close. When Steve started asking questions about Thomas and Sarah, he'd had to think quickly. He'd listened as the men talked. Luckily, Lex Larsen had commented on the absence of Sarah and Thomas earlier, before the alarm had been raised. He had waited until all the men were talking and then started dropping comments about seeing them together. He'd added trumped-up lies about the time that they were seen and the fact that they were seen heading northeast. He sneered with contempt thinking about how easy it had been to manipulate the story. They'd bought every detail hook, line, and sinker.

When he received his assignment, he had lingered over saddling up his horse, pretending to work on the straps of his saddle. He had stayed in the barn, listening to the pounding hoofs of the search party as they rode away. There was no need for him to join in the search; he knew where Thomas and Sarah were. He didn't have any fear that they would stumble on the cabin today. The search had been going on for days now, and they still hadn't found it. He was confident they never would. It was too remote, and the turnoff to that particular logging road was difficult to see and easy to miss, even in daylight. Besides, by the end of the day it would all be over anyway, so it wouldn't matter if they did manage to find the cabin. By that time, there would be nothing remaining for them to find.

His determination to destroy Bree had been strengthened that morning. He had stood back, watching as she threw herself into Steve Sheridan's arms. She should have turned to *him* for comfort, not Steve. She would pay for that mistake, just as Steve would pay. He would never see Sarah again. That would be his price for the role he played in Bree's betrayal.

He had watched the play of emotions cross Bree's face as she'd been left alone. He knew that she was frightened, and he knew that he was the reason for that fear. But he had recognized the courage that kept her upright, the fortitude that kept her functioning. She had more grit than he'd given her credit for. For some reason, her show of courage made him angry.

It was time to teach her another lesson. All he had to do was lie low for a couple of hours. Smiling wickedly, he dismounted from his horse and prepared to implement the final stages of his plan.

Chapter 52

"Sarah, Thomas is waking up!"

Sarah stirred at Shari's soft voice. Feeling her way in the darkness, she crept across the cold, hard floor. She fought back her anger and dismay. It was incredible that the children had survived so long in this dank and smelly hole. The stench was overwhelming, and Sarah found herself gagging back the bile that threatened to rise in her throat.

She seemed ultrasensitive to smells these days, and she was starting to suspect why. After Bree and the children came to the ranch, Steve had mentioned to her that he would like to try again for a baby. A few days ago, she had started wondering if the miracle they had prayed for had happened, but at the time, her suspicions were only a niggling hope at the back of her mind. So she hadn't said anything to him. As the days had passed, however, and she started to experience a few more symptoms of pregnancy, she was almost positive. The thought of finally having a baby had thrilled her, and she had intended to tell Steve soon, once Brock and Shari were found and life on the ranch had settled back to normal.

Now she found herself wondering if she would ever have that opportunity. *Stop it!* she berated herself silently. *If these children could survive in this spine-chilling place for as long as they have, then so can I.*

Sarah felt Thomas's legs under her searching hands, and as she scooted around him, Shari turned on the flashlight.

Its light was very feeble, and they had all agreed not to use it unless necessary. Shari and Brock were used to being in the darkness, and just having the two grown-ups with them had given them hope.

Shari shined the light across the old man's wan features. His eyes opened painfully, and he stirred, groaning from the ache in his head. "Shari? Honey girl, I thought I was dreaming, but it really is you!"

Thomas's voice was weak but clear. He had awakened a time or two previously, but he had been incoherent and confused. "Hey there, mister. What kind of adventure have you gotten us into?" At the sound of Sarah's voice, Thomas opened his eyes a fraction wider, the wrinkles on his face deepening with consternation.

"Miss Sarah?"

"Yes, it's me."

"Hi, Thomas. I'm here too!" Brock's voice sounded frail in the darkness.

Looking back up at Sarah, Thomas felt his eyes start to water as realization dawned. "Miss Sarah, what's going on?"

With sadness in her voice, Sarah told him as much as she knew. During the hours since she had been thrown into the cellar, she had quizzed the two children about what they knew. She had almost cried when they told her about the night they had been taken, how frightened they were, and how they had been brought to the cabin and left in the cellar.

"They've been here this whole time?"

Sarah nodded solemnly.

"How? I mean, how have you survived this long?" Thomas's trembling voice asked.

Shari spoke up, "We just remembered what you told us."

"What I told you? About what?"

"About Jesus and Heavenly Father. And we prayed and we knew that we would be okay."

"An' we sang songs, too."

"Did you, buddy? What songs did you sing?"

"Jesus songs. And Shari tol' me Jesus stories."

Sarah and Thomas both felt an overwhelming sense of tenderness listening to the two children. Their simple testimonies of faith brought hope back to the old man and to the woman who knelt with them in the ebony cocoon of the old cellar.

Chapter 53

"Bree, are you sure you'll be okay?" Tina's voice was filled with concern as she loaded the last of the breakfast dishes into the dishwasher.

Bree was wiping down the counter, and she smiled at her friend. Tina went to the door leading into the dining hall and called to her children, who were sitting at one of the tables coloring. "Jenny! Nate! C'mon, it's time for school." Tina hurriedly shooed her children out the front door. "Go on, you two. You'll be late for school. Now, scoot!"

"I'll be fine, Tina. I'm going to stay here and get some baking done." Bree waited until quiet descended on the kitchen in the wake of the departing children. "I feel like I need to keep busy, and baking up a bunch of goodies to feed everyone is just the thing."

"I don't want to leave unless you're sure you'll be okay. I know that Steve and Sheriff Hambly have been adamant about you not being alone."

"Everyone is so busy that I think they'd be surprised at how often I'm left on my own." Bree paused as she contemplated her own words. "But you know what? It's okay. And it's going to be okay. I feel so much better knowing that everyone who is available is out looking for Brock and Shari. Besides, Deputy Odham is here. He's so good about doing rounds and checking in with me every few minutes. He's never very far away."

"If you're sure," Tina expressed her doubt. "I'll be back in an hour or so, and I can help you with the baking. It shouldn't take me too long at home to finish up my chores. I need to go get Tommy ready to go for the day. I put him back to bed before coming over here, and he was out like a light. He had an asthma attack this morning, and they always tire him out. Mary's oldest daughter is with him. I need to go relieve her so she can get to school."

"I need to know something, Tina, and I want you to be honest with me. Are you changing your plans for the day . . . because of me?"

"Well, I was going to run in to town and do some errands, but it sounds like we have some baking to do, so I'm going to stick around here!"

Bree looked at her friend, a stab of guilt causing her to wince slightly. "I don't want you to do that!"

Tina hastened to reassure Bree, "It's okay, honey. I can run in to town any day. My errands aren't that urgent." Tina thought about her youngest, Tommy, who was out of the medication for his breathing treatments. She had used the last of it that morning. She was usually very conscientious about refilling his prescription before he ran out, but with everything that was happening on the ranch, she just hadn't had time to run in to town. Tina said a silent prayer that he would be okay until the next day.

Seeing Bree's concerned look, Tina said, "I mean it, Bree. It's okay."

Bree walked Tina to the door and gave her a big hug before waving her off. "Thank you, Tina, for everything."

"You're sure welcome, honey. I'll be back in a little while, and we'll bake our little hearts out this morning!" Tina left, comforted by Bree's assurances, her mind turning to her son.

Chapter 54

Tina wiped her hands on a tea towel as she headed for the front door, summoned by a loud knocking. Wondering who could be stopping by, she smiled in recognition when she opened the door. "Good morning! What a surprise!"

"Morning, Tina." Smiling and removing his hat and holding it politely in front of him, the visitor said, "I just stopped by to check on Bree. Is she here with you?"

"No, she's over at the cookhouse. She seems to be doing fine. In fact, she decided that she needed to keep busy, and she's over there doing some baking. I'm actually just about to finish up here and go over to help her."

"Is there anything I can do to help?"

Tina shook her head slowly, thinking about the medication for her son.

"Come on, I can tell there's something. Don't be afraid to ask."

"Well, I'm supposed to keep an eye on Bree, but . . ."

"Yes?"

Deciding it wouldn't hurt to ask, Tina blurted out, "My youngest, Tommy, is out of his asthma medicine. I really need to run in to town and pick it up for him. This fall season is the worst time of year for him, and I'd hate for him to need a breathing treatment and not have his medicine."

"Tina, of course you need to get his prescription. You go ahead. I can hang around here and keep an eye on Bree."

"You're sure?" Tina smiled her relief. "Thank you so much. You're the best!" Impulsively, she reached up and lightly kissed the tanned cheek of the tall man standing in front of her. "I'll just dash off right now. Oh, wait, I better run over and tell Bree that you're here to keep an eye on things."

"No, I'll do that. You and Tommy need to get going."

Just then, Tina's three-year-old son galloped out of his bedroom, his rosy cheeks and sparkling blue eyes the picture of health.

"Hey there, buckaroo!"

Tommy stopped in front of the cowboy and grinned up at him. Tina laughed, scooping the little boy up and tickling him. His giggles filled the air while his mother got him into a jacket. She stopped and smiled, her gratitude and relief evident in her glowing countenance. "Thank you so much. You don't know how much I appreciate this."

"Oh, it's my pleasure. Really. Take your time. There's no need for you to hurry back."

"If you're sure, I do have a little shopping."

His smile reflected the pleasure he found in her words, but his countenance hid the wicked excitement building in his black heart. "You take all the time you need. Bree and I will be just fine."

Chapter 55

"Sarah, can I have a drink of water?"

Brock's soft voice wavered in the inky cloak of darkness, and Sarah felt a prickle of tears stab the back of her eyes as she had to answer, "I'm sorry, baby. The water's gone."

"Oh."

Thomas squeezed Sarah's trembling fingers, sharing her pain as she had to deny the boy's request. "It'll be okay, lil' buddy. We'll get you a great big drink of water as soon as we get out of here."

"Okay, Thomas." Brock's simple words of trust touched the old man, and he bowed his head as he murmured another prayer of supplication. His faith never wavered, but he hurt at the understanding that his promise might not be fulfilled.

"How 'bout singing us another song?"

"Not now. I'm tired."

"Too tired to sing your favorite song?"

"Yeah."

"Well, okay. I'll sing it. You just listen."

The heavy silence was broken a few seconds later by Thomas's aged voice voicing the words of Brock's favorite Primary song. Shari couldn't resist, and she joined as they sang about popcorn popping on apricot trees.

Thomas smiled when he heard Shari. She giggled when Brock could no longer refrain and his young voice sang with them.

Sarah listened with tenderness as the three voices concluded the simple song.

"Thanks, Thomas."

"Oh, yer sure welcome, kiddo."

Silence descended on the group, and soon the sound of the children's soft snores filled the air. Shari was curled up against Sarah, and Thomas cradled Brock in his arms.

"Thomas?" Sarah's voice was soft so as not to disturb the sleeping children.

"Yes?"

"Aren't they remarkable?"

Thomas knew that she was referring to the two children. "Yeah, they are."

"I can't believe they've survived this long. This place . . ." Sarah paused, closing her eyes and trying not to breathe in too deeply. The air in the cellar was heavy with the cold and the dankness of unwashed bodies.

Thomas grunted his understanding at her unspoken words.

"How did they do it?"

Thomas felt his old heart soften at the genuineness of Sarah's question. He knew that the spirit of the children's testimonies had softened her. Their faith was so simple and pure. He felt his own testimony grow as he began to tell Sarah about the power that had helped the children survive as long as they had. Their situation hadn't changed; the darkness and the discomfort of their surroundings remained. But as Thomas bore testimony of God's love and the spiritual light that had encircled the children throughout their ordeal, the Spirit touched Sarah's heart and she, too, felt the warmth of its comfort. Thomas's quiet voice filled the air, and the peace of God's love nurtured Sarah's heart until she felt completely enfolded by the Spirit.

Chapter 56

The kitchen was warm and steamy, filled with the mouthwatering aroma of baking bread, cakes, and cookies. The counters were filled with cooling loaves, frosted cakes, as well as Bree's favorite, cinnamon rolls. She broke off a piece of one of the warm buns, chewing it thoughtfully, enjoying the moist, spicy-sweet treat. She then turned to the sink in order to finish up the last of the dishes and utensils used during her baking spree. Her cheeks were flushed, and the tendrils of hair that escaped her ponytail curled and danced off her neck while she hummed a simple tune.

Her mad bout of baking had spent a good portion of her anxieties, and she felt surprisingly calm and relaxed as she finished wiping out the sink. With a damp hand, Bree pushed aside the bangs brushing her forehead and stood back, gazing at the pastries lining the kitchen counters. She glanced at the wall clock and saw that it was well past noon and wondered where Tina was. *She must have gotten busy at home. I hope Tommy is okay.*

Bree sighed. It was going to take several trips to get the products of her morning's work upstairs to the overhead pantry. With a resigned shrug, she gathered up an armload and headed up. Just as Bree reached the storeroom, she heard the sound of a door opening below.

Pausing, Bree pushed a strand of hair behind her ear and smiled. Clearing her throat, she called out, "Tina, I'm upstairs. I'll be there in a minute."

Bree waited a moment and then shouted again when there was no answer to her greeting. "Tina?"

The silence from downstairs remained. Frowning, Bree dumped her load of goodies onto a shelf in the pantry. She walked toward the stairs, calling again, "Who's there? Tina? Deputy Odham?"

Starting hesitantly down the stairs, Bree grasped the handrail, her fingers tense and white-knuckled. She reached the bottom door and pushed on it, suddenly frightened by the sensation that someone was waiting on the other side of the barrier.

The door creaked open, and she haltingly stepped through. "Oh! Hi!" Bree breathed a sigh of relief and smiled at the familiar figure standing across the room. "I thought you were Tina Larsen. She was supposed to meet me here. How come you didn't say anything when you heard me call?"

"I didn't hear you."

"Oh, probably because the door was closed. Hey . . . would you be willing to help a tired cook carry all that stuff upstairs?" Bree waved her hand toward the counter.

"Sure, Bree, I'd be glad to help."

Bree smiled gratefully and walked toward the man, her earlier nervousness melting away, replaced by a sense of comfort in the presence of someone she trusted.

Chapter 57

Michael Reilly dismounted his horse and led it into the hazy interior of the barn. He was tired, on edge, and ready for sleep. He had been grateful to return home for a few hours of rest, having skipped his earlier rotation. He was lifting the saddle down from the back of the tired gelding when he heard a strange sound from deep inside the large barn. Frowning, he grabbed a blanket and started rubbing the heaving sides of his horse, but when the sound turned into an unmistakable human groan, Michael jumped, the fabric falling to the floor.

Quickly striding toward the back of the barn, Michael followed the moans. He rounded the furthest stall partition and paused, his jaw dropping in astonishment. "Deputy Odham, what happened?"

Michael knelt on the floor next to the crumpled figure of the law enforcement officer. The deputy struggled to focus his eyes on Michael's face, his features contorted with pain. "Someone hit me."

"Who? Who was it?"

"Don' know." The deputy's words were slurred and barely coherent. "Hit me from behin'."

"How badly are you injured?" Michael was running his hands over the fallen man's arms and legs, searching for injury.

"Don' worry 'bout me."

"Did you call the sheriff?"

"Couldn't. He took my radio. Got to find him." Deputy Odham's face constricted as a wave of pain washed over him. He gasped, "Bree . . ."

Michael paled and stared at the injured deputy. Deputy Odham murmured, "Find her. Find Bree."

Jumping to his feet, his heart pounding frantically, Michael said, "I'll get someone here to help you as soon as I can." He then spun on his heels and ran from the barn, his mind shouting Bree's name.

Chapter 58

"There, that's the last of it!" Bree smiled at the tall man standing behind her. "Thank you so much for your help. I hadn't realized I had baked so much."

"It's been my pleasure, Bree. I would do anything for you."

Missing the strange innuendo in the man's deep voice, Bree turned back to gaze at the pantry shelves filled with baked goods. "There should be enough here to feed the troops for days." Her voice dropped. "Hopefully it won't be needed." Bree swallowed the familiar surge of sorrow that had been buried beneath the surface of her morning's activities.

"Oh, it won't be needed. I'm sure of it."

The sinister tone in the man's voice caused Bree to turn and look at him questioningly. "What? Do you know something?"

"I know everything, Bree." The man was twisting an object in his hands.

His movements drew Bree's startled gaze, and she gasped. The knitted fabric of her favorite scarf was stretched out of recognizable shape, but its glowing color mocked the blanched paleness of her face. The last time she had seen the scarf had been the night she had been stalked on the mountainside, the night she had run from an unseen predator. The scarf had been left on that mountainside, entangled in the thorns of a wild rosebush.

Slowly she transferred her gaze back to the features of the man standing in front of her, horror and disbelief frozen in her eyes. Shaking her head, her lips stiff, she murmured, "No, no, I don't believe it. It can't be you!" Bree backed away, crying out when she bumped into a wall, cornered by the figure of the man looming over her. He reached for her, wrapping the tattered strands of the scarf around her neck, the color reflecting the terrified blue of her eyes.

Chapter 59

Suddenly, the heavy wooden door leading up from the cookhouse kitchen below swung open. The ensuing draft at the foot of the stairs caused the dangling lightbulb hanging in the stairwell to swing, mottling the walls with dancing shafts of light. Bree felt like she was in a scene straight out of a horror movie, but the loud bellow of rage that came from the man rushing up the stairs was very real.

Michael's appearance startled Bree's captor, and he weakened his grip on her. She pulled away from him, but the strength of her movement sent her sprawling backward. She lay crumpled against the wall while a nightmare unfolded before her eyes.

Bree watched Michael lunge for the man, panic making her head spin. Her scream ripped the silence of the room when she saw Ben Laird raise his hand, the dark gleam of hard metal flashing. Bree's cry was interrupted by a red flash shooting from the barrel of the pistol, the accompanying report thundering through the rafters. Michael's forward assault was checked midstride by a bullet ripping through his flesh. A second shot brought him to his knees and a third threw him backward, where he lay sprawled in a heap. A hysterical cry ripped through Bree, and she automatically reached out a trembling hand to touch the pale, motionless man, her heart breaking.

Without warning, Bree found herself being wrenched to her feet. Before she could say anything, she felt strong hands pushing her. She stumbled down the narrow flight of stairs, attempting to assimilate all that had just taken place. She felt like she was on an out-of-control carnival ride as Ben Laird continued to pull her behind him until they reached the ground floor. When her feet touched the tiled floor at the bottom of the stairs, she began to struggle with superhuman effort, refusing to be pushed any further. Her breath was coming in great, labored sobs, and she turned a tearstained face up toward the man standing beside her. She barely recognized the contorted, angry features of the ranch foreman, her fear mounting when she saw the glittering hate reflected in the dark orbs that were the eyes of the man holding her in his grasp.

They stood facing each other, the silence of the room mocking the clamor of racing hearts and gasping lungs. Bree felt Ben's anger, tangible and powerful. Her knees felt weak, and she thought they might give out any minute. Reaching out to him, Bree silently entreated Ben to explain what had just happened.

Without another word, Ben lifted Bree into his arms and carried her outside, ignoring her struggles to get free. He hurried across the graveled driveway and came to a stop beside his dusty, mud-splattered pickup. With great care, he opened the door and deposited Bree on the wide front seat. She fought to escape his hold, and with one solid whack, he hit her in the face, causing her to collapse against the back of the seat. He then reached across her and securely buckled her seat belt. She averted her face from him, and he leaned close and gently caressed her cheek with a soft touch. "The time has come, my darling. We were meant to be together, and we'll never be apart again."

Ben drew back before locking and slamming Bree's door shut. He ran around to the other side of the truck and climbed behind the wheel. Bree was in a daze, fighting waves of nausea. She felt like her head was spinning, and her face throbbed from Ben's vicious slap. She turned to face him, but Ben averted his gaze. Even though her lips felt numb, Bree managed to exclaim, "Where are we going?"

"Sit back and be quiet. What's the matter, darling? Are you afraid?"

Bree stared at his stony, remote profile. The truck suddenly hit a large rut, and she found herself bounced against the hard metal frame of the pickup. With a gasp, she wrapped her arms across her stomach, waves of pain coursing through her body. Biting her lip in an effort to smother a scream, Bree was unaware of the taste of blood in her mouth.

"How did you do it, Ben? Why did you do it?" Her last question reflected the tortured confusion that had driven out all hope.

Ben leered at her, his eyes masked and inscrutable. He laughed harshly, the sound ringing in Bree's ears, causing flashes of memory to clash with the confusion. Suddenly, her mind cleared, and she was back in her house, the darkness swallowing her in its clutches as she fought for her life. The sounds of her screams mingled with the laughter of the man holding her down. The room had been lit up by the strobe effect of lightning, and Bree saw his face, distorted and terrifying but suddenly recognizable.

"Why? WHY?!" Ben's shouts broke through Bree's recollections. She stared in petrified fascination at the anger and hatred contorting his features. "Why! Because I loved you! But you never knew that, did you?! You never once thought about what you were doing to me! It was always those brats . . . and Thomas . . . and the Sheridans. And Michael." Ben's voice was suddenly calm, devoid of expression. "They're all out of the way now, my darling. They'll never again get in my way. Do you remember that night you were followed in the woods?"

Visions of her blue scarf, tattered and tightening around her neck, made Bree lift a hand to her bruised throat. "Of course I remember."

"That was so much fun for me. I thought if I frightened you badly enough, you'd turn to me. I wanted to be the first person you saw, the first person you'd turn to for comfort."

Bree was silent, dumbfounded by his confessions.

"But you didn't. It was always Michael. Even my nephew, Chuck, got closer to you than I ever did. I wanted you to turn on Michael, to see him for what he really is, to see his temper. He can't be trusted."

"And you can!" The words flew out of Bree's mouth before she could stop them.

"Shut up!" Ben's hand flew out and caught Bree on the side of her face. She fell against the side window, her cheek stinging and her eyes filling with tears. She bit her lip, unwilling to give him the satisfaction of seeing her cry. She closed her eyes tightly as he continued to rant.

"Just shut up! You don't know me. But you could have. I loved you from the first time I saw you. But it's too late." Ben's words faded and he fell silent, his face grim and his eyes unexpectedly sad. "It's too late."

Chapter 60

After what seemed like hours of driving through the thickly forested mountains, the pickup finally rolled to a stop. Bree had lost track of time. She had listened to Ben's demented muttering until she thought she would go insane. Finally, lassitude settled in on her, paralyzing her thoughts and emotions. She no longer knew nor cared where he was taking her. She just wanted the ride to be over. She was bruised and broken and lost in a haze of terror. The faith that had promised to see her through the difficult times was buried beneath the fear and despair.

She watched helplessly when Ben jumped from the truck and walked away. Grappling with the door handle, Bree pushed, and with a cry, she tumbled to the ground. She was unaware of Ben when he paused in front of the dilapidated, old cabin.

* * *

Ben turned and looked back at the crumpled figure lying in the dust and grass of the mountain clearing. With an indifferent shrug, he walked up the rickety steps and unlocked the rusty padlock bolting the front door shut. He knew she had nowhere to go. If she tried to run, all he had to do was follow her. With a swift kick of his booted foot, Ben pushed the door open. He blinked in the dimness of the unlit interior.

With a satisfied glance around, he turned and went back outside. He laughed out loud as he watched Bree. Her efforts were pathetic. She *was* trying to get away. Fine. He'd play along—but not for long.

The game was ending, and he didn't have the time or the patience to let her drag it out for too long. He stepped back into the cabin and partially closed the door, then stood near the window, his face pressed up against the grimy glass to watch Bree's futile endeavor to escape.

* * *

Bree determinedly placed one hand in front of the other and managed to crawl two feet forward. Forcing herself to stop crying, unaware of when the tears had begun to fall, she took several deep, cleansing breaths. With slow, deliberate concentration, she pulled one foot up under her and slowly started to rise. If she could just get on her feet, she thought she could make it to the nearby cover of dense underbrush and thick mountain foliage.

Finally, she stood. Panting and sweating with the exertion, Bree looked over her shoulder toward the house. Freezing in terror, she peered at the cloudy window set high in the wall of the cabin. Was that a face watching her through the marred glass?

Blinking rapidly to clear her vision, Bree looked again but saw nothing. She figured it must have been the reflection of the sun glinting on the windowpane. With a sob of relief, Bree turned and stumbled into the forest. She hadn't gone far when she suddenly found herself falling to the ground, her vision going black, her head reeling and her senses blanking out. With a sigh, Bree collapsed, her mind and body shutting down in defense against the trauma and stress.

* * *

Ben stood at the window, watching her pitiful attempts. He saw her glance back at the cabin, and he also saw the sudden awareness on her face as she caught a glimpse of him through the cloudy pane of glass. He stepped back a pace, out of Bree's vision but still able to watch her attempt to escape. She was so pathetic. He would give her another minute or two, and then he would follow her. It was time for him to wreak his revenge. She had so much to pay for. In his demented mind, she had betrayed him in so many ways.

This afternoon in the attic, fear and horror had ravaged her. Ben had seen it in her face. Even then, with Michael lying at her feet, bloody and unconscious, she had turned to him with love and compassion. Ben had felt the cold anger he lived with every day turn to a fiery furnace of hate as she had reached out to Michael's dying body. Even in death, Reilly had bested him and had kept her his. But no more. Ben would force her to forget.

He watched Bree's stumbling figure disappear and let his mind wander back over the past. He had come to the ranch a little over six years ago. He felt as if life had only truly begun, however, when Bree entered his life this past spring. She was so young and lovely. Even now, it took his breath away to think of her, an innocent young girl fighting bravely to overcome the trauma of the death of her parents and to establish a home for herself and for her younger brother and sister. She had been like a lovely young star, bringing beauty and grace to the rough man's world of the ranch.

He had wanted to gather her into his arms, to protect her and to offer her the strength of his love. But she hadn't even noticed him. She had been so wrapped up in her relationships with the brats and the Sheridans. Even old Thomas had outdone him. And then Michael had come between them. Ben's thoughts burned with jealousy as he remembered the open adoration and pure love reflected in her lovely face, the adoration that was directed at everyone but him.

He had tried to be her friend, to draw closer to her, but she had resisted. To be sure, she had always been kind and had treated him with the same casual friendship with which she had treated all the other ranch hands. But he had wanted more—he had expected more. Soon his love and patience had turned to resentment, and as the months had passed, the resentment had turned to obsession and, finally, to hate.

The hate was driving him mad and destroying his soul. His rage extended to all whom Bree loved. Brock and Shari had been the first to pay for sharing her love. Then it had been Sarah and Thomas. And finally, Michael. He didn't have to worry about any of them ever again. It was time for him to go to her. The game was over.

He entered the forest, pushing through the dense cover of underbrush, following the trail of crushed grass and broken branches easily.

He didn't have far to go. Rounding a thick outcropping of brambles, he saw her. She was lying silent and still, her body sprawled in the thick grass. Her face was pale, devoid of any color. Even her lips were white, blending with the blanched parchment of her face. Her clothes were stained with sweat and blood, her legs and arms scratched and marred from the punishing whip of stiff, thorny branches.

Bending over her, Ben scooped Bree into his arms. She was limp as he turned and headed back toward the cabin. He held her tightly in his arms, her head lolling back over his forearm. Her hair was hanging in long, tangled tresses. The burning color of her hair mocked the pale, lifeless pallor of her cheeks.

Ben's icy heart began to smolder with the excitement of revenge as he walked through the forest glade. He crossed the clearing, intent on reaching the dilapidated cabin. He strode through the narrow door and dumped Bree onto the rickety old cot, then strode across the room and grabbed a rag off the table sitting beside the old, potbellied stove. A pan with a little bit of water still sat on top of the stove, a remnant from his previous visit. He plunged the rag into the water and squeezed out the excess. Returning to Bree's side, he knelt on the floor and smiled when he saw signs of her return to consciousness. He used the cloth to wipe her face, and as the application of water cooled her feverish skin, her eyes began to flicker.

Bree was brought back to sudden wakefulness and turned her eyes to Ben, hoping to find in him a measure of mercy.

Ben looked into her eyes and said, "Hello, darling. I've been waiting for this moment for so long." He stroked her cheek with a trembling hand. His emotions were flooding his thoughts, propelling his actions. Without another word, Ben rocked back on his heels and reached behind him. He grabbed several lengths of strong rope out of his back pocket. With deliberate slowness, he brought her hands and wrists together in front of her, binding them and tightening the rope so that it bit cruelly into the softness of her flesh. Bree winced but found the strength to withdraw emotionally.

The muscles around his eyes hardened, and he silently cursed at Bree for appearing so self-possessed. If she would only give him some sign, some indication that she cared, Ben knew that he would let her live. But there was nothing. He grabbed a handful of her hair and pulled, his strength causing Bree's head to snap back with a painful jerk. A gasp escaped her lips, and she clenched her teeth, refusing to give him the satisfaction of hearing her cry out.

"Why, Bree? Why couldn't you love me?" Ben's voice cracked as he released her hair. Her silence spurred his anger, and he removed Bree's sturdy work shoes and thick wool socks. He bound her ankles, again causing the rope to bite into the tender skin. He saw her wince and tightened it even more, gaining a measure of satisfaction from the whimper she couldn't suppress.

Bree felt a lump of nausea form in her stomach when he rose and faced her, his face unreadable. His eyes glittered with a hate-driven excitement, and Bree found herself unaccountably spellbound.

Her parched mouth opened, and she tried to find the words to ask him what he wanted from her. "Ben, please." Bree's plea was hoarse and cracked. "Don't do this."

Looking into her tortured, pain-glazed eyes, Ben felt triumph well in his heart. He said nothing, but instead only watched her, feeling overwhelmed by the maelstrom of hate and love. He turned away from her, his shoulders rounding forward, his head dropping into his hands.

Bree watched him clasp his head, and she heard the choking sounds coming from his throat. He sounded like a trapped animal, tortured by jaws of steel that inextricably bound him. Finally he dropped his hands and lifted his head.

He turned and faced her, looking directly into her eyes as he backed away. He kept his gaze locked with hers until he bumped into the door. Reaching behind him, Ben pulled it open and backed over the threshold. A few seconds passed before he whispered in a gruff voice, his words carrying across the stillness of the room, "Good-bye, my darling. Happy death."

Before he closed the door behind him, Ben paused again. He then turned and said with calculated cruelty, "Just so you know, you're not alone."

Confusion warred with the agonizing fear on her face. "What?" Bree whispered.

"You're not alone. Just thought you'd like to know." With that, Ben closed the door.

* * *

Panicked realization broke through the trance caused by Ben's words. Brock and Shari! Twisting her head to look around, Bree shouted, "Where are they?"

Ben padlocked the door and smiled when Bree screamed, her voice echoing around the barren, empty cabin. Several minutes passed before the muffled revving of a truck engine penetrated the haze of disbelief surrounding Bree's senses.

Finally, with dawning horror, Bree realized Ben's intent. This was the ultimate torture. He wanted her to feel the despair of betrayal and desertion as he left her to die, alone and bereft in the cabin. What greater torture could he inflict than to walk away from her, leaving her physically bound and emotionally tortured after informing her that Brock and Shari were somewhere close? He had left, knowing that by so doing, he would drive her to the brink of madness. She felt as though she would sink into the black abyss of insanity as she screamed and cried, alone in the dark mountain cabin, unable to reach Brock and Shari.

Looking helplessly about the cabin, Bree didn't have the strength left to fight. The potbellied stove was cold and lifeless while the chill of the evening air slowly penetrated the evaporating warmth of the day. With one last cry, her will almost depleted, Bree cried out Brock's and Shari's names.

* * *

"What was that?" Thomas furrowed his brow at the unexpected intrusion of sound.

"That sounded like Bree!" Brock exclaimed.

"It couldn't be," whispered Sarah.

"It is Bree! I heard Bree's voice!" Shari insisted.

The two children, excited and enlivened by the familiar tones of their sister's voice, started to shout, tears cascading over their grimy cheeks as they continued to call out Bree's name.

"Thomas, do you think it's possible?"

"I heard it too, sweetheart. Her voice seemed kind of far away, but it was Bree."

Sarah closed her eyes before joining her shouts with those of the children.

Thomas bowed his head in a silent prayer. After a few seconds, he, too, raised his voice and began to shout.

* * *

Bree lay curled on her side, her emotions spent and her spirit broken. Her bound hands ached, and she longed to stand up and stretch her cramped legs. She was too broken to even cry.

Bree was on the brink of unconsciousness. Just as her eyes were starting to drift shut, closing out the physical walls of her prison, a distant sound disturbed the stillness surrounding her. Bree gasped.

Life crept back into her eyes and her heart. She heard voices. And they were real, not some figment of her tortured imagination. Brock and Shari were calling to her. She heard their voices, and even though she couldn't be sure, it sounded like her name being shouted over and over.

Struggling to sit up, Bree used her right elbow to maneuver herself into an upright position. She swung her bound ankles over the side of the cot and found herself sitting on the edge of the rickety old bed. It seemed forever before the fog of despondency cleared from her mind. She felt a sensation of warmth wash over her, and she whispered, "Shari? Brock?"

Regaining her strength, Bree said their names out loud and felt the flickering flame of her faith rekindled. With her heart beating strongly and her spirit soaring, Bree began to shout their names.

She paused and then she heard a faint reply.

"Bree, we hear you!"

Laughing out loud, Bree began to fight the rope tied around her wrists.

While Bree struggled to free herself, gleeful pandemonium broke loose in the dark cellar below. Shari and Brock had their arms around each other and were laughing and shouting as they bounced on their knees. Sarah and Thomas were crying and laughing as they, too, rejoiced.

"She's here. She's really here!" Shari giggled over and over again.

"I knew she'd come. I just knew she would!" Brock shouted.

A few minutes later, their first surge of exhilaration fading, Brock turned to Thomas and asked, "Why doesn't she come open the door?"

"Well, I don't know. She's close, but maybe she hasn't found the cellar door yet."

"Oh." Brock's voice was solemn as he thought it through. "How long do you s'pose it'll take her to find us?"

Sarah answered, "It could be a few minutes. Let's take turns calling to her until she comes."

"Sarah? Thomas?" Shari's voice was a question in the dark.

"Yes, punkin?" Thomas answered.

"Can we say a prayer?"

Thomas felt his eyes soften as he answered the child's response, "Yes, baby. We most definitely can say a prayer."

They clasped hands in a circle, and Thomas, Sarah, Brock, and Shari joined their hearts and their souls in supplication to their Heavenly Father. Thomas's voice was deep and strong as he concluded, "We thank thee so much for bringing Bree to us. Please let her be safe and help her find her way to us. Please let us be reunited with our loved ones soon, and please keep them safe until then. We love thee and thank thee for lighting the darkness of our imprisonment with thy love." He closed in the name of Jesus, and the others joined in a fervent, "Amen."

Chapter 61

The ranch yard was a swarm of commotion with Sheriff Hambly organizing the cowboys and deputies to commence an all-out manhunt for Ben Laird. The flashing lights of an ambulance filled the darkening skies with strobes of blue and red. Michael Reilly reclined on the gurney, his face pale and his hands shaking as the paramedics ministered to his gunshot wounds. Deputy Odham was lying on a gurney beside him, awake and listening to the surrounding activities but resting quietly.

The blast of gunfire from Ben's weapon had knocked Michael off his feet. He had lain stunned, watching Ben escape with Bree in his clutches. Michael had fought the nausea and the pain of his wounds, unsure of how seriously he was injured. Dizzy, he had groped his way to the stairs, stumbling down the flight until he broke through the door into the kitchen. He had managed to stay upright long enough to make his way to the wall phone, his hands shaky as he dialed 911. The emergency operator had patched him through to Sheriff Hambly's mobile phone.

Upon learning the details of Deputy Odham's and Michael's encounter with Ben Laird, the sheriff had quickly signaled all the searchers and headed with them back to the ranch. He had also summoned an ambulance for Michael. The group of lawmen and ranch hands arrived just minutes before the ambulance arrived. They had found Michael collapsed on the kitchen floor, conscious but weak from the loss of blood. He was sitting upright against the wall of the kitchen.

He'd had the presence of mind to grab dish towels to stem the flow of blood from the gunshot wounds. The first bullet had hit

Michael in the left arm, causing a burning flesh wound. It bled profusely but showed no signs of having hit a major artery. The next bullet caught him in the rib cage, carving a deep groove along the left side of his torso, but it had miraculously avoided his abdominal cavity. The third bullet, embedded in his left thigh, was causing him immense pain.

When the sheriff and his men entered the kitchen, guns drawn and cautious of a possible ambush, they found Michael sitting on the floor attempting to staunch the flow of blood from his wounds. Ben had shot him at a point-blank range. Michael knew that the foreman was a good shot and could only thank whatever power had intervened on his behalf and caused the gunshots to go astray. Otherwise, he'd be a dead man, and Ben would be free to disappear with Bree. No one would ever know what had happened to Sarah, Thomas, and the kids.

While the paramedics worked on him, bandaging his arm and side, Michael argued that he was well enough to rejoin the manhunt. He became fixated on tracking Ben down, since it was only through Ben that they had a chance to find their missing loved ones.

"There you go, Michael. You're sure you don't want something for the pain?"

Michael looked at the young woman who had dressed his wounds. "No, thank you, Carla. I'll be fine."

Dismissing her concern, Michael tried to rise to his feet, hugging his injured arm to his side, the support offering some comfort from the throbbing ache that accompanied his injuries. Yet his injured leg refused to carry him, and he collapsed back onto the gurney.

Steve and Lex were by his side immediately. Steve gently pushed him back onto the gurney until he was lying flat. "Son, you're not going anywhere other than the hospital."

Michael started to argue, but Lex broke in and said, "The paramedic said that you're going to need surgery to get that bullet out of your leg. So you just lie there and let them do their work. They'll get you to the hospital and get you fixed up—"

Steve finished Lex's sentence, "So that when we bring Bree to visit you, you'll feel up to giving that girl a big hug and kiss."

Michael smiled wanly, his eyes absent of humor. "I'd have to be dead not to want to hug and kiss her."

Steve's face was solemn as he said, "You almost were, son. You're mighty lucky Laird's shots weren't on the mark."

"I know, Steve." Michael's face tensed as a wave of pain washed over him. He felt faint and light-headed, and his voice reflected his debilitating injuries. "I guess I better let these medics get me to the hospital." His voice broke with emotion. "You go find them, Steve. All of them. And please," he paused to swallow the lump of pain and heartache choking him, "bring Bree back to me."

Steve acknowledged the young man's request with a slight nod of his head. "We will, son. We will."

Steve watched until the ambulance workers had loaded Michael and raced off, lights flashing and siren blaring. They had been warned that a return run to the ranch would probably be necessary, and they had promised to have the dispatcher send another ambulance and team of paramedics to the ranch, ready to be called into service.

After the ambulance disappeared into the distance, Steve joined Sheriff Hambly, Lex Larsen, and the other men. "Sheriff, what are the plans?"

"We're just about ready to head out. I've got an all-state APB out on Ben and his truck. One of the men," Sheriff Hambly pointed at Jonathan Smith, "indicates that there are a couple of deserted cabins high up in the mountains, farther out than we've been so far."

"That's right, boss," Jonathan said. "They used to be used by the loggin' companies, but they've been deserted for years now. I know Ben knows they're there. Me and him came across them one year when we was cuttin' down some trees for firewood. Only problem, I don't rightly remember where they are."

"Sheriff, do you honestly think Laird would be so stupid as to take them someplace close like that?"

"I don't think Ben is stupid at all. But when you consider how quickly he was on the scene last night after Sarah and Thomas disappeared, I think that bears looking in to."

Breathing deeply, Steve nodded. "You're right. What else do you have planned?"

"We've got a map here from the forestry department. It does a pretty decent job of showing the logging roads. Unfortunately, it doesn't indicate any cabins. But we can still grid out the search area, and I think we can cover it pretty quick."

"Where do you want me to search?"

Looking at the big man, Lou Hambly answered. "Why don't you ride along with me and Lex?"

Steve glanced at his ranch hand and unsmilingly nodded his agreement.

"I've paired each of your men with a deputy. I think we're ready to go. The deputies all have their mobile phones so we can keep in touch. Okay, men? Everyone set?" the sheriff asked.

At the nods of agreement, the sheriff said, "Let's roll."

Just then, a strange look of awareness crossed over Steve's face. "Where's Chuck?"

"Who?" asked Sheriff Hambly.

"Chuck Laird, Ben's nephew."

Silence greeted Steve's words. The men looked at each other and were forced to admit that no one had seen the young man. The sheriff looked at Steve, "Do you think he's involved?"

Steve shook his head. "I don't think so. He's a hotheaded kid, but I don't think he'd do anything to hurt Bree. He has a serious crush on her."

Sheriff Hambly rubbed a weary hand across his chin. All he needed was another missing person. Sighing deeply, he dropped his hand and asked, "Does everyone know who Chuck is?" At the affirmative answers he received, he continued, "Okay then. Add him to our list of missing persons and keep your eyes open for him. Let's move."

Each squad of searchers took with them sack lunches and thermoses of coffee and water. They also had high-powered lanterns, flashlights, maps, toolboxes, blankets, and guns with boxes of extra ammo. The faces of the men involved were grim and tense. Those who knew Ben Laird were struggling with feelings of disbelief mingled with anger and dismay. Steve Sheridan, especially, felt himself wallowing in mixed emotions. Mixed with the fear, anger, confusion, and disbelief was the sense that he had failed his wife, Bree, the children, Thomas— everyone—by not seeing through the facade of Ben's friendly concern. He climbed into the passenger side of Sheriff Hambly's jeep, pausing for Lex, who crawled into the backseat.

Steve gripped the map handed to him, his eyes narrow and steady as he studied the lines and squiggles representing the dozens of logging roads that covered the mountains. He felt himself settling down to the task at hand. He was determined that nothing would keep him from finding Sarah, Bree, and the others. Steve wasn't deeply religious, but he believed in God, and even though he hadn't done much praying in his life, Steve found his heart turning to God and asking for His help.

Sitting next to him, Lex Larsen silently bolstered Steve's heaven-sent plea with a prayer of his own. Lex not only believed in the Lord, he trusted Him. He knew that Thomas was a man of great faith, and he knew that Brock and Shari had recently embraced the knowledge of their Heavenly Father's love. Lex's faith told him that Thomas and the children, wherever they were, would have used their under-standing of prayer to help survive the awful circumstances.

Ben Laird's evil designs had set in motion a pattern of faith and prayer, and as determined searchers scoured the mountain and night-fall cloaked it with deep purple shadows, the light of God shone in the hope-filled hearts of the three grown-ups and two children captive in the solitary cabin.

Chapter 62

Ben pulled his truck to the side of the road and sat huddled in the cab. When he had left the cabin, his emotions had been frenzied. He knew that he had cast Bree into a pit of anguish that would destroy her spirit. He had driven away knowing that she would die alone and bereft, as bereft as he had felt all these months because she didn't return his love.

Ben's mind cleared and suddenly veered in a new direction. The realization that the mountains were probably crawling with search parties hit him. Even though there was a lot of mountain to cover, it was inevitable that one of the searchers would eventually stumble across the cabin. Cursing, Ben remembered that he hadn't been alone when he'd discovered the cabin. Would Jonathan Smith remember the isolated, deserted cabin? Swearing out loud, he knew he had to go back.

Ben's head hurt. He couldn't think. Everything had been going so perfectly, but now it was all going askew. His paranoia exploded, and he agonized over what to do. If he waited much longer, he might get caught. He knew he was running out of time. But if he drove away, he would never rid himself of the hateful knowledge that somehow, Bree might escape or the search parties would find her. He had to make sure. He couldn't leave yet.

With sudden insight, he knew what he was going to do. Jumping out of the cab, he vaulted himself into the truck bed. He had a can of gasoline strapped to the tool rack, and he knew how he was going to kill Bree. Then he could leave, free from the imprisoning torture of his obsessive love for her.

Chapter 63

Chuck Laird was riding his horse along a narrow, winding trail. He had been following the path for the last half hour, and he was starting to get nervous. There was an eerie feeling about being alone in the deep and dappled shadows. While he loved the ranch and being in the mountains, he had never ridden so far beyond the contact of other humans. He was so deep into the forested wilderness that he hadn't heard the signal summoning all of the searchers back to the ranch. He had, instead, continued on, marking the trail as he went so that there would be no chance of becoming lost.

He was grappling in his saddlebag for the food he had packed when he heard a curious sound in the distance. It was the revving of a truck engine. Puzzled, he refastened the flap on the saddlebag and unwrapped a candy bar. He consumed it quickly and spurred his horse forward. Two minutes later, he was surprised when the trail led out onto a narrow but serviceable road.

He spurred his horse into a gallop and felt perspiration break out on his forehead at the sound of an idling vehicle somewhere up ahead. When he rode into the clearing surrounding an old, deserted cabin, he was startled to see his uncle's truck sitting in front of the old house.

Ben wasn't in sight, and Chuck suddenly felt fear creeping up his back. *It's only Uncle Ben!* Chuck's attempt to reassure himself didn't work. There was something wrong. He felt it.

Drawing closer to the house, he dismounted and left his horse grazing on the sparse grass growing at the side of the clearing. With deliberation, Chuck walked toward the cabin. He thought he heard voices from inside. *That sounds like Bree!*

Chuck ran forward but suddenly stopped as his nostrils were assailed by the sharp, acrid, and unmistakable odor of gasoline. *What's going on?* His fear suddenly building, Chuck spun around wildly, searching for the source of the smell. He saw a dark trail in the dirt around the cabin and then noticed the periodic splash marks on the walls of the cabin.

Realization hit him. *No! Not Uncle Ben!*

Just then, a man ran around from the back of the cabin, a large, metal gas can dangling from his hands. He didn't see the boy watching him as he flung the last of the gasoline toward the front door. The liquid splashed onto the old, weathered wood, and Chuck was again overcome by the stench.

"Uncle Ben! No!"

Ben spun around, astonishment etched on his face and anger burning in his eyes. "Don't try to stop me, boy." Ben's voice was surprisingly soft yet forceful with rage.

Chuck stared, his face white with grief. "Why, Uncle Ben?"

His whispered question was lost on his uncle. Ben came to a stop in front of the boy, and Chuck looked into his uncle's eyes. He was unable to believe what he was seeing; his mind rejected the fearful truth, and he was totally heedless of the mortal danger facing him.

Ben dropped the gas can, ignoring the metallic clank when it hit the ground. He stared at his nephew, his eyes devoid of familial affection as he withdrew the pistol from the holster strapped around his waist.

Chapter 64

Bree continued to work at the rope tying her hands together. Her skin was raw and open in places from the friction, but her fingers were finally able to awkwardly grasp the knotted ends. She had been fighting the taut strands for what seemed like hours, and she was finally making some progress. Her slender hands and wrists were agile as she twisted and worked the cords. The knots were loosening.

The sun had set, casting the mountain in total darkness, before Bree finally exclaimed, "There!" With a cry of satisfaction, she shook the ropes from around her wrists. Without taking the time to rub out the numbness in her fingers, Bree immediately set to work on freeing her ankles. It took a few minutes, but finally she was able to move.

Crying out in pain as pins and needles shot up her legs, Bree stamped her feet, trying to restore circulation. Pausing in the dark, shivering against the chill, she listened closely. Brock's and Shari's voices had faded away into occasional cries. Bree could have sworn she heard deeper, mature voices as well. She wondered if Sarah and Thomas might be with the children. But where were they?

Before the feeling came back to her legs, Bree was exploring the interior of the cabin. The door was heavy, locked, and impenetrable. The only window was high on the wall, almost beyond her reach, and no moonlight shone through the grimy pane of glass. Bree's eyes were slow to adjust to the raven-dark night.

Maintaining control of her rising panic, she methodically began inspecting the walls and floors of the cabin. It was slow work, but she was determined to find some way out. As she worked around the room, Bree bumped into the potbellied stove. Dropping to her knees, she crawled behind it, wedging herself between the cold iron and the rough-hewn surface of the log walls.

Her fingers became sensitive to the texture of the wooden floor, and she was able to feel the infinite number of cracks and grooves in the old wood. Just as she was about to move on, her fingertips brushed something, a minute difference in the feel of the wood. It wasn't a crack or a natural groove, but rather, it was an indentation, and as her fingers explored further, she detected the cold touch of metal deeply embedded in the indentation. She fingered the metal, tracing its hard, cold surface until she identified its circular shape.

Settling back on her haunches, trying to relieve the pressure on her kneecaps, Bree continued to work at the metal ring, certain she had found the handle to some kind of trapdoor. Maybe there was a basement of some sort lying under the floor of the cabin. *Probably more of a root cellar*, Bree thought to herself as she managed to get a fingernail under the lip of the ring.

Swearing softly, her fingernail ripping, Bree ignored the minor discomfort and continued to work her fingertips under the ring. It was old and rusty, but finally she managed to lift the tab. Holding her breath, she tugged as hard as she could. She heard a faint creak but could feel no discernible movement. She tried again, but this time there was no response to her pull.

"I just can't seem to get enough leverage."

Sitting back on her heels, Bree pushed her hair away from her face. *There's got to be an answer,* she thought to herself. Reaching out to tug once more, she clenched her teeth and sucked in her breath, pulling with all her might. Sweat popped out on her brow, and she felt like the capillaries in her face would burst with the exertion.

Snorting with disgust, Bree dropped her hands to her lap and let her chin fall forward until it rested on her chest. Wearily she leaned against the cold, solid mass of the stove. As she brought a hand up to rest against the burnished, iron surface, Bree lifted her head, her mind suddenly enlightened with comprehension.

"The stove! It's sitting on top of the trapdoor." Bree was more convinced than ever that she had found a door leading into some kind of cellar. But she couldn't open it because of the weight of the stove.

After scooting backward and bumping into the wall with her right hip, Bree scrambled to her feet. Blindly reaching out, she grappled for the top of the stove. Once she had a good grip, she tried rocking it. It wouldn't budge. Moving her hands higher, she found the smaller diameter of the stovepipe. Taking a deep breath, Bree pushed on it as hard as she could.

She grunted with the effort and felt like her lungs would burst while she continued to push. Finally, with a loud, metallic clamor, the surprisingly sturdy rounds of pipe came crashing down. Bree jumped up and down and shouted out with glee.

Quickly calming herself, she knelt down and found the broken tubes of pipe and one by one, she flung them across the room. Standing up, she wedged herself between the wall and the stove. Using the wall as leverage, Bree braced her arms and firmly pushed against the stove. After what seemed an eternity, her efforts were rewarded, and she felt the slightest movement.

Five minutes later, drenched in sweat, Bree was able to sit down between the wall and the stove and use her legs to push. The added strength of her legs caused the stove to screech when it scooted across the floor. She continued to apply pressure with her feet, tightening all the muscles in her legs and abdomen. Suddenly, she felt the opposing force of the stove give way as it rocked backward. It seemed to hang suspended for several seconds before crashing to its side, causing the floor and walls of the cabin to reverberate.

Bree collapsed against the wall, breathing hard and wiping away the sweat pouring down her face. Laughing, she looked up toward the ceiling and whispered, "Thank you!"

Quickly, she dropped to her knees, her hands out in front searching for the small ring. Bree heard voices that were suddenly much clearer and much closer than they had been before.

"Bree? Are you up there?"

"Brock!" Bree felt her heart flutter with tenderness when she heard the clear voice of her young brother. "Oh, Brock! Yes, baby, I'm here!"

Down below, the two children and two adults erupted with cheers. Their voices shouted up to her, and even though she couldn't make out the words, she knew that not only were Shari and Brock okay, but Thomas and Sarah were, too.

"Hang on, guys. I've got to get this trapdoor open! Can you push while I pull?"

* * *

Thomas, his dirty, weathered face creased in smiles, reached high overhead, following the sound of her voice. Sarah and the children had been sleeping when he first heard the scrambling and scratching sounds coming from the far corner of the root cellar. He had traced the sounds with his ears and, standing beneath the corner where Bree was working, he silently whispered grateful words to his Heavenly Father. Bree was up there, and she was working hard to get them out.

He quietly urged Bree on, recognizing the sounds of her efforts to scoot something heavy across the floor. When the loud crash resounded throughout the cellar, Shari, Brock, and Sarah jumped like they'd been shot. At first they were frightened, but as soon as Thomas explained what was happening, they started to shout to Bree.

With all the strength he had, Thomas placed his hands on the roughly hewn boards that formed the ceiling of the root cellar. He heard Bree command him to push, and he did. With a sudden crack, the old trapdoor flew upward, sending a shower of dirt and debris cascading over the four people standing below.

* * *

Bree was crying as she collapsed on the floor and reached through the hole. She felt four sets of hands grappling for her fingers, catching hold and squeezing. "Oh, my. Oh, my." Bree was crying so hard the two words were barely recognizable.

Suddenly, a watery beam of light shone through the darkness, and Bree found herself staring down into the beloved faces she hadn't seen in such a long time. Brock and Shari were crying too, staring up at their sister. Bree smiled down at them and whispered, "Hey, you two!"

"Sarah, give me a hand and we'll boost them up," Thomas instructed. Soon Bree was joined first by Shari and then by Brock.

The two children threw themselves at her, wrapping their arms around her and burying their faces against her chest.

"I love you, Bree!"

"I love you too, sissy!"

"I missed you so much, Bree!" Brock's voice was muffled as he cried into her shirt.

"Oh, buddy, I missed you too. And I love you so much!"

Bree cradled Brock and Shari, kissing the tops of their heads over and over again. Finally they raised their faces to look at her, and she transferred her kisses to their cheeks and noses and foreheads.

It seemed like she couldn't hold them close enough or long enough, but Bree finally drew back and said, "Okay, you two. We need to get Sarah and Thomas up here."

Thomas and Sarah grinned up at her when Bree's face appeared once more in the opening of the trapdoor. "You guys ready to get out of there?"

"The sooner the better, Bree!" Sarah smiled up into the girl's lovely face.

Before she could reach a hand down to her friend, Bree heard a disturbance at the front door. "Someone's out there!"

"Who is it, Bree?"

"I don't know. Hush!" Bree firmly responded to Brock's frightened query.

The two children sat huddled next to Bree, listening to the furtive sounds coming from outside the cabin.

Thomas's voice drifted up. "This can't be good."

Sarah nodded her agreement. Whoever was out there was being too stealthy. "Do you think Ben's come back?"

"I'm sure of it."

Brock and Shari started to whimper as Bree reached for them and gathered them close to her. If he came back in, she would never let him separate them again. They sat silent and tense for several minutes. Finally, the sounds from outside died away. The night was again quiet and still.

"Whoever was there is gone."

Bree turned back to reach a hand down to Sarah but stopped when Shari said, "I smell smoke!"

"So do I!" Brock echoed.

Bree turned her head. "I smell it too."

Just then, a dancing streak of orange flashed past the window.

"Oh no!" Bree's quiet whisper was drowned out by the shrieks of the children. "The cabin's on fire!"

"Bree! Hurry! We have to get up there!"

Scrambling, she reached down to Sarah. Thomas boosted Sarah up as Bree pulled. As soon as she could, Sarah used her hands to help hoist herself up out of the hole. Turning back to the opening, she reached down and said, "Come on, Thomas. Give us your hands."

The two women grasped the old man and pulled while he used his legs against the wall of the cellar to help boost himself through the door. It was hard work, and Sarah and Bree gasped with relief when Thomas, with aching slowness, finished pulling himself through the opening.

By then, the smell of smoke was thick and overpowering in the confines of the small cabin. Bree could feel the heat of the flames that had yet to eat through the wooden structure. It wouldn't take long before the hungry fire broke through the barrier.

They had to get out. Already the children were choking on the smoke writhing through the cracks in the walls.

"There's only one window! Over there!" Bree pointed.

The glow from the inferno engulfing the front stoop lit up the inside of the cabin with an eerie, red fluorescence. Soon the thick, black smoke would obliterate even that small bit of light.

"We've gotta try and break the window out."

"With what, though?" Sarah answered Thomas's cry with her question.

"What's that?" Thomas pointed to a dark oblong shape lying on the floor under the window.

Bree, following his pointing finger, exclaimed, "The stovepipe!"

"That'll work!" Thomas yelled, dashing across the floor, his aged legs a surprising source of speed and strength as he snatched up the heavy metal pipe and began smashing it against the windowpane. The glass cracked with the first blow, and it took five heavy hits to completely knock the glass out of the window.

"Come here, kids. You first."

Grabbing Shari by the hand while Sarah took Brock, Bree dashed to join Thomas at the window. Picking up the little girl, Bree and Thomas hauled her up to the window. "Okay, sissy, it's gonna be a bit of a drop on the other side, and you'll have to roll quick and get away from the fire. I know it's scary, but it's the only way out."

Petrified, Shari nodded obediently as she felt herself being pushed through the window. With a cry, she hit the burning porch. Without thinking, she curled herself into a ball and rolled toward the edge, where she had a much softer landing on the dirt. Jumping to her feet, she dashed several feet away from the burning structure.

By the time she stopped and turned back to look at the cabin, Brock was already on his feet running toward her. Bree came next, and when she fell to the porch, her weight caused the singed and weakened boards to crack as she fell through. With a desperate howl, Bree shot to her feet and jumped clear of the porch as flames licked at the cracked tinder.

Trying not to think about the danger, Sarah pulled herself through the window, Thomas pushing her from behind, and she followed Bree off the porch. Sarah turned and watched in horror when the flames that suddenly engulfed the porch directly below the window illuminated Thomas's face.

"Thomas!" Their combined voices were a tortured cry in the night as the roar of the inferno drowned the sounds of his screams.

* * *

"Sheriff! I smell smoke!" Lex's voice alerted the driver of the jeep.

Sheriff Hambly stopped the vehicle, and the three men climbed out and stood sniffing the air. The normal scent of the forest carried the distinct, caustic smell of smoke.

"Look!" Steve pointed down the road. At a distance, the dark mountain was lit by an orange glow. "Something's on fire!"

"Back in the jeep!" Lex barely had his door shut before Sheriff Hambly was hurtling down the road, hitting the ruts at top speed. The men hung on, oblivious to the pounding discomfort as they were flung around inside the cab. Their attention was centered on the infernal orange light.

Chapter 65

Ben stood hidden in the surrounding forest, beyond the reach of the savage flames engulfing the cabin. Tears streamed down the angular planes of his cheeks. His hands clenched at his side as he realized the fulfillment of his dreams. He gave no thought to the crumpled, lifeless body of his nephew lying facedown two feet away from him.

He dropped to his knees and wept into his hands. Then he saw her. She was floating through the dancing flames, coming to join him. He had killed her, and as the fire set her spirit free, he captured it and secured it within the walls of his insanity.

Suddenly, he heard voices. The cries of children penetrated the mist of his madness, and he raised his head. His eyes fastened on the unbelievable sight of the two children wrapped in the arms of the two women. They were crying and shouting as the overhead supports of the cabin porch collapsed in a sparkling shower of embers.

"Noooo!!" Ben jumped to his feet. Confusion warred with his madness. It couldn't be!

She had escaped. She was standing there, unharmed, flesh and blood, with her arms around one of the brats.

Just then, a horrific cry came from the front of the cabin. A frightening, flame-engulfed form came hurtling through the wall of fire surrounding the front of the building.

* * *

The children screamed as the fiery apparition dropped to the ground at their feet. Bree and Sarah jumped forward and started to beat at the flames with their hands.

"Stand back!" The deep voice of her husband penetrated the haze of fear that drove Sarah to help Thomas. The panic-stricken women and children had not noticed the arrival of the sheriff's jeep, but as Steve's voice registered in her mind, Sarah grabbed Bree's arm and pulled her back. He and the two other men used a tarp to smother the flames, pounding it against the ground as they wrapped Thomas in its folds, choking off the oxygen feeding the flames that seemed to engulf the old man.

Shari and Brock were crying hysterically. Bree dropped to her knees and took them in her arms. She knew that the sounds of Thomas's screams would haunt her dreams for years to come.

"Bree, kids, I think he's okay!"

Bree looked incredulous as Sarah's reassurances overrode the children's cries. She stared in amazement as Steve and Lex helped Thomas to his feet.

Brock and Shari broke away from Bree and threw themselves across the clearing, not stopping until they had their arms thrown around their old friend.

Bree followed them until she, too, was hugging Thomas. Thomas, wincing from the pain, smothered the groan of agony welling in his chest. He closed his eyes, hugging the two children and Bree tightly until the physical anguish caused him to take a trembling step out of their embrace.

Meanwhile, Sarah ran across the clearing toward the tall, imposing figure of her husband. Steve saw her coming and met her halfway across the clearing. He opened his arms, and Sarah found herself lifted and held tightly against his chest as he cried her name.

Setting her on her feet, Steve tightened his hold and captured Sarah's lips in a long kiss. They broke apart, taking deep, gasping breaths.

Steve cradled Sarah's head in his hands, her soft blond hair flowing around his fingers. He said, "I thought I'd never see you again. Oh, Sarah, I love you so much!"

Sarah whispered, "I love you too. I didn't think we'd ever be together again."

"The baby? How's the baby?" Steve's frantic question startled Sarah.

"You knew?"

"It's true, then? I only suspected . . . hoped . . ."

"Yes."

"Please, tell me. Is it okay?"

Sarah began to softly weep. Wordlessly she shook her head. "I don't know. I think so. Oh, honey, it has to be okay!"

Steve silently gathered her close and kissed her soundly, their union strengthening their prayers that their unborn baby was safe.

* * *

Sheriff Hambly was speaking into his portable phone, "We need an ambulance and fire trucks up here ASAP! Logging road 214. I don't care, Leah!" Quieting his voice, he continued, "Leah, I'm sorry I shouted, but listen to me. We're on logging road 214. There's a structure on fire, and we have folks who need medical attention." Listening for a moment, frustration etched on his weary face, Sheriff Hambly shouted, forgetting his resolve to be patient with his elderly dispatcher, "Leah, get them up here! There are logging maps somewhere around the office. Find them!"

Disconnecting with his flustered dispatcher, Lou turned back to the group huddled together beyond the heat of the flaming building. "Ben Laird? Where is he?"

"I don't know, Sheriff. After he set fire to the cabin, I don't know where he went."

Lex responded to Bree's answer by saying, "He couldn't have gone far. His truck is over there."

Pointing, Lex drew all eyes to the abandoned pickup sitting on the far side of the clearing. As they looked in the direction of his gesturing hand, shouts erupted in the night air, increasing the commotion. Racing engines vibrated through the night when three trucks loaded with men pulled into the clearing, illuminating the surrounding area with beaming headlights.

After the reinforcements piled from the trucks, Sheriff Hambly shouted, "Leave them headlights burning!" In the confusion of the next few minutes, he tried to organize the men to make assignments for continuing their manhunt.

Steve, meanwhile, was attending to Thomas. Sarah and Bree had waved away his ministrations to them, insisting that the old man needed his help more. Stepping away from Bree and the children, Thomas collapsed to the ground, overcome by the smoke and heat. He lay on the ground, his breathing labored and his face as gray as ash. His clothing and hair were singed from the intense flames. Bree backed away with Brock and Shari, trying to give Steve room to work with Thomas. He had the old man wrapped in the tarp, not sure how seriously he was burned.

* * *

The fire continued to roar, threatening to spread to the surrounding forest. In the commotion, no one noticed the staggering figure creeping out of the forest. At first his furtive movements blended with the quaking shadows of the forest, but as he stumbled toward the light of the flames and the beams of the headlights, his silhouette grew.

The diabolical figure loomed over the unsuspecting crowd. Ben had watched the sheriff's men fan out, searching the forest surrounding the clearing. Yet somehow, they had missed him. Two deputies had passed within arm's reach of him when they had plunged into the dark woods.

Ben waited, the raging in his mind quieting while he watched the men disperse. Soon, the sheriff, Steve and Sarah, Bree and the kids, and the injured old man were the only people remaining in the clearing. He watched Bree holding the children and hovering over the old man, and Ben felt his anger take on new life, resurrecting the storm of hatred and obsessive love. It dispelled the confusion and disbelief that had swamped him when he had first realized that Bree was alive. Soon the furious anger was burning as destructively as the flames consuming the old cabin. He began to walk toward her. He would be taken, but that didn't matter. He may die that night, but he wouldn't die alone.

Chapter 66

"I'll be okay, Steve." Thomas's voice was weak as he fought the waves of pain coursing through his body. "I don't think I'm burned much." A paroxysm of coughing choked off his words.

Steve grasped the old man's shoulders and helped him sit up, tears streaming down Thomas's leathery face. Finally, with a gasp, he was able to draw in some life-giving air, and Thomas leaned weakly against Steve, closing his eyes.

Steve supported Thomas's back as he looked up at Sarah and Bree, who were standing over them, concern and worry etched on their grimy faces. "Hope that ambulance gets here soon!"

Thomas opened his eyes to respond to Steve's remark. Before he could open his mouth, though, his eyes traveled from Steve's face to the two women standing over them. He smiled up at Bree and Sarah. Suddenly, a movement caught his attention.

Thomas squinted his eyes as he gazed into the darkness beyond the ring of dancing firelight that filled the clearing. Realization dawned in his aged eyes. He reached out a hand, trying to stop what he saw coming.

* * *

Bree and Sarah were unaware of the man rushing at them from the canopy of trees behind them. Gone was the unnatural stillness that had kept him safe from the eyes of the searchers. Gone was the cold, deliberate calculating that had masterminded his plan to destroy Bree. Gone was any hint of love or tenderness toward the young woman who was his target.

Instead, raving madness and demonic dementia propelled him forward, his eyes blazing with insanity. In his hand, Ben gripped the handle of his pistol. Rushing toward Bree, he fired, the shattering report echoing off the mountaintops. The flashing sparks from the barrel of the revolver repeated as he fired again.

He was screaming as he ran, firing erratically. His first shots went wild, but as he drew closer, the frenzied shooting became more accurate and more dangerous.

Ben's fanatical attack was a severe contrast to the slow response of the seven people in his line of fire. Sarah pushed the terrified, screaming children to the ground and fell on top of them, protecting them with the shield of her body.

Sheriff Hambly clumsily grabbed for his revolver while Steve lurched to his feet. Bree stood frozen in place, coming face-to-face with the man who had tormented her and tried to destroy her.

"I only wanted to love you!" Ben's words screeched through the air. He came to a stop five feet away from Bree. He was panting, his body shaking from the power of his deranged emotions. "But no more. You'll never betray me again, Bree!" He raised his arm, and his last words bit into the night, "Why couldn't you love me?"

The eruption of his gun was accompanied by a loud howl as Thomas lunged to his feet and threw himself at Bree. He knocked her off her feet, the bullet exploding into the barricade of his back.

Answering reports from the sheriff's gun ended the life of the man who had wrought such havoc in the lives of those who lived on Sheridans' ranch. Ben fell forward, summoning one last ounce of will by reaching out a hand toward Bree, the fire of hate fading from his eyes.

Chapter 67

An unnatural silence descended on the group of people standing in the garish light of the burning cabin. The surrounding forest seemed to dance, the mad fluctuation of firelight teasing and taunting the shadows of night. Bree suddenly felt her knees give out, and she fell to the ground in shock. Reaching for Thomas's silent form, she used her other hand to cover her mouth, smothering the sobs threatening to erupt.

She felt Brock and Shari kneeling next to her, leaning against her, crying for their fallen friend. Bree watched Steve drop to the ground next to Thomas, his hands gently searching for the wounds that had caused the old cowboy's fall. Sheriff Hambly was stooped next to Ben's lifeless body, making sure the threat from the foreman was truly gone.

Steve glanced at Bree and the children, his eyes reflecting their pain. He then shifted his gaze to Sarah, who was standing next to him. "We can't wait for the ambulance."

In a swift, decisive move, Steve scooped the old man into his arms, picking him up as easily as he might lift a child. He called to Sarah to pad the back of one of the trucks sitting on the edge of the clearing with the blankets that were folded and stored in Sheriff Hambly's jeep. Bree jumped to her feet and ran after Sarah. Brock and Shari stood by and watched, tears streaming down their cheeks.

Sarah urged them into the cab of the truck and watched Bree climb into the bed of the pickup, sitting so that Thomas's head rested in her lap. Sarah climbed into the passenger side of the cab, drawing the children to her while Steve slid behind the wheel. They left the burning cabin behind just as a flurry of movement and shouts of dismay heralded the discovery of Chuck Laird's body.

The mad drive down the dark mountainside was a nightmare for Bree. Steve drove quickly, cursing each time he hit a rut in the road and glancing in the rearview mirror at Bree and the still form of his old friend. Bree cradled Thomas's head in her lap, his blood seeping through the wad of material she was holding against his wound, trying to staunch the flow.

Bree's mind blocked out the horrible events of that night— Michael's confrontation with Ben, her fear of the ranch foreman, and the agony of leaving Michael behind, knowing he was seriously injured. Bree shuddered recalling how she had felt when Ben's mad obsession had been revealed, the ensuing drive through the forest, and, finally, being left to die in the cabin.

She forced down the bile that rose in her throat at the memories of how the joyous reunion with the children, Sarah, and Thomas had turned frantic with the discovery of flames, smoke, and heat as they fought to escape the burning cabin. And then to watch Ben run toward her, the gun in his hand pointed at her heart. More than anything, Bree knew that she would never forget the image of Thomas throwing himself in front of her, the look on his face reflecting the love he felt for her as he collapsed from the bullet in his back.

"Bree?" Thomas's voice whispered.

"Thomas? Oh, Thomas!" Bree caught her breath, gazing into the shadowed face of her beloved friend.

"The children?"

"They're fine. They're sitting up front with Steve and Sarah."

"Good. That's good." Thomas's voice trailed away, a sickening wave of pain robbing him momentarily of consciousness.

"Thomas!" Bree's voice was anxious with sudden fear. "Thomas!" she whispered his name again, gently rubbing his shoulder. "Oh, please! Wake up!"

Thomas's eyelids flickered. His tongue probed his dry, cracked lips. A moan escaped his throat, and he once again opened his eyes. His voice was so faint that Bree had to lean close to him, the softness of her cheek brushing the whiskered coarseness of the old man's face.

"Bree, tell the kids I love them."

NO! Bree's shout of denial remained locked in her thoughts. Her voice was calm even as her mind raged with fury. "You can tell them yourself. Later . . . at the hospital."

"No, you tell them. And Steve and Sarah." Tears leaked out of Thomas's eyes, and he sucked in a deep breath. "And Michael. Tell my son that I love him!"

Bree was sobbing openly. "No, Thomas! You can tell him!"

Thomas weakly shook his head. With one last surge of strength, he reached a hand up to stroke Bree's cheek, to wipe away the tears bathing her face. He smiled, his eyes twinkling despite the pain wracking his body. "Oh, honey, it's gonna be okay. Your faith brought you through this night. It'll take you into the future."

Bree turned her face into the palm of Thomas's softly aged hand. She kissed his fingers and then grasped his hand with both of hers. She held on to him. "I love you, Thomas. Thank you so much for adopting the kids and me. They're going to miss you so much!"

"I know. But they'll be okay. They're strong. Lean on them and let them teach you." Thomas's voice was growing weaker. He swallowed and fell silent for several moments.

Bree understood without being told what Thomas meant. Her brother and sister had already shown a remarkable reservoir of strength and faith. She knew that they had much to teach her.

Thomas drew in a ragged breath and continued, "Trust Michael. Let his friendship guide you."

Bree managed to control her overflowing emotions. A sense of deep calm descended on her, and she smiled warmly, the tears drying on her cheeks. "I will, Thomas. I will."

"He's strong. Just like his mother." Thomas's eyes closed, and his face relaxed into peaceful lines of relief. His hand went slack, and Bree gently laid it across his chest as Thomas's spirit rose to heavenly heights of release.

Bree felt warm tears again coursing down her face, her heart torn and exhausted as she said good-bye to her good friend. Deep in her soul, she understood the tremendous gift Thomas had given her that night. He had not only endorsed her friendship and possible future with his son Michael, he had literally bestowed upon her the gift of life.

Finally, wiping away the tears, her throat aching with grief, Bree gently scooted away from Thomas and laid his head on the blanket. She rose to her knees and turned toward the glass barrier of the pickup's rear window. Gazing through the window, its surface rippling as if with rivulets of water, Bree realized that she was crying again. She watched Brock and Shari through the cloud of sadness, and, biting her lip, she forced herself to rap on the window.

Four heads turned toward her, four faces reflecting the grief etched on her own features. No words were needed. Steve slowly stopped the truck, and the night enfolded Thomas's companions in a blanket of mourning.

Chapter 68

The next few hours found the victims of Ben's maniacal spree being examined, nursed, and sheltered in the safety of Sun Valley's community hospital. Bree was exhausted, but she stood by, anxiously watching the young doctor who was examining Brock and Shari.

"They're both dehydrated and in need of some good food and lots of rest. I'd like to keep them here overnight for observation."

Bree nodded her head, suddenly choked up and unable to verbally answer his query. The doctor took the gesture for her assent and left the exam room to make arrangements for the night's stay.

Bree was just sitting down in a chair when the curtained door stirred and parted. Steve and Sarah entered, their faces creased with worry. The lines smoothed when they saw Bree and heard her reassurance. "They're going to be fine. The doctor wants to keep them for the night, though. He said they're dehydrated and in need of rest and food."

Steve sighed and ran a hand through his hair. He closed his eyes, clasping Sarah to his side. Sarah felt tears trickle down her cheeks. She started to hiccup, gulping her tears that mingled with laughter when she saw the answering moisture on Bree's face. "We're a fine bunch, aren't we?"

Bree started to laugh too, but her laughter soon turned to heartrending sobs. Sarah stepped out of Steve's arms and went to the girl. She knelt and put her arms around Bree, and they cried for several minutes, finding comfort in the knowledge that they were safe.

Steve stepped over to the stretchers containing the two sleeping children. He had gained control of his outward show of emotions, but his face was still gray with shock. He pushed Shari's lank hair off her forehead and leaned down to press a kiss against her grimy cheek. He stroked her face before turning to Brock. "Oh, buddy!" He stifled a moan, his hand gentle as it rumpled the little boy's hair. He kissed Brock also, then turned and looked at the two women crying in each other's arms.

"Okay, you two. What's next?"

Sarah dropped her arms from around Bree, drying her face. She looked up at her husband and said, "I suppose we should go home and get some rest."

Bree was shaking her head. "I'm not leaving here. I can't leave them." Her voice was quiet but firm with determination. "I can't bear the thought of being separated from them again." Her voice broke as she continued, "Not after just finding them."

"I don't want to leave either," Sarah said. "I want to wait until Michael wakes up."

Bree's head shot up. "Michael?" Images raced through her mind of him collapsing on the attic floor, his body broken by bullets. She had quelled any thought of him in the ensuing events. But hearing his name, Bree realized her grief, and her face crumpled from the fear that she had lost him forever.

Sarah looked stricken. "Oh honey, I'm so sorry. I forgot that you didn't know." Earlier, during the frantic drive down the mountain-side, Steve had filled Sarah in about Michael's encounter with Ben, his subsequent injuries, and the fact that he was alive.

"He's okay, Bree." Steve's voice was gentle. "Before we came in here, we checked on him. He's asleep, doped up on some pretty strong pain medication, but he's going to be fine."

"I want to see him!"

Just then, the curtains parted once again and the doctor stepped into the cubicle. "I have a room ready for these youngsters." Two orderlies and a nurse followed the doctor. "These guys will help get them transferred. Bree," the doctor looked at the pale, exhausted girl, "I've made arrangements for a cot to be set up in their room for you. I figured you wouldn't want to leave them tonight."

Bree whispered her thanks to the thoughtful doctor, pushing away the worry she felt for Michael. She had to see to the children first, then she could go to Michael.

"Sarah, honey, why don't you and I head home? We can come back early in the morning and see how everyone is doing. You can see Michael then. I'm sure they have him doped up after his surgery."

Sarah sighed wearily, "Okay. Bree, can we bring you and the kids anything?"

Bree looked at Sarah, grateful for her thoughtfulness. "Some clean clothes. For all of us?"

"Of course. We'll bring some for Michael too, even though he probably won't need them for a few days."

Bree followed Sarah and Steve out of the room, letting the orderlies and the nurse have the space they needed to prepare the children for their transfer to the pediatric wing of the hospital. Just as they entered the lobby of the emergency ward, Sheriff Hambly walked through the double doors followed by Lex Larsen and Jonathan Smith. "Steve, Sarah, Bree. How are the kids?"

"They're going to be fine," Steve answered. "They're going to stay the night here, though, just to be sure."

"What about Thomas?" Lex's voice was tight with anxiety.

Steve clapped a hand on the man's shoulder, his fingers trembling. "Thomas died on the way down off the mountain."

Lex closed his eyes, his lips quivering. Sheriff Hambly tightened his mouth, his face lined with stress. Jonathan Smith was too weary to wipe away the tears trickling down his cheeks.

He was the first to speak, however, his voice quaking with emotion. "Any word on how Michael's doin'? I been purty anxious 'bout that young man."

Bree felt her heart turn over with tenderness at Jonathan's concern. Her heart reflected his anxiety a hundredfold. She answered him, "I haven't seen him yet, but from what I hear, he came through surgery fine and is sleeping."

Jonathan swept a weary hand across his red-rimmed eyes, "Thank you, Lord." His quietly whispered prayer of gratitude was echoed in the hearts of all his friends.

"Steve, there's something you need to know." The sheriff's words were charged with feeling and caused Steve, Sarah, and Bree to stare at him, renewed fear reflected in their eyes.

"What is it, Lou?"

Sheriff Hambly sighed deeply, hating to impart bad news. "It's about Chuck. Chuck Laird."

Bree felt her heart constrict, and she heard Sarah gasp with dawning realization. Steve's face looked grim as the sheriff continued, "We found his body just after you left the cabin. He'd been shot. By Ben."

Bree and Sarah started to cry again, their emotions raw from the trauma of that night's events. Steve cursed, closing his eyes.

Bree's grief for Chuck was intense. It didn't matter to her that Chuck had changed, turning into someone she found unlikable. The knowledge that he had died at the hand of his uncle, a man he should have been able to trust, nearly broke her heart.

Bree dried her tears and shared a hug with Sarah and then Steve. She bid the sheriff, Lex, and Jonathan good-bye and watched as they all left before turning and making her way to the elevators. When she reached the second floor and found the room assigned to Brock and Shari, Bree discovered that they were settled in and still sound asleep. She stood at Shari's bedside, brushing the curls away from her face before gently kissing the soft cheek of her little sister.

When she leaned over Brock's bed and kissed his forehead, he awoke and sleepily smiled at her. His eyes sparkled with the trust, love, and faith that had kept him alive during his ordeal. He reached up and wrapped his arms around Bree's neck and held her close for several seconds. His arms went limp, however, as fatigue overtook him and he fell back to sleep. Bree gently tucked him in. She was so tired, but before she rested, there was one more thing she needed to do.

A few minutes later, after running a comb through her hair and dabbing some lotion on her face, Bree hurried down the hall, taking the elevator to the third-floor surgical ward. She followed the signs leading to patient rooms and soon found number 316. She paused for a moment outside the door and then knocked quietly. She listened, and when she heard a muffled "Come in," she pushed the door open.

Michael, lying in a bed, was the sole occupant of the room. His hair looked darkly damp and was combed straight back off his forehead. He had a two-day growth of stubble on his chin, but somehow he managed to look younger than ever. It was hard to believe he was twenty-seven years old. His blue-gray eyes focused on Bree, and his face lit up with recognition.

Bree ran across the room and dropped onto the edge of the hospital bed. She ignored Michael's hands, gently pulling him close. He wrapped his arms around her, unmindful of the tug from the IV lines stretching from his right arm to the bag of fluid hanging above his bed.

Bree buried her face in the crook of his neck and felt answering moisture against her cheek, his eyelashes fluttering against her skin as she cried in his arms. They cried for Thomas and the grief they shared over his death. They cried with relief that the children and Sarah were safe. And they found comfort in their shared embrace.

Chapter 69

One week later, Bree shepherded Brock and Shari across the softly lit room. Hauntingly sweet music played softly in the background, and the ambience of the room reflected the peaceful sadness filling the hearts of the mourners filing through the viewing room.

Bree had been hesitant about allowing Brock and Shari to attend the viewing, but Steve and Sarah had counseled her to allow them to go. "They may be young, but they need the same kind of closure you do." Sarah's wise words had finally convinced Bree.

The children preceded her in the line, and Bree felt herself choke up when they came to a stop in front of the simple casket that was the final resting place for Thomas's physical remains. They were silent for several minutes, their faces pale and unsmiling. Finally, Brock reached out and laid his hand against Thomas's pallid, waxy cheek. The sight of his small, softly dimpled hand against the leathery, seasoned face touched Bree's heart, and she began to cry as Brock turned to her and buried his face against her side. His shoulders shook with the tears he could no longer hold back. Bree reached for Shari with her other hand, and the three Nelsons stood together, sharing their love for Thomas Reilly and their grief over his loss.

The children had told Bree how the songs and stories they had learned at church had helped them through the lonely, dark hours of their imprisonment. Bree knew that it was Thomas's example that had helped her find her own faith. In the end, he had given her the gift of life.

He had taken the bullet meant for her, and Bree knew that she would always remember how she had sat cradling his body, crying for the life he had been willing to give so that she might live.

"Bree, kids," Sarah's soft voice filtered through the mists of sorrow encircling the Nelson siblings. She reached out a hand and laid it on Bree's shoulder. Bree lifted her head and found herself wanting to curl into the warmth of Sarah's comforting gesture, but she forced herself to stand upright, her arms resting around the slight forms of her brother and sister.

"It's time for us to go into the chapel. The services are going to start in a few minutes."

Bree followed Steve and Sarah down the hall of the LDS church. The sensation of homecoming surprised Bree. She had never been in this place before, but somehow it felt familiar. She recognized that this room of worship had the same spirit of holiness that had resided in Thomas's home.

While the soft voices of her friends and family filled the air with the essence of togetherness and the prelude music gently soothed her spirits, Bree let her thoughts wander. She felt as if she had a lifetime of memories stored up from the past six months. While the horrifying events of the last two weeks had nearly destroyed her peace of mind, her family, and her life, dozens of images warmed her heart, healed her spirit, and dispelled the devastation of Ben Laird's evil designs.

She saw herself twirling on the dance floor of her senior prom, enfolded in a cloud of chiffon, held in the strong arms of her friend Chuck. The boy who had held her close that night, offering his friendship and his loyalty, was the boy she wanted to remember. Bree wondered if the subtle, insidious aura of his uncle was what had changed him to a man who selfishly sought to force her into a different kind of relationship. Bree felt that she had forgiven him, and thoughts of his life being snuffed out so cruelly by the hand of a trusted family member twisted her heart with sorrow. Tears glimmered in her eyes as she heard his voice, full of enthusiasm and vitality, telling her about his plans to join the Air Force and see the world. *Good-bye, Chuck. I'll miss you. I'm sorry I couldn't be what you wanted me to be. But I was always willing to be your friend.*

Bree blinked her eyes, and the images in her mind shifted. She saw the welcoming smile on Steve Sheridan's strong, kind face when he opened his home to her and the children. She saw Brock's young pride when Steve shook his hand like a man, and she saw the dimples in Shari's smile when he held her hand and led her down the hall to meet Sarah. Bree felt again the comfort in Steve's friendship and the strength in his determination to safely guide Bree through the harrowing days following the children's disappearance.

Sarah's beautiful face and loving smile filled Bree's mind. *If I were to go away today, I would carry with me forever the picture of Sarah's smile.* Turning her gaze to the woman sitting next to her on the wooden church pew, Bree felt a rush of gratitude unlike any she had ever felt before. Sarah was her confidant, her comforter, her sister . . . her friend.

Additional pictures of events on the ranch flashed through Bree's mind. Lex and Tina, Jonathan and Mary, as well as all of the other ranch hands, mingled in a collage of laughter, love, and friendship. The whirlwind of remembrances caused Bree to experience a moment of dizziness. It was all too much to comprehend.

When her thoughts finally settled, Bree felt her heart constrict. In her mind she saw the face of Ben Laird, strong and handsome, laughing and teasing with her, causing her to blush and smile shyly with his outrageous compliments. She shuddered to think of the months that had gone by, months of seeing him on a daily basis and not knowing who he was. She had never suspected that hidden behind the smiles, the twinkling eyes, the merry words, was a heart filled with obsessive love that later changed into hate and vengeance.

Bree closed her eyes, holding them tightly shut as the whirlwind pictures in her mind turned gray and ugly. She felt like she wanted to clap her hands over her ears. She heard Ben's voice—seductive, cruel, devoid of human emotion as he called her *darling* over and over again. *No! It's over. He's gone. He can't hurt me anymore. He can't hurt Brock or Shari. I won't let him control me another minute!*

Bree opened her eyes, her lips taut with determination, and as she did so, she felt a small hand grab hold of her fingers. She looked down into the eyes of her little sister. Shari was gazing up at her, her dark blue eyes and pert nose a mirror reflection of her older sister. Bree smiled at her and felt the golden glow of Shari's answering smile dispel the ugly images that had been flooding her mind.

Bree transferred her gaze to Brock and felt like laughing out loud at the sight of his ginger hair and freckled face. *I am so lucky! I love Brock and Shari so much!*

In her mind, Bree heard the warmth of Thomas's laughter and felt her own lips curve into a smile, the dimple in her right cheek deepening with humor and affection. *Thomas! How wise and brave and good you were! Do you know how privileged I was to know you? Can you even begin to comprehend how much you have given me? You've given me faith, hope, life!*

Bree almost whimpered as her heart constricted, her tremendous joy intermingled with her sorrow causing her to gasp with an emotion that was so deep it was almost painful. *I love you, Thomas! Thank you . . . for everything . . . for my life . . . for Michael.*

* * *

Michael was watching Bree and had been watching her for a long time, his fledgling love deepening as he watched the flood of emotion-packed memories play across her expressive face. He watched the sorrow of the day mingle with happiness and joy.

He followed the path of her gaze as it traveled from Sarah and Steve, to Brock and Shari, and then to the casket containing the body of his father. Michael felt the breath catch in the back of his throat when Bree turned toward him and settled her beautiful blue eyes on him.

* * *

Bree clearly read the open adoration in Michael's eyes. He smiled at her, and Bree felt her pulse quicken, her spirit responding to the love reaching out to her. Bree knew that her future was settled. It would be spent with the Sheridans, Brock and Shari, and Michael. They were her family.

Bree knew that she still had issues to face and that the future was going to have its challenges. She, Brock, and Shari had been through too much, and they had only started on the road to recovery. But the words, the feelings, and the testimonies she had heard from Michael, the Larsens, and others had opened the door between her heart and heaven. She knew in whom she could trust, and she knew that she was loved. She also knew that she no longer had to be afraid, and that she was no longer alone.

Sitting among her loved ones, her fingers clasped in Shari's, Bree felt her face grow peaceful and reflective, memories of her parents gently sweeping through her mind, blending with images of Thomas and the wonderful lessons he had taught her. She remembered his whispered words on the night she had run to him through the cold and snow and how he had sat with her until she drifted to sleep. The testimony he had shared continued to touch her heart, and as she closed her eyes to join the congregation in a prayer of comfort and supplication, she heard again the sacred verse he had quoted to her that night. Just as they had then, she found that the words still had the power to touch her soul with healing grace. *Peace I leave with you, my peace I give unto you: not as the world giveth, give I unto you. Let not your heart be troubled, neither let it be afraid.*

Bree felt at peace. The only difference between the present and the memories of that night were that she could now look her loved ones in the eyes. She could touch them, hold them, and know that they were safe. Her peace and her faith were finally anchored. Quietly she turned her eyes to the rest of her family and smiled, encircling them with her love.

About the Author

Lorraine Taylor grew up a navy brat, which instilled in her a love for seeing new places. She currently lives in Caldwell, Idaho, where she serves as the Primary president. She has eleven nieces and nephews, scores of Primary children she has taught, and students who have filled her life with laughter and love. She currently provides occupational therapy services to elementary students in the Caldwell public school system.